# NOTHING IS INFLAMMABLE

# NOTHING IS INFLAMMABLE

## SIMON LOGAN

PRIME BOOKS

**Prime Books**

www.prime-books.com

# CONTENTS

# NOTES TOWARDS THE DESIGN AND PRODUCTION OF THE PROTOHUMAN

### Chapter One
*Wherein the lone mecha-scientist, Dziga,
introduces himself and his work.*

My name is Dziga and this is my work. This is my life.

Since January I have resided in this lab, my cage. There are five rooms in the facility, all of which are mine to do with as I wish. The lighting is intermittent and pus-yellow, the walls and ceilings crumbling and full of exposed wires and pipes. I have all the equipment I could desire and each piece is broken or damaged. I have every chemical I need.

This is how I work.

I spent the first few weeks I was here exploring every inch of the place.

There are porcelain tiles on the floors and walls of some of the rooms, cracked and filthy with a greasy residue. There are two immense, rusted autoclaves in one room a little further along the corridor that occasionally work well enough to sterilise my equipment. There are several storage cupboards, the shelves within haphazardly filled with beakers, pipettes, Bunsen burners, racks, storage jars, large bottles, tiny micro litre tubes and rows and rows of chemicals.

Damp stains the corners of the ceilings in most rooms and particularly in the corridors that join the complex together. There are cracks here and there from which insects and small rodents crawl out. And there is a persistent smell of chlorine in the air.

Everything has a sepia tint.

The main room from which I work apparently used to be three separate rooms that were knocked into one before I arrived. The uneven edges of the dividing walls that were hammered away are still visible; they give the impression that the building is trying to regenerate itself, like an insistent weed.

This room, which I use as my primary research chamber, is therefore about thirty feet long by fifteen feet wide, cluttered with my tools and implements as well as the litter of small experiments that I am indulging in. There are windows along one wall but, like all the others in the lab, they are clouded by years of chemical silt that has worked its way into the glass' very pores.

I have no wish to look outside anyway.

I work in an appalling silence. I am alone here, except for Judas of course and, if you count it as an entity, the Protohuman. Occasionally Jakobsen or Dmitri visit but apart from that I am left to my own devices.

There is more to my life and my lab than this, of course, but this description will suffice for now. More important than the building is my work. And this is how it started.

In the last century William Levitt and his company began building what would become the community of Levittown on Long Island in America. Over the next four years a total of 17,447 homes were built, effectively creating a town through the will of a single man. 75,000 people ended up living there—75,000 that had no choice but to recognise William Levitt as somewhat of a god, for without him their little society would never have existed.

He managed this feat by being one of the first to realise the awe-inspiring power of rationalisation if it were used in this way. His company built each home to exact specifications, using exactly the same materials in exactly the same quantity in exactly the same way in every single house they built there. There was no need for anyone to think about how a wall should be put up or where—this had already been decided. Each wall was put up in exactly the same way.

This homogenisation is the only way such a accomplishment could have been achieved, for if Levitt had decided on how to build each house individually he would probably still be building them today. Only by deciding on the best way to do something and eliminating all other choices could it be done.

The trend was reflected elsewhere, carried by TV screens and telephone cables and modems. Everything could be scientifically managed and controlled to ensure the utmost efficiency.

Burger sizes, coffee flavours, movie plots, musical melodies, health care, marriage, even creativity.

It was all subject to the four-pronged mechanisation process—efficiency, calculability, predictability and control.

Except something passed through, something vital.

As I had read about Levitt and others like him while in the asylum it seemed to me that they had all missed what could be the real purpose, the real power, of scientific management.

It was then that I had formulated the theory of the Protohuman.


And this is the Protohuman.

It is chained to the wall merely to keep it upright. It watches me whenever I watch it. It occasionally wears a lab coat like mine to preserve its decency and because it bears enough resemblance to a real human being to require it.

Once, it was human just as I am. But with each day and each stage of my research it grows further and further apart from our species and into the realm of something new.

I leaned towards the Protohuman and it copied the gesture. I could see the reflection of myself in its eyes, repeated on to infinity. The scars of the past stages of the experiment were bright white on it's skin, healing perfectly.

There was a commotion from the far side of the room, screeching and the sound of metal being hammered against metal. I turned from the Protohuman, sensed it sink back onto the wall as I left it and went to Judas's cage.

The cage hung from the ceiling, suspended by a thick, rusted chain with a hook on the end that looped through a catch on the top. I have placed a broken steel girder under the cage to steady it and stop it swinging too much when Judas bounced around inside.

"Jealous?" I asked the creature.

It slammed against the metal bars at my proximity, teeth bared—but it's been almost a week since I've fed it and soon it slumps to the cage's floor, exhausted. It had lost even more hair since the last time I looked closely at it. Its scrawny body seemed to be curling up day by day like a piece of fruit left in the sun, the skin visible between the uneven clumps of fur left wrinkled and covered in sores.

It barely resembled a proboscis anymore.

I poked a finger through the bars and stroked its balding head, soothing the poor creature.

"You hungry, Judas? Mmm? Hungry?"

I turned to the chest freezer fitted into the corner of the room. Steam poured out and there was a pneumatic hiss as the lid lifted. Chunks of raw meat—shoulders, legs, great slices of torso—lay within next to racks of test tubes and packs of frozen vegetables. I removed a loose nugget of fatty red meat turned pink by the sub-zero temperatures, took it to the microwave oven on a bench opposite.

The device was as old as everything else, the LCD display cracked and empty. Most of the buttons were missing, exposing the black pads that lay beneath. I had scribbled numbers in chalk on the pads but they were practically rubbed away to invisibility so I punched in numbers at random. A strip of electrical tape was all that held the door shut—I removed it, placed the meat inside, then taped it shut again. I hit the wide START button and watched the meat become illuminated by a yellow glow.

It fascinated me, watching the stuff soften and redden as it circled around and around. Juices soon began to roll out of the carcass's pores, blood and water like tears.

I felt sick.

*Sitiophobia—fear of eating, or food.*

The microwave came as close to a ping as it could manage and the light shut off. Judas crawled to his emaciated feet, aroused by the smells when I opened the microwave door. I picked the piece of meat up with a pair of tongs, keeping them at arms length and trying to avoid the trail of stink that came off of it.

Judas began lazily hitting his head against the side of the cage in dazed excitement. I pressed the offering to his bars and he pulled it through eagerly, spraying blood into the air then falling backwards against the cage as he sank his teeth in.

I listened to the sounds of him tearing the meat apart hungrily, unable to watch. My stomach turned, my throat spasmed. Judas's eating always sounded to me like a blocked drain trying to clear itself.

I left him to it.

I had work to do—you see, there was the problem of bleeding.

For whatever reason, I had been finding it increasingly difficult to stop the Protohuman from bleeding constantly when I delivered fresh wounds as part of a new surgery. This had only been a problem formed of late and I considered that it had something to do with my over-eagerness with it's body, not giving it enough time to recuperate.

Unable to find any coagulants amongst the array of compounds in my cupboards I was forced to formulate one myself. It was a crude attempt but it seemed to help a little, turning the blood that spilled from the creature a darker red.

Despite this it continued to leak, however, and my efforts to sew up its wounds tight. More often than not I came away from my time with the Protohuman as smeared in its blood as it was. My lab coat was encrusted with day-old haemoglobin that I could only get rid of by waiting for it to crisp up and then brush off.

As Judas finished his meal I stood by the Protohuman before a large blackboard that was set into the wall, the kind you'd find in old-fashioned classrooms. I used the device for scribbling equations and thoughts on whenever I felt the need. At the present moment I had illustrated a large-scale drawing of the Protohuman's cerebral cortex, filling in some areas and annotating others.

On the Protohuman's shaven head I had drawn in black marker dotted lines to delineate the various sections I was currently studying.

My theory—the less decisions that have to be made on an individual basis the more efficient the decision process becomes. If a method of performing an act can be shown to be the best one then there is no need for anyone to use a different method. If one thought can be proven to be the most efficient then there is no need for anyone to think any different.

I took the scalpel I had in my hand and pressed its dull, rusted blade to the Protohuman's stubbled head. I had to press down hard to get it to cut, finally tearing the skin more than slicing into it. The creature flinched suddenly, making me jump and I loose the thread of the incision. The chains that held it rattled, kicking up dust from where they were attached to the wall.

I watched a single rivulet of blood trickle down its scalp and forehead and felt a similar bead of sweat tickle mine. I brushed it away absentmindedly, a quiet aggression ticking over in my stomach.

To deflect the anger I turned to the chalkboard and scribbled hard with the chalk across the drawing of the brain—

Pain is an efficiency. The human reaction to it is NOT. We MUST move BEYOND this. The Protohuman will not SUFFER as I do.

I stopped, fingers aching from pressing so hard, panting with exertion as I stared numbly at what I had written. With my sleeve I rubbed out the final portion—as I do.

I replaced it with—as we do.

I placed the chalk back in its holder and noticed it was stained pink. I looked at my fingers, the fingers that had wiped the bead of sweat away.

It was blood.

I rubbed my thumb and forefinger together curiously and when I looked up at the Protohuman it was looking back. There was a smear of red on its head from the incision and something cold and frightened reflected in its eyes.

To distract myself from its unnerving attention, I decided I would finish tidying the lab for Jakobsen's visit.

## Chapter Two
*Wherein Dziga meets with Jakobsen, his mysterious benefactor*

The letter had come a few days previously, deposited in the metal wire rack that was fitted against the front door to the lab complex. I knew who it was from and what it would be about before I had finished climbing the steps that led up to the door. There was only a small handful of people who knew I was here and only one who would write to me.

Jakobsen had said that he would be coming on Wednesday morning and despite his usual calm, gentle manner it always flustered me when I knew he would be visiting to the lab. I'm not quite sure why.

Certainly he couldn't criticise me for the condition or tidiness of the lab for the place was a shambles before I had ever been brought here and besides he never seemed interested in looking around to see what I was doing. Perhaps it was my own discomfort at not knowing what he was there for that encouraged me to create something for me to focus on.

So whenever I knew he was coming I would spend days and nights re-arranging things, putting jars and beakers that I had been using back in whichever cupboard had space for them, wiping down spillages if I could find a rag to do so. I would even scrape the shit out of Judas's cage, though often there would be no need for if I avoided feeding the monkey long enough it would begin eating its own faeces.

I was careful not to clear up too much for fear that I would look like I wasn't doing any work while I was down here. But again, I had received the distinct impression from Jakobsen that he was as interested in my work as he was in the lab's cleanliness.

Which, of course, raised the question—what *was* he interested in?

He had come for me, given me a lab that was mine to do with as I wished, endowed me with all the equipment that he could acquire for me and asked almost nothing in return except that he be allowed to pay me these little visits. Dmitri was suspicious of the man's motives—he had made that only too clear to me on the handful of occasions he come to visit me—but I felt in less of a position to question the man considering what he had rescued me from.

And if he could take me from there then didn't it follow that he could put me back again?

That thought terrified me more than death itself.

So Jakobsen was to come—and this is what happened when he did.


The man was always clean-shaven and smartly dressed, a rarity in my experience. We sat on ratty, torn sofa chairs in a small room at the back of the lab complex, one which I had prepared especially for us. Aside from the chairs, the only other pieces of furniture in the room were a low, scarred coffee table and a frameless painting hung on a syringe embedded into the wall to keep it up. I had once, some weeks ago, locked myself in the room to try and work through a problem I had encountered in my work. I had tried to remove the scribbles and sketches from that time but had been only vaguely successful. Illustrations of pieces of anatomy and the tail-end of equations littered the tea-stain walls.

My attempt at homely.

"How have you been feeling of late, Dziga?"

We both held mugs of watery coffee in our hands. I noticed how the steam from mine rose in thick, clumsy clumps while that from his ascended like rose-angels.

"Good," I told him. "I have been much better."

"That's good to hear." He paused to look around the room. "And your work?"

"Also good." I watched the coffee steam obsessively, unable to look directly at him. Eye contact was a problem for me. "I am making good progress. I can prepare a report for you should you wish."

"That won't be necessary. Here . . . I have your newspapers."

He produced from inside his coat a brown paper bag that had been taped shut at one end and handed it to me. I took it graciously, and placed the bag beside me, not wanting to appear too interested.

"Is there anything more you require?"

I disliked asking him for things. He always seemed eager to give me whatever I wanted or needed but I couldn't help but wonder that all of this, all what he was doing for me, would one day be turned back on me and I would owe him it all in return. I didn't know if I would be able to repay.

"Some chemicals. I have a list." I removed the scrap of notepaper from my coat pocket and handed it to him. Our hands almost touched; I saw how precise his nails were. I also saw the scar on the underside of his wrist.

*Haptephobia—fear of being touched.*

"I'll have them to you by the end of the week."

"I'd be most grateful."

A silence followed. I felt him studying me. The room's ceiling dripped yellow moisture from a pipe that showed through in one corner. It was the only sound.

"Would you like to see it?" I asked him to break the silence. It had been several weeks since his last visit and I was eager to prove that the project was coming along.

Jakobsen smiled placidly. "Of course," he said.

I rose eagerly, glad for a distraction. We left our coffee untouched on the table and he followed me down the long, thin corridor to the main research chamber. Bubbling sounds came from within, chemicals boiling themselves into bold new substances from within a small network of tubes and Pyrex pipes next to the doorway. The counters were mostly clear save for a few small experiments I had allowed to continue running and I had replaced a broken light bulb to better illuminate the place.

I had covered Judas's cage with a large piece of black fabric and drugged the creature to avoid him interfering. I could hear his soft, laboured breathing from behind the cage's curtain.

I went straight to where the Protohuman lay chained to the wall and stood before it. Jakobsen remained on one side, always a little uneasy around the creature. His face crumpled slightly into a frown as the gaze went from me to the Protohuman and back.

I had wiped the blood from its head away and washed it as well as I could before Jakobsen's arrival, ensuring it looked as presentable as possible.

"You are being careful with it, Dziga?"

"Of course. It's my life's work. It's my life. Very careful."

Jakobsen nodded slowly. "It wouldn't be good to cause too much damage to . . . it."

I was surprised that he should be concerned about such a thing. "Of course, Mr. Jakobsen. I would never harm it."

I watched Jakobsen peer at the creature and I knew he was looking at the ice-white scar tissue visible in places.

"My experiment must continue, you realise, Mr. Jakobsen. Eggs will be broken. But I would never harm the creature beyond what is necessary."

There was a long pause before Jakobsen turned to me, smiling now. "Of course, Dziga. I know. Forgive me."

I shrugged, feeling in no position to offer anything but gratitude to the man. "Do you require to see my written results? I have constructed an interim report for you . . . "

Jakobsen waved a hand as I knew he would. "That won't be necessary. I just wished to check that you had everything that you needed. I am glad your work progresses, however."

I nodded. "Yes, Mr. Jakobsen."

Jakobsen frowned. "Dziga, I feel like you are wanting to tell me something. You seem . . . agitated."

I shook my head, quickly looked elsewhere in the room. I still hadn't decided whether to say anything to him or not for I had been told I was prone to moments of paranoia and I didn't want to alarm my benefactor and possibly trigger my return to the hospital. But surely not *all* paranoia was unfounded?

"Dziga?"

"Mr. Jakobsen, I have . . . suspicions. Or . . . not suspicions. Feelings. I . . . Things . . . "

Not making sense. Not making sense.

*Act calmly, Dziga, do not give him cause for concern!*

Jakobsen began to reach out to me with one long, textured hand but I withdrew instinctively as an abused dog would from its owner.

"I worry that we are not as cautious as perhaps we should be," I finally managed. "About my work."

"How so?"

"There are people who would see what I am doing and want it for themselves. People who would be willing to . . . do things to get it."

"You fear for your life?"

*Always* I thought but did not verbalise. Shrugged instead. "It is always scientifically reasonable to assume that knowledge uncovered by one is of greater value to another just as it is of less value to the majority. And I fear my work is of more value than most."

Jakobsen seemed unconvinced. "You are safe here, Dziga. Very few even know you are here. I brought you to this lab because of its isolation; nobody could know about your . . . work. Has something happened?"

"Nothing of noticeable import. But I worry that those who would seek to usurp my work would work in ways subtle enough that perhaps even I would not notice. Samples have gone missing. And . . . one of my equations was altered while I slept one night."

"Are you sure?"

I sensed the tone hidden in Jakobsen's voice, that tone of examination and assessment that was usually wrapped in a stark white lab coat and framed by wire-rimmed glasses and the jagged spikes of cranial charts.

"No. I could have been mistaken."

Jakobsen nodded, folding his arms. "I shall look into further security measures for you, Dziga, if it will make you happier. You need not be fearful here, however. I will not let any harm come to you."

I bowed my head, anxiety crawling within me like insect larvae. "Thank you, Mr. Jakobsen."

As we walked to the door minutes later, the visit over, Jakobsen touched my shoulder. We stopped at the foot of the steps leading to the front exit.

"No more episodes, Dziga?"

I breathed hard because his question reminded me of before, of what he had taken me from.

"No, Mr. Jakobsen," I lied. "No more episodes."


The visits always left me shaken.

Being down there in the lab, so completely alone, it was like I had become utterly detached from the world, as if I were a thread unravelled from a shirt or an astronaut tumbling through space. It was so easy for me to feel that there was nothing else except me, the lab, Judas and the Protohuman but every time Jakobsen or Dmitri came to see me it brought the world and everything inside it crashing back to me.

How much further must I retreat before I felt truly safe?

I almost felt like I was back in the asylum, chained to the wall as the doctors examined me endlessly.

I emptied a brown glass jar of pills onto the counter top and popped three into my dry mouth, my hand shaking as I tried to take a sip of water from a beaker. I steadied myself against the wall and felt the pulse racing through my head slowly begin to calm down.

But it wasn't enough.

I hated Jakobsen for showing no interest in my work. I hated the memory of a world full of noise and crowds that pressed against your ribcage and stopped you from being able to breathe. My claustro-phobia began to set in like a great black spider crawling up my back and over my head.

At times like this it was like I had received a sudden dose of the world, more than even a normal, functioning being could handle and I had to retreat further. I rifled through the workbench drawers, pulling them open and slamming them shut, rattling their contents until I found a cloth bag. I took out the bag and removed from it one of several syringes filled with a viscous, faintly blue substance.

My life was one great long molecular chain, chemical after chemical after chemical.

I didn't want to—but it was all I had ever known.

My hands still shook as I rolled up my sleeve and fought to find a vein—not difficult considering how hard my blood was pumping. I sank the needle into my arm and felt the room turn liquid.

breath, sweat particles visible on his brow even through the bubble. I noticed that he had put on quite a bit of weight since the last time I had seen him, the macrobiotic mush that Eva fed him obviously full of useless fat that now sat on his jowls and chest.

There was a low whirr as part of the bubble mechanism settled beneath him and we came to a halt. Dmitri breathed asthmatically inside for a few moments, releasing himself from the straps and boots. The floor of the bubble was a four-foot square of tempered steel with a thin layer of some type of foam pasted onto it that, one through the intricacies of a small set of tracks that encircled the inside of the bubble, was always underneath him no matter how much the device rolled over on itself.

I sat on a stool by one of the workbenches, my hands clasping the front of the seat.

"Can I get you anything?" I asked my brother. I knew better than to expect him to take up any offers of food or drink but manners had been drummed into me by my mother on a deeply subliminal level.

"Nothing," Dmitri told me, breathing out long and hard, his chest finally settling. "It gets very hot in here."

"Perhaps you should consider putting the air vents back in," I suggested. He had removed the gauze strips that had once been at the top of the bubble to allow cool air in but had become paranoid about what other particles might find their way in and so had sealed himself completely. His air supply was now controlled by a rusted $O_2$ tank bolted to the bubble's iron bracework that had to be replaced every week or so.

Dmitri looked at me in that odd way only he could, a bizarre mixture of sheer terror and incomprehension. "That would not be a good thing," he said flatly, his voice watery and vacant once it had been filtered by his bubble.

The skin squeaked slightly against the porcelain tiles on the floor as he turned to Judas's cage next to him. The monkey was quiet and shrivelled inside, always a little wary of Dmitri's attention.

"He looks ill," Dmitri said, tilting his head in a way that would mean his breath would not steam the view in front of him.

"He's fine," I told him. "I take good care of him."

Judas moved a little closer to the bubble, poking one emaciated finger through the cage's bars and touching the skin tentatively. It stretched softly under the pressure and I could sense Dmitri's discomfort. It would take a lot more than Judas's gentle prodding to pierce that skin, I would imagine, but even the thought that he might be exposed to unfiltered air and the microscopic legions that lived within it was enough to make Dmitri withdraw.

I watched my brother cautiously, suddenly a little irritated at his presence—perhaps because of him questioning my ability to take care of Judas, perhaps something more.

"I didn't realise you would be visiting," I said.

"I have been on business in the west. My train stopped off nearby and I thought to visit you."

"There is a *train* running to our village again?"

Dmitri looked at me, puzzled. "Of course not. Brother, I live in the city now, everybody travels by train—even my children!"

He seemed delighted by the idea but I was not so sure. It didn't seem so appealing.

"Of course. I forget."

Dmitri looked over his shoulder at the bare wall where the Protohuman had been before I'd moved it to the O/R, at the shackles hanging out of the brickwork like dead worms or severed limbs. When he turned back to me there was a deeply sad look in his eyes, distinguishable even through the warp of his bubble-skin.

"It's in another room just now," I explained. "Do you wish to see?"

The sad look intensified. "No, Dziga. I do not."

Abruptly, I felt uneasy but was unsure of the logic of it. Something about my brother's presence, for the first time, had shaken me. Perhaps it was the hangover from the drugs I had taken a few days previously, or the distraction of what I had heard on the radio.

I guiltily glanced at the device sitting on the worktop beside us as if it were a black market lung that I had been caught with. I licked my dry lips.

Dmitri moved awkwardly around the counter top, pausing to read a scattering of equations and chemical formulae on the chalk board at the bottom of which, in large, thick lettering, was the number 101.6 I watched as he studied the scribbles, shaking his head.

"What is this? What are these formulae?"

"Mere scribbles," I lied. I felt unable to say anything just yet, even to my brother, about the messages. I hadn't mentioned my attempts to make contact with whatever chaotic forces guided me to either Dmitri or Jakobsen, preferring to keep that line of enquiry secret and safe until I knew where it would take me and because of this interruption I would have to wait even longer.

"How is Eva? And the children?" I asked him by way of distraction.

"Well," he replied, seemingly reluctant to draw himself away from the chalk board. "These seem familiar . . . "

"They are nothing, brother—I insist. At least nothing that should concern a mathematician of your calibre."

Dmitri's $O_2$ tank had a rubber hose that came out of its neck with a plastic mask on the end, now fixed firmly to his face. His breath steamed inside it, his eyes slow and heavy now and he cautiously took it away. A thread of beaded saliva was caught on his lip then snapped.

"I have a new job now, Dziga. I work for the Government. I travel all across the country."

He took another draw on the oxygen mask, droplets of sweat now visible on his forehead but I knew better than to offer him water or any other substance not first filtered and purified by his machines at home.

"I'm worried about you, brother," he said suddenly. He looked at me in the same way that he looked at a needle bleeding with the substance it contained.

"Why should you be worried?"

"Is this really want you want, Dziga? All this? The lab?"

I didn't fully understand his question. What was the alternative?

"You don't have to be here, you know. We could . . . arrange for something else."

"What else?"

"It doesn't matter. You could come to the city and live nearer me. I could look after you."

"But I am already looked after." The words left a slightly bitter taste in my mouth considering the feeling that had been growing inside me that although there were forces working with me there were those working against me. Perhaps I hoped to convince myself at the same time I would convince Dmitri.

"Brother, I have supported you as much as I have been able to. Long after mother burned all your belongings, long after the doctors left you cold and alone in their research halls. When your head was shaven and split. I try not to judge you, Dziga but I am worried about you."

"But I am closer now than I have ever been."

"Closer to what, Dziga? You can't go on harming yourself like this."

"I'm not harming anything, Dmitri—I'm helping."

I felt something beginning to sink inside me as if my brother's confidence in me was sliding into the mire in my chest. This was when I knew that I needed him, a thin strip of cartilage that kept the blood flowing between myself and the world.

"Do not worry about me, Dmitri."

When he looked at me, I knew he could see my resilience, or perhaps my desperation. My work was all that I had had for so long, if it had not been for that I dread to think where I might be now—and he knew this. Dmitri nodded wearily inside his bubble. A machine part lifted on one of the metal struts, clicked behind a small burst of steam. "Okay, brother. But I want you to know that at any time, any time, if you wish to get out of here, out from under Jakobsen's thumb, I will find somewhere else for you to go. There will always been somewhere safe to take you."

"I don't understand. Why would I . . . ?"

"You don't owe Jakobsen anything, remember. What he gives you, he gives you of his own choice."

"Jakobsen? But it was you who brought me to him."

"I know, I just . . . ." He came towards me, the plastic flesh pressing against me and it was warm. I believed I could see tiny translucent veins running through it, carrying watery, chemical blood. "I only ask one thing of you, brother—just be careful."

## Chapter Six
*Wherein Dziga returns to his work*

As soon as my brother had left, I had rushed back to the lab and turned the radio back on.

Static.

I was certain the dial was still at the correct setting but adjusted it anyway, searching for the voices I had heard before and whatever pirate broadcast was their source—but there was nothing. I reached the end of the dial then worked my way back again, slowing as I passed 101.6 yet there wasn't a single broadcast.

The whole thing was bland static!

I wondered if perhaps there was an electrical storm outside or a smog cloud that was causing interference but could see nothing through the bleary windows.

I switched the device off, silently cursing that Dmitri's unexpected intrusion might have caused me to miss my message.

Why had he come anyway? He usually informed me before he was going to visit, why not this time?

His sudden concern for my welfare puzzled me.

My own feelings of what others would term paranoia had become as much a part of me as leather restraints and powdery medication and certainly Dmitri was no stranger to it himself. However so far he had shown nothing but confidence in Jakobsen and my position in the lab—so why the change? Nothing had happened, nothing was different.

It certainly was curious.

However I had more important things to concern my time with for the foreseeable future.

And so for the next few days I worked with the blare of null radio transmissions in my ears as I listened for the voices again and went back over the newspaper clippings to see if there was anything I had missed.

*I didn't get the message* I whispered to the newsprint.

I continued to take readings and monitor the Protohuman's progress but with a certain level of distraction and, dare I say it, disinterest. Each procedure I carried out seemed to emphasize my feeling that my work should be moving on, that the next stage was awaiting me—and that in turn would bring me back to the radio and the message.

A terrible dread began to swell in me by the dawn of the third day that I truly *had* missed the message. I attempted to soothe myself by referring to the theory that a natural, chaotic system was repeated and reflected both microscopically and macroscopically and thus the message was *there* and could not be missed even if certain manifestations of it were.

And then it struck me.

Perhaps no further attempts at contact were being made because it had already been initiated—now it was my turn to reciprocate.

I pondered the idea as I prepared a snack for Judas and myself then selected one of the few newspapers that were still entirely intact, flipped through the pages until I reached the section *Advertisements—Personal*. It seemed logical to me that if contact had been started in newsprint then that would be the most efficient way to continue with it and as it seemed unlikely I would be able to place an article in the newspaper a personal advert would be the most sensible option.

Of course.

I ran my finger along the variety of messages and requests that lined the double-page spread, everything from assertions of love and/or hatred to thinly veiled calls for revolution from anarchist splinter groups to announcements of the sale of discounted hardware. It seemed like every human emotion and inspiration had been drained into a vat of ink and then stamped onto the paper.

At the very end of the spread was a black square with white text detailing the requirements for further adverts. It allowed up to 150 words for free and requested that details be telephoned in before 4pm to guarantee inclusion in the next edition.

There was a telephone in the lab but I had barely used it in all my time there. Although my fear of the machines had been assuaged by the doctors back at the hospital when I had been convinced that my every thought could be read by whom so ever might wish to listen, lingering doubts remained.

My mother had once said that no fear was irrational at heart, though it may manifest itself inaccurately, that fear was our spiritual reaction to danger that went far beyond instinct or learned reaction. I considered this as I stared at the phone, all that stood between myself and . . . and whatever lay ahead for me.

I couldn't.

I had taught myself to remain calm when it became necessary to contact either Jakobsen or Dmitri but to speak to a stranger? What if it *was* possible for them to see into my mind? At least Jakobsen and Dmitri already knew most of my thoughts—what good could come of someone I had never met read my thoughts? I shivered at the prospect.

I would have to ask one of them to do it for me. If they questioned my logic or motives I would just have to invent an excuse for I felt sure that neither of them should be privy to my attempts. Not yet, not until I knew more.

So I would code the message.

My first thought was that I would ask Dmitri, who would do anything for me and had certainly fulfilled some more abstract requests in the past, but I discarded this approach. I discarded it not because I felt like my brother had lost faith in my work as he had implied upon his last visit but that this would in fact be the perfect opportunity for me to test Dmitri's own misgivings—and in turn, those of my own.

*Could I trust Jakobsen?*

Later that night, after speaking with Jakobsen, I returned to the operating room and the Protohuman. Around us were portable drawer units of varying size, shape and build pulled close so as to remain within easy reach. The table was an adjustable one, such as you might find in a doctor's office, but the electrics had failed some time ago and the headpiece was stuck at a 35 degree angle. A large angle poise lamp loomed overhead like a curious carrion beast, only a few working bulbs remaining.

Metal trays flecked with rust sat on every surface, stacked high with bladed, spiked, pronged and toothed instruments. Wires grew out of some of them, connected to a main circuit set into the wall behind me, most of the sockets of which were black and charred, blown long ago.

The light from the lamp overhead was harsh and coated the Protohuman in a kind of glaze as if it were made of glass. I ran my fingers across the old-style leather restraints encircling the creatures' limbs and for a terrible moment I saw that it was I who lay on the table as Dr. Beveridge stood over me, about to place the electro-shock cap on my head.

*Tomophobia—fear of surgical operations.*

I pulled suddenly against my restraints. The Protohuman pulled against my restraints. Against its restraints. To get away from that cap. To get away from the memory of that cap.

I . . .

There was a sudden spark of electricity from the circuit and a blue-white line shot out in front of me like a heartbeat on a cardiogram. A small puff of smoke crept out of one the machines, lit neon green by a readout monitor and I quickly shut it off. It smelled like singed hair.

I left it for a moment as I gathered my bearings, feeling as if I had begun to float somewhere backwards at great speed before the power surge, then switched the machine back on.

Nothing.

I flicked the switch again—on, off, on, off.

Still nothing.

I mused that soon I would be stuck in a lab full of dead machinery and wet slops of rotting food, shook my head, left the room.

Jakobsen had agreed to place the advert for me when I had spoken to him. He had asked me several times to repeat the simple message that I had dictated to him for inclusion in the newspaper.

"Infinite mass," I had said. "Infinite reflection."

My benefactor hadn't asked me the purpose or meaning of the message, which both puzzled and relieved me. Relieved since I wouldn't have to lie about my first attempt at contact with the outside world., puzzled because I felt he *should* have been questioning me. Nonetheless he assured me the call would be made and also agreed to have that particular newspaper delivered to the lab every day for the next two weeks at least, longer if I requested it. I had made no mention of Dmitri's visit and had tried to appear as aloof as I possibly could in order to conceal my suspicions regarding Jakobsen I had also asked him not to mention this to anyone else, even my brother and he had again agreed without question.

I remained wary of his straightforward compliance but was willing to go along with it for now while it suited my needs—though cautiously.

Lets see how he fared against the forces of Chaotic logic if he indeed did wish to betray me.


The next morning the paper was delivered through a convoluted system of slots near the front door. Its arrival is announced by a series of thunks and metallic creaks and I waited until they had finished before retrieving it from a bin built into the wall.

I hurriedly took it through to the lab, glancing at the Protohuman who was once again chained to the wall, and spread it out on the worktop. I flipped to the adverts and after a brief scan located my own.

INFINITE MASS. INFINITE REFLECTION.

Just as I had requested.

I found myself smiling broadly for this was *progression*. I was still uncertain as to what we were progressing towards but it was progression nonetheless. Did this mean I could trust Jakobsen after all? Perhaps.

Perhaps the man had no grasp of what I had asked of him and complied through ignorance. His little mad pet acting up again.

Either way I would remain cautious. *Someone* had poisoned my food and there was only a limited number of people who would have access to my supplies and enough knowledge of myself and my work to make it worth their while trying assassinate me. Better, however, to appear ignorant to the attempts in the hope of encouraging my assailant to reveal themselves when they realised their failure thus far.

I returned to my work, trying to put aside my excitement at my engagement with whatever forces were working around-me with-me and how this might speed up the whole process, running another few assays I had plotted out previously to pass the time. Again such minutiae seemed inconsequential now but I felt it important to maintain my momentum as well as the appearance that my work was advancing as normal so as not to raise any suspicions.

I fed the Protohuman some of Judas' meat and left the radio on as I worked, fixed to the frequency of 101.6 though no voices returned. I checked the newspaper every morning right after it was delivered for three days. I studied the other adverts, not knowing exactly what I was looking for but feeling certain I would know when I found it.

On the first day I read and re-read proclamations of personal grievances, messages for secret society and religious sect members, lovers' requests and other meaningless drivel. I hadn't realised I had truly expected to have found a reply the very next day until my disappointment at not doing so collapsed on me like an architecturally faulty roof. I sat later that night as I was drifting towards sleep with my head clasped in my hands, staring down at the spread, desperate to find a response.

"I heard you," I said to the pages. "I listened like you asked and I heard you. Where are you now? What will you have me do?"

I was awakened on the second day by the noise of the latest paper being delivered and found myself still slumped over the previous one. I quickly rushed to the bin-contraption to recover it and just as I had done the day before, opened it on the adverts.

Again I scanned every advert, feeling my way through the random words and expressions for some sort of response but nothing, *nothing*. The page was cold to me.

I slammed my fist on the table.

Why were they not responding? It wasn't a case of whether those who would seek to contact me would read the paper or not because I knew these forces weren't as literal as that. I was in touch with them on another level—the level of Chaos and mathematics where universality applied and everything reflected everything else.

Dolls within dolls within dolls.

The radio remained on—and the broadcasts dead.

Silence.

In frustration I abandoned a small experiment I had begun the evening before to re-measure the Protohuman's pain threshold and burned the results so far, dropping the charred mess into a bin while Judas screeched excitedly in his cage. I prepared myself a hot protein drink that I filtered thoroughly using purely chemical ingredients and decided to take a break from my work.

I retired to the back room I had taken Jakobsen to and sat in the sofa chair, watching the steam rise from my drink. Each ribbon of moisture was unique, each twist and turn seemingly random but in fact utterly precise. The steam could not rise in any other way than it did.

I took comfort from this.

In lieu of anything else to do, I paged through the rest of the news-paper, trying to distract myself with stories of political riots and royal scandals. I was briefly entertained by a series of small articles on recent scientific innovations in the field of engineering and in addition ended up reading a piece regarding a group of makeshift surgeons who were performing increasingly radical operations on willing participants. They called themselves artists and the article spoke of a great building full of such creators working within a latticework of needles and blades. There was an accompanying photo of a male and female, both with penetrative, kohl-smeared eyes.

"There is infinite reflection in humanity," one of the group was quoted as saying, "and we hope to enhance that."

I smiled to myself even as I felt sleep begin to descend upon me. The Chaos thread truly did run through everything.

On the third time I was more leisurely when retrieving the paper.

The quote from the newspaper article had reassured me that whatever messages awaited me would, in time, reach me as they should and so on the first sweep I had actually missed the advert. It was only as I checked once again, almost ready to put the paper away and return to my studies, that it caught my eye.

It looked like a string of letters and numbers, utterly random like the fragments of a literary nail bomb and yet as I dragged my eyes slowly along its I spotted a sequence which almost seemed to glow before me.

C3H5N3O9.

Not random, of course, for nothing was random.

A chemical formula.

I looked backed at the chalk board, at the formula that had so interested Dmitri when he had visited.

$C_3H_5N_3O_9$.

My face flushed and I suddenly felt as if I was surrounded by creatures that I could not see nor hear nor smell, beings of another nature that were watching over me, breathing their words through the airwaves and into my test tubes.

Judas cried out from across the room.

I circled the advert with a pen and immediately set about with what I knew was the next step.

I mixed the compound quickly and easily, as if I had already done it one hundred times before.

For once I had all the materials I needed, both chemical and technological, and so it was a mere hour after I had first commenced work that I poured the grey-green liquid into a fresh hypodermic syringe.

I tidied the notes that lay on the counter, dropped some semi-thawed meat into Judas' cage [which he promptly ignored] then crouched before the Protohuman.

Its eyes were darker than I remembered, its facial bones more pronounced. It didn't seem to be responding particularly well to the cocktail of vitamins I had been feeding it since discovering that my food supplies had been contaminated but then I no longer thought that that truly mattered.

I held up the syringe before us and looked into the smeared, awkward liquid within. I imagined there to be one hundred thousand futures in there, each molecule a further letter in the words of guidance being handed to me.

The creature regarded with me with a strange expression that was somewhere between hurt and puzzlement as I pressed the needle into its arm and in that moment I believe we were so close, my creation and I, that I too experienced the stinging kiss of the metal and I had to grit my teeth as I forced the concoction into its veins.

I float, I float.

Move like the injection through the veins and arteries of air and chemical stench in the lab, everywhere at once. I stop and look down at my arm and a needle mark glows there as if my blood were phosphorous. The Protohuman holds out its arm to me, displaying a matching wound and the eyes of a homeless man about to be beaten senseless.

My body is mercury, dense and immoveable and yet constantly in motion, my bones swimming around inside me and I try to stand but it is a useless effort. I reach out to the Protohuman but though it reaches back my hand moves through its hand and I wonder if I am now a ghost, a discarded being.

*What is happening to me?*

The Protohuman leans back and takes its chains between its fingers, holding them up for me to see. Accusing me? It turns its wrists upright and shows me that there are no locks on the iron cuffs, that its bondage is a sham, and opens them one at a time. It discards the chains and stands before me, rising like a god, towering over me and it gives me its hand and I find that now I can stand, though unsteadily.

It is a foot taller than me and its chest broadens before my eyes. I can hear its mighty heart beating behind the bones of its rib cage.

I stare into its face and realise it has no features—no lips, no eyes, no nostrils, nothing. Its head is like an egg, like a clean palette.

And yet still it watches me.

"What is happening?" I ask it.

But I don't. I don't ask it.

I try to. I want to.

I can't speak.

I touch my face and its as if an electric shock has just jolted through me when I find that I too have no features. Panicking, I trace my entire head but find nothing. No bumps, no grooves, no indentations.

And the world goes dark for I can no longer see. I have no eyes.

I have no breathing orifices. I cannot breathe.

I am still holding the Protohuman's hand and I grip it suddenly as my lungs threaten to burst.

"Help me," I try to say but can't.


When the darkness receded and my vision returned I was lying sprawled on the floor of the lab.

I was able to move freely once again and as I picked myself up was horrified to find that the Protohuman was gone, its chains hanging limply from the wall like stripped DNA strands. I spun around, utterly disorientated, trying to hard-focus on the room as it blurred and re-blurred before me. I steadied myself on the worktop, tried to control my breathing.

Recalling my hallucinations, I ran my fingers across my face and was relieved to find that my eyes, nose, mouth were all intact. But if I had imagined it then where was the Protohuman?

By my foot was the syringe, the plastic chamber crushed and splintered and a small trickle of its contents pooled beside it.

I tried desperately to remember what I had done then noticed the chemical formula scrubbed on the chalkboard.

The newspaper.

The messages.

The radio.

My work.

I rushed out in the corridor, praying to see my creature lying on the ground or propped up against a wall, praying that it had not abandoned me.

Room to room.

And nothing.

Then a bang, the thump of metal. I stopped where I was, in the doorway of the storage cupboard I had earlier recovered the radio from and peered down the corridor.

*THUD.*

Coming from the door.

Someone was banging on the door.

I remained utterly still, noticing movement beyond the tiny, bleary window and my heart jack hammering in my chest.

*THUD.*

I started forwards, hesitated.

*Jakobsen* I thought to myself. *Jakobsen intercepted my messages and has now betrayed me. Drugged me and stole the Protohuman and now returned to finish me off.*

"Leave me!" I shouted as the thuds became louder, harder, faster.

I quickly looked around for a weapon but before I could find anything I heard the door's locking mechanisms undoing themselves just as the Protohuman had undone its shackles. I grabbed the first substantial implement I could find, a small claw hammer of the type I used to break up Judas' meat, and tried to conceal myself in the cupboard. As I closed my door, those who came for me opened theirs.

Theirs because there was clearly more than one of them from the sounds of their heavy footsteps echoing along the corridor. There was a pause as I imagined them to be peering into my main workshop and I heard Judas screeching terribly.

I would *not* allow my work to be vandalized like this!

As the footsteps began again, I raised the claw hammer ready to strike.

Outside the cupboard, they were *right outside the cupboard*!

I watched their devilish shadows sweeping across the crack of light by my feet and silently cursed them for what they were about to do and what they had already done.

The handle turned and I tightened my grip on the hammer.

Suddenly the door swung open and light spilled in and I lashed out and possibly hit something but in the same moment my arm was grabbed and I was torn from my the storage cupboard and pushed into the opposite wall. I collided with the hard concrete as my legs were held, then large hands pressed down on my shoulders and abdomen. The hammer was pulled from my immobilized hand as someone leaned over me.

At first I thought it was the Protohuman because of the clean-shaven head but then the face came more into focus. It glittered with piercings and a pair of bright green eyes. Its pate was covered with sprawled markings.

"Dziga," the face said. The man said.

He leaned back and I could see the rest of my assailants. They were both male and female but all had shaven heads and dark-smeared eyes.

"What do you want?" I asked them.

But they didn't answer.

Instead they pulled me to my feet and dragged me along the corridor, struggling to hold onto me as I kicked and lashed out at them but those that carried me were too strong and I shouted out for Judas as the open door got nearer and nearer.

Beyond, I glimpsed the billowing smoke of the factories and the razor-light of the heavy rain that was falling.

"NOOOO!" I screamed. "Please!"

My lungs began to close up in panic at the sudden realization that I might be taken from the security of the lab but no amount of struggling could break me free. I kicked and kicked and kicked and managed temporarily to get a leg free and block myself from going through the door but the limb was quickly recaptured.

My head was swimming with blood and dirty oxygen, lights flashing before my eyes and I felt unconsciousness descend on me like a vampire.


My life had been a series of cages, I mused. Some were bigger than the one before, some smaller.

Some dingier.

From my mother's womb to the steel cot to my bedroom to my first makeshift lab in an abandoned railway shack. From the local hospital to the asylum and from room to room in there. To my lab.

And now to a gurney in a vehicle of some sort.

My captors were huddled around me but appeared as nothing more than disfigured shadows in the darkness. I listened to the sound of the wheels thumping across whatever ground we were travelling and made the decision to remain still and quiet for now.

If they had simply wanted to kill me then they could have done so by now and I did not want to provoke them.

The vehicle come to an abrupt halt and once more I was gang-lifted out of the van's slide door. The gurney's wheeled legs snapped into place beneath me. I tasted the steely, rotten air but instead of the usual din of factorial machinations there was a near-silence that made me wonder if I had just been transported into some sort of industrial afterlife.

*They're taking me back to the asylum* I suddenly realized and *then* I started to struggle but the leather restraints around my wrists, neck, abdomen and ankles held me in place. I tried to call out but found that I couldn't speak, as if my vocal chords had been paralysed. Instead, my mouth flopped open and closed like a dying fish.

One of my captors leaned over me, a girl whose age was distorted by her shaven head and the tribal tattoo that crawled around her ear. She held a black-nailpolished finger to her similarly dark lips and motioned for me to be quiet and still.

With a desperate familiarity my vision was fixed straight up above me so that all I could see at first was the glittering, smoggy sky and the glare of the moon. This was quickly replaced by a corrugated metal roof with a strip-light set into it and we were moving again but vertically this time.

An elevator.

I tried to look around me as much as I possibly could but the restraints were too tight and soon my eyeballs ached from the effort. I caught glimpses of my kidnappers but nothing more.

The familiar mechanical sounds of great wheels turning against threads of thick wire echoed in my head and inside myself I was screaming to get out.

A bell rang and then I was being wheeled along another corridor but what I saw above me was nothing I had seen from the asylum. In my years there I had come to memorize what I imagined to be a large proportion of my former prison from my corpse's point of view, though of course I had no idea of how much bigger the building might have been. For all I knew I could have been restricted to a small wing yet it felt as if I had been wheeled through every inch of the place.

Above me now, however, was not the endless patterns of stained white and cold blue tiles, the rusted pipes and loose electric cabling but a solid mesh that allowed me to glimpse the levels above us. From the noise the gurney made I suspected the floor beneath us was of the same construction, as if the entire building was merely an architectural sketch, unfinished and exposed, the railings and struts a fine skeletal bonework.

I could see people moving around up there as high as three floors or more if I squinted.

*What was this place?*

Often my view was blocked by large pieces of equipment that haemorrhaged wires from their undersides or furniture that was wrapped in plastic. I heard the noise of medical equipment, the buzz of electricity.

Finally we came to a stop and the gurney was snapped into place in holding blocks. My captors shuffled around me, turned on a great white light and shone it down upon me.

I was blinded by its luminescence until one of them leaned over me, silhouetting himself.

"Welcome, Dziga," he said softly. "We've been eager to meet you."

## Chapter Seven
*Wherein the Chaos forces make themselves known*

I held the cup of water in my hands but did not drink from it. Most poisons were invisible.

My restraints had been undone, one end of the gurney tilted so that I sat upright and my captors were gathered around me just as the doctors and research students used to be. They all wore dark clothes with sleeves that came past their wrists and had small holes in them which their thumbs emerged through. Their shaven heads glistened in the stark lighting that spilled in through the latticed ceiling and floor, their curious tattoos like living creatures.

Behind them a woman shuffled around amongst a series of cabinets attached to the wall. She wore a tight white latex uniform and stockings, heavy cream-heeled platform boots and I glimpsed a large red cross just below her breasts.

"We've been reading through some of your notes, Dziga," one of them said. He held a small stack of curling, worn papers and I recognized my own writing.

I found myself following the wiry pattern of his tattoo around his skull and over his ears then down his neck. Spiralling.

A Chaos spiral.

I glanced at the others and found similar patterns in their tattoos.

"Do you have instructions for me?" I asked them.

"Instructions?"

"A message. Directions. For my work."

The man paused, laid down the papers.

"We were hoping that perhaps *you* could direct *us*."

I regarded them cautiously, still uncertain of why they had taken me and what their intentions were. Their interest in my work was logical both if they were summoned by whatever Chaos energies inspired me and if they were part of a conspiracy to steal my work. I would not allow myself to be intimidated or take advantage of either way.

"What have you done with the Protohuman?"

"It's safe," a girl said, stepping forward. Her eyes glittered amongst the kohl like gems embedded in coal.

"You have it?"

"It's safe," the male repeated. "We're here to help you, Dziga."

"How?"

"That's what we need you to tell us."

"I don't understand."

They didn't appear to be armed but the fact was they had forcefully removed me from my lab and brought me here. The room had only one window but I knew we had come up at least a couple of floors, having used the elevator, and therefore I couldn't be certain of the safety of the drop if I tried to escape. In addition, all impressions I got of the building were that it was huge, from the endless echoes of distant machinery and human babble to the production-line quality of the interior's construction, and I knew it would be next to impossible for me to get out that way.

The man leaned close and I thought I saw his tattoo squirming on his pate. "The airwaves, Dziga. We listened to them too."

My eyes widened and some of my fears distilled. "It was you on the radio?"

The man shook his head. "No, it wasn't us. But we heard. It spoke to us too."

"Who *was* it?" I asked, sitting up with sudden interest.

"We aren't certain," the girl said. Behind her, the fetish nurse finished what she was doing and left the room, closing the door delicately behind her. I could hear her footsteps for almost a minute after she left, like distant gunfire.

"There's something else out there, isn't there? Something guiding us?" I asked them. My excitement grew not just because I was now more able to relax regarding their intentions but also because my theories were being confirmed.

"We believe so," another of the males said carefully. He was shorter and stockier than the first, with broad lips and a tongue piercing that glistened in his wet mouth as he spoke. "We believe we have been brought together because the time has come for us to combine our abilities."

"You are scientists, too?"

"Of a sort," the first male said, placing a hand on my shoulder as I began to sit up. "Please, stay where you are, Dziga."

"Why? I don't understand. What is this place?"

A look was exchanged between those gathered around me that made my excitement waver momentarily.

"Our paths have crossed. Our work has crossed. Independently we have been working towards the reinvention of the human species—an evolution."

"*Yes*," I responded enthusiastically. "My work . . . I have been making some great progress lately!"

"As have we. We are part of the collective that established and runs this building but our work diverged some months back when we received our first message."

"What is the nature of your work?"

"Simply put, modification of the body to enable modification of the species. We started like all the others in this building, working for purely aesthetic reasons. But then the messages began and since then we have been experimenting, going further."

"You are no longer restricting yourself to aesthetics?"

"The exact opposite, in fact," the girl said. She looked no older than nineteen and as she slid herself alongside the men I saw that the tattoo spiralled off her shaven head and reappeared upon her stomach where the tight-fitting black garments she wore separated and exposed flesh.

"Aesthetics are the key to our work," the larger man began. "What we see is the key to what we are."

"But sight is just one sense. The new human species should evolve from ALL senses and introduce new ones!"

"No, Dziga. Our work says that this is not true. There is only one sense, it merely functions on several levels. Reality need only register on one of these levels for it to permeate throughout all of them."

"A Chaos spiral," the young girl said, lifting her t-shirt to expose her stomach further and tracing the unending curve of the tattoo that swarmed around her belly button. "Everything is the same."

I nodded for it *made sense*. "The perfection of Chaos is that it was too simple for us to understand, not that it is too complex."

"Exactly. Rationalisation is merely the removal of all perceptions of reality except for the sole true one. Our work is not to create—but to *un*create."

My heart pounded with the excitement of this sudden clarity. It was as if someone had revealed to me the value of an unknown variable in a simple but solvable equation. The answer was perfect and precise.

"We're here to help you with the Protohuman, Dziga," the bulkier man said, moving closer.

"Help me? How?"

"Uncreation," was the reply.

"I don't understand."

They moved closer to me and I felt myself leaning back further into the bed to maintain our distance.

"As we said, sound, image, touch—they are all a manifestation of a single sense, a single emotion. If we change one, we change them all."

"Change how?"

I found myself looking at the exits once more as they drew in around me.

"Uncreation, Dziga. You have created an identity for the Protohuman. We must undo that."

"Identity? I don't . . . "

My feet were grabbed again and my restraints reapplied. I couldn't see who by.

"I won't let you touch the Protohuman. It is *my* work."

"It is *not* your work. It is beyond any of us. And we already have the creature."

I tried to sit up but they forced me prone, one large hand slamming down on my chest and my wrists were placed in bondage once more. I saw the young girl pull on a pair of black latex gloves that went up to her elbows and pick up a needle filled with a substance that looked the same as the one I had been told to mix. She sparked the needle, throwing a small spray of the liquid into the air.

"Leave it alone!" I barked, pulling desperately at the restraints. "I won't let you touch it!"

The bulkier man leaned over me. "We don't need your permission, Dziga. This goes beyond us. We don't need your permission, we don't need Jakobsen's permission, we don't need *any* of it."

I screamed as the girl shoved the needle into my chest and all I saw as consciousness faded was the movement of other modification artists moving around above me. My vision blurred and I watched one of them kneel on the grating and peer down at me.

Lab coat and greying, frizzy hair.

He looked just like Dr. Denovich from the asylum had.

## Chapter Eight
*Wherein Dziga realises Jakobsen's betrayal and decides to act on it*

As I stared back at myself in the reflective surface of a handheld mirror I ran my fingers across what the Engineers had left of my face. It was smooth, abnormally flat where my nose had been, and thick like old scar tissue. My eyes were sunken black holes, my mouth a sunken red one. My ears were ragged, raw at the edges.

This wasn't me I was looking at.

This was someone else. Something else.

I had no recollection of the procedure, nor of being returned to my lab. I was filled with vague, blurry memories like the images that clouds form if you look at them long enough, little sparks of recall jolting me every now and again. The rumble of their van mixed with the hum of drills that I might or might not have been conscious of as they worked on me. Their chatter, their whispered arguments about where to make the next cut and how deep to go splintered with the drum of my own heartbeat.

I remembered a diagram.

Shining metal implements.

My face throbbed rhythmically, the open flesh successfully coagulated now and whatever substance they had put on it soothing the pain. I could still feel my nerves burning just beneath the skin of translucent gel, menacing me with a pregnant agony.

Had I felt the pain at the time?

I remembered our discussion. I remembered the bonds. I remembered nothing.

I stared down at the Protohuman, prostrate on my OR's gurney before me and it reflected my own disfigurement. It too had a face full of scar tissue and blood, its features reduced to anonymous concaves and a pair of dull eyes peering back at me from dark pits.

Had they operated on us both one by one? Or both together in harmonious mutation?

A blood bubble formed and burst on the edge of the Protohuman's mouth where its lips used to be. I held out one of the painkillers I has recovered from a broken bottle in one of my supply cupboards but it wouldn't open its mouth to take one. I hadn't taken any either.

I did not know what the Engineers had intended by doing what they had, though I had spent most of the three hours since I had regained consciousness analysing going over it.

We had come together so that our concurrent research projects could combine, that was clear, but I was still unconvinced as to the intentions of the forces that did so. In equal place in my mind was the idea that this could either have been a sabotage attempt upon me and/or my work and the idea that this was the necessary breakthrough for my creature and I to achieve mutual evolution.

And then there was a third option—perhaps it was both.

Like one of the Engineers had said, this was beyond any of us. This wasn't in our control.

Perhaps there *had* been a betrayal that had been partially stifled by the forces controlling the Protohuman's development, a conflict of desires that entwined with one another and resulted in the outcome that I now stared at in the mirror. God and Nature and Man all battling with one another.

And all over my beautiful creature.

As I leaned over it, some of the analgesic gel dripped from my face, a small lick of pain bubbling where it had fallen from.

I smiled, if it could still be called that, and picked up the small stack of papers laying on the instruments tray. The sheets were crumpled and water-rippled, stained with fingerprints of dried blood from when I had looked at them earlier. Most were scribbled notes but alongside them were sketches of the human face and its musculature. I had made them whilst back in the asylum and possibly in the midst of a course of shock therapy treatments and they had somehow made it into one of the many boxes of my papers that Jakobsen had brought into the lab for me.

And had been there ever since.

I flipped through the pages until I was about halfway through them then stopped. Before me was a tracing of a male face from a physiology textbook. The features had been etched out with variously nibbed pens and alongside it, some scribbles.

*A focal stage in our species' evolutionary genesis will be the shedding of identity, for if each and every being is operating at the best possible levels of efficiency then there will be no need for it any more.*

And next to it.

*Individuality is an inefficiency.*

I had forgotten about the notes until soon after coming to, my reflection instantly triggering a recognition with a train of thought had been lost inside me for years. I had established the concept along with so many others during the process of my investigations, an infinite mass of tangled threads, knotted and spiked like barbed wire wrapped around a prisoner of war, and yet somehow this particular strand had emerged of its own free will.

Except there *was* no free will.

There was only the machinations of the universe.

Or the machinations of humans.

My collaboration with the Engineers was, I am sure, a definitive moment in the production of the Protohuman and yet I also felt certain that something else had taken place. Just as the Engineers, or the Chaos forces, or whomever, had sent me messages through the newspapers and the radio now I was being sent another message.

A threat.

And that threat must have come from someone who had access to obscure scribbles that had been locked away for so long that even I had forgotten about them. The notes had been confiscated and no doubt analysed by the doctors at the asylum and then packed away with the rest of my work, stored until my release therefore it could only have been someone from the hospital—or the man who had acquired the release of myself and my work.

*We don't need Jakobsen's permission*, the bulky Engineer had said.

Later I sat at my workbench in near silence, the only sounds that of the radio whispering empty static like cosmic blood flow and the occasional dripping of a tap. Judas was curiously quiet around me now, contemplating me somewhat fearfully, reaching out to touch me a couple of times before retracting hurriedly. He seemed fascinated by the slow movement of blood and gel across my non-face.

I listened to see if any more messages would assemble themselves for me but had decided that whatever process had been initiated by the previous rounds of contacts had now finished. For now, I was left to work alone again.

I thought of the Engineers and wondered if they had returned to their own experiments, their work now accelerated as mine had been. I imagined them to be stripping the faces from many more subjects, piling up useless pieces of flesh in a plastic bucket.

I had treated the Protohuman's raw features several times with antiseptic gel to keep it clean, stroking the substance on and admiring its new beauty as if it were my own. And, of course, it *was* my own.

The Protohuman and I were brothers and that was how it should be. Two completely different creatures moving closer and closer to the same strata of perfection.

I would not allow anything to stop me now.

Jakobsen's intention must have become entangled with those of the forces directing my work and what had resulted from this conflict was a mixture of the two. The development of the Protohuman required that it lose its identity but my own disfigurement was never part of the plan. Or not part of my plan.

And yet now that it had occurred it seemed like it was a vital part of the experiment.

I felt incredibly calm at the realisation that this betrayal—an attempt at murder, or sabotage, or perhaps just vicious assault—had become assimilated into the Protohuman project, had become a further advancement of it. It had taught me that the Protohuman and I should evolve simultaneously and it taught me that I was being watched over by something more powerful than mere jealousy or hatred or whatever it was that Jakobsen sought to betray me for.

I stroked the Protohuman's non-features, as bloody as my own.

Jakobsen must have intercepted my messages somehow, even if he hadn't been able to understand them. He might have been able to decipher enough to allow him to act, perhaps realising just how far my work was coming, perhaps feeling able and ready to steal the project from me and have it completed by some other rogue hack. Or even to let it complete itself.

I looked at Judas, curled awkwardly on the floor of his cage, one scabby arm hanging out from between the bars. He had seemed fine up until a few hours ago but now his breathing was laboured, his pupils fully dilated and I thought once more of the poisoned food.

Jakobsen had given me the supplies, along with everything else in the lab.

And everything he had given to me, he could take away.

Or so he thought.

So I called him and requested that he visit me.

And this is what happened.


I sat at my workbench, nervously working my hands as my chemicals bubbled around me. Laid out before me was the small canvas bag that I had been given by one of the many men that come to us after Nadia had killed herself. When unrolled it revealed a set of polished scalpels and surgical instruments, the kind the travelling doctors that visited our town every so often would carry. They were all rusted now and there were several gaps where instruments had been lost or broken beyond repair. One, however, remained well-maintained. I removed it from its holder, letting the light of the Bunsen flame lick across it, then placing it next to the syringe I had looked out earlier.

It had been Jakobsen's machine that had answered my call the day before. I had left a brief message, relieved that I wouldn't have to talk to the man. I had had my script written out because I had never been good at improvisation. I needed time to plan, to prepare for every eventuality. There was nothing that couldn't be solved by the implementation of simple or extensive calculations.

I looked up as Judas suddenly hissed from within his cage, slumped against the metal. He didn't seem to be getting any worse the past few hours, implying the doses of poison that had been injected into my food supply had been small enough to need repeated ingestions over a long period of time. So this betrayal had been a well thought-out, planned affair meant to escape my attention.

And as I sat there, as I had been sitting there, I began shifting around the particular variables involved in this little sum. Side to side. Positive to negative.

Jakobsen and Dmitri, the Protohuman, blood, poison, honour and scientific integrity. And theft.

My face itched beneath the thick layer of petroleum jelly and I mused that although I might have been moving towards the nu-evolution for now I continued to bleed like a normal, deficient man and needed help to get through the healing process. I traced a finger along the ridges where my eyebrows once were, tongued the hole that was my mouth as I listened to the crunching footsteps of someone approaching the lab through the thick layers of hard snow that had fallen. Judas began whining and got to his feet as there was a knock on the door.

I placed the syringe and the scalpel in my lab coat pocket. Drops of sweat had formed on the back of my neck and hands. I moved slowly into the hallway and saw the outline of my visitor through the mesh that covered the small window at the top of the front door.

"Who is it?" I stood well back as I asked, the question fully aware of all that was around me as I had been since the Engineers had opened my eyes.

"Dziga? It's Jakobsen. I came as quickly as I could."

I studied the man's shadow through the glass, fingered the scalpel in my pocket, then began removing the locks on the door. I refrained from opening for a moment, stepping back. A second passed then the massive steel hinges creaked as Jakobsen entered the lab.

"Dziga."

I stood directly in front of him as he emerged from behind the door, the bare bulbs that lit the passageway throwing a sick light across me.

"Dziga what . . . *dear God* . . . "

The colour drained from his face, his knuckles whitening as he gripped the door.

I said nothing, just stood there.

Let him see me. Let him see what he had done to me. I knew this was all a ploy, part of his little game. I would play along with him—for now.

"Dziga your . . . your *face*. What has happened? What have you done to yourself?"

A globule of petroleum jelly dropped from my chin and spattered against the floor. "Would you care to join me?" I asked, my words slurring slightly due to my newly-reconfigured features. I turned from him calmly before he could answer me, hands in my lab coat pockets, and strolled into the workshop. The heat from the Bunsen burners washed over me and I could almost feel it drying my skin. There was a pause then I heard Jackobsen come after me.

He gripped his briefcase in both hands, unable to take his eyes from me.

Did he know they were going to do this to me? Did he ask for this specifically? From his reaction, for I do not believe the man to be that good an actor, I surmised that his instructions to the Engineers, if that had been the nature of his interference as I believed it had been, were vague enough to allow them to be creative. He wasn't even decent enough to take a personal interest in my disfigurement.

"Thank you for coming so quickly," I said to him, then gestured at the workbench. "Please, sit."

He hadn't looked at the Protohuman yet, seemingly entranced by me. I tapped the stool beside me to encourage him.

In the corner of the room, Judas battered the side of his cage wearily. The skin on his arm had peeled away in places where he had been scratching himself.

"Everything is fine," I assured Jakobsen. I was distantly beginning to enjoy this game now that I felt I had control. "Let me explain. Please, sit."

Jakobsen's eyes ran all over me. "I'll stand. If you don't mind."

I shrugged. "I've made some tea. Would you care for some?"

"Tea?! Dziga, what is this!?"

I looked at him suddenly and immediately he shut up.

I lifted the jug I had filled with herbal tea and poured it into a beaker then held it up for him. He took it from me somewhat dreamily, making sure not to touch my hand and I began to realise how this simple alteration of my outward self had completely altered me entirely in his eyes. What was I now, to him? What had he meant me to become when he ordered the Engineers to operate on me?

I was truly a creature of science.

"Drink it," I told him.

He stared down at the beaker, seemed to consider the liquid inside it.

"Go on."

He shot me a look and then put the beaker back down on the bench as quickly as his enforced calmness would allow. He wasn't expecting this confrontation, wasn't expecting me to have figured out what he was up to. But I'm no puppet.

He thinks he could just come here to *gloat*?!

"Dziga, I'm worried about you. I think maybe . . . "

Of course he wouldn't drink the tea. He was proving to me that he knew every foodstuff in the lab was tainted. I shook my hand at him. "There is no reason to worry. The experiment is coming along beautifully."

"It's not the experiment that concerns me."

"Really. Then perhaps you would do well to cease interfering."

"Interfering? I don't understand."

"The Engineers."

He looked at me blankly. "What . . . Engineers?" he stuttered.

I remained silent.

"I spoke to your brother, Dziga. He is very concerned for you."

I smiled inwardly. "How so?"

"I think I was wrong to bring you here. I don't think you were ready."

I felt anger rise inside me. Not only was he trying to undermine my experiment but he was also planning to put me back in the hole he took me from. I could see it so clearly now, the depth of his betrayal. He has been using me all this time, removing me from the asylum purely to begin the development of the Protohuman so that he could steal it from me when it was near completion.

I was indebted to no one. He had tricked me.

"So that is your plan? Not to kill me but to force me back into the asylum?"

"Kill you? Dziga, I would never . . . "

"Of course not, not yourself." I smiled, waved the air as if to clear this line of thought. Take my time. "I've had a small breakthrough in my work," I said, watching steam rise from the tea. "Would you like me to tell you about it?"

Jakobsen was shaking his head, his features creased in mock-sorrow. "Dziga, please—don't you see that the project isn't what matters to me? I brought you here so you could get *better*. Perhaps I did the wrong thing."

"No, no, Mr Jakobsen, don't diminish what we are accomplishing here. I think my work was *exactly* why you brought me here. Tell me, have you got others ready to finish the project once I am out of the way?"

His fingers flexed around the briefcase handle. He flinched as Judas suddenly screeched for one quick moment. I was aware of how the petroleum jelly would give the illusion of my face squirming wetly on top of my skull.

"This is the face of your betrayal," I told him.

"What betrayal? Dziga, please . . . "

He stepped forwards and I retreated equally from the desk, ready to see the glint of a knife or perhaps even a pistol. His plan was falling apart, he knew now that he wouldn't be able to convince me to go back to that place, no matter how scared he might make me.

"So are you ready to finish the job yourself? Are you willing to get your hands dirty with my blood?"

"Your *blood?* Dziga, this is all wrong. Please, let me help you."

He dropped the briefcase and started towards me but before he could draw his weapon I had drawn mine. I threw myself at him without a thought for what I was doing, both of us tumbling backwards and crashing into a stack of culture plates overgrown with spores. As we hit the ground I thrust the syringe into the soft flesh at the back of his neck. Blood sprayed at me in one quick gush and he cried out. I grabbed him by the hair as he arched upwards, then slammed his face back down to the hard flooring.

"Dziga . . . !"

Spoken through crushed teeth and spittle.

"You will *never* take the Protohuman away from me!" I shouted at him, slamming his head down again.

Judas began screeching in his cage, rattling around in excitement, the supporting pole crashing to the ground. Did he smell the blood? Could he taste my violence?

I slammed Jakobsen's face into the floor again, my rage mutating into something more beautiful just as I and the Protohuman were too. Judas shrieked, his cries accompanied by the creaking metal of his cage, as it swung freely and Jakobsen struggled as if in slow motion beneath as I twisted the syringe in his neck. He coughed blood at the broken shards of the culture plates.

"*Dziga, please . . .* "

There was an almighty crash and Judas went silent but I didn't look back, just kept slamming Jakobsen's collapsing head into the concrete. His blood flew in bright strands through the air each time I pulled his head back for another strike. He wriggled and almost got loose, pulling away enough for the syringe to be pulled from my grip, wedged in his neck. I sat back, letting him crawl out of his own bodily fluids and reached calmly into my pocket for the scalpel.

I put the blade to his neck then looked up as I glimpsed something out of the corner of my eye. Judas was sitting on the floor, free of the cage he had torn from its holding in the ceiling, and was lurking behind one of the benches, notably perplexed by his freedom. His weary, milky eyes watched me in return as I took Jakobsen's hair in my hands and exposed his neck, placed the blade against it.

"Welcome to freedom, Judas," I said, then drew the scalpel across my betrayer's throat.

Jakobsen jerked for a few moments, then his struggles stopped. I let him drop back onto the fragments of plastic plates as Judas emerged cautiously from behind the workbench.

"Go on," I told him, panting from my exertion. Jakobsen's blood dripped from my new face. "Go!"

He jumped at my shout, sprinted past me and out into the hallway. I listened to the sound of his elongated nails skittering across the hard floor and his wild squawking confusion, the thuds of him crashing into the walls on limbs that hadn't been used in years.

And then stared down at Jakobsen's corpse, slumped beneath me.

I stood and watched his blood congeal before my eyes, time accelerating like a heartbeat during a cardiac arrest and imagined that if I stood there long enough I would see him turn to maggots and then dust.

What have I done?

Another blob of pinkish gel dropped from my face to the ground beside Jakobsen's corpse, exploding as it hit the growing puddle of his blood.

*What have I done?*

His tongue was swollen in his mouth, emerging like a fat purple bug from between bluish lips.

Eyes bulbous and blank and staring right at me.

They'll come for me, I suddenly realised. Jakobsen must have had others helping him in this conspiracy against me [his interference with the Engineers confirmed that] but I had no idea the extent to which this might be true.

Judas' cries echoed through the long corridors of the lab as he desperately tried to come to terms with a world in which you couldn't see the bars of your cage and my mind raced with his frenzied rampage from room to room.

Jakobsen was a clever and devious man to have tricked me thus far and I knew he would not have come alone to my lab, my little cage, without some sort of back up plan. I didn't know who or when they would come but I felt certain that I would not get away with Jakobsen's murder. I began pacing the lab, shouting at Judas to stop his screeching as I tried to formulate a plan. My face itched terribly, the petroleum jelly slipping from me as if my features were once again melting away in some further step of my evolution.

I couldn't go. I couldn't leave.

No matter how dangerous it might be for me to stay I couldn't even begin to contemplate going outside, into the fumes, the crowds, the infections. They would find me there, as I stumbled from street to street to street, find me and destroy me because of the power of my work and what I was creating. And even if I were to leave, how would I be able to take the Protohuman with me? He was growing weak since I had avoided feeding him anything but intravenous vitamins which I had scavenged from my chemical supplies. Most of the time he just hung on his chains, his face dripping onto the floor in front of him in little clumps of bloodied jelly.

I would have to act now.

I hurried to one of the back rooms and pulled out several sheets of thin, battered steel that I had attempted to use with the now non-functioning x-ray machine my benefactor and betrayer had endowed me with. I heard Judas down the hall, no longer screeching as he hunted in the cracks in the walls for insects to feast on, and dragged the sheets into the corridor. I began to seek out anywhere and everywhere that could be a potential entry point and bolt the sheets over them with a nail gun—the door and windows of course, the cracks around the rim of the front door, vents, ducts.

What else? *What else?*

As I worked I cycled through the different fates Jakobsen might have in store for me. Might they already be waiting for me, the assassins and thugs he had no doubt arranged? As I shut myself in I kept expecting to see their lurid faces peering back at me through the dirty glass, or their skittering shadows tracing the walls as they came to finish the job.

I listened. I listened.

Judas skittered around me, occasionally flashing past a doorway or appearing at the end of the corridor before disappearing again.

My heart rate increased with each minute that passed, a biological pulse that manifested itself on my face like a wet lung.

The windows, all shut off. The door, barricaded.

The water supply, a tank sealed within a metal holding at the rear of the building. I severed the supply pipe, limiting myself only to the water that was already in the storage chambers and pipes within the lab.

As the lab was originally a war bunker the roof was constructed of foot-thick concrete slates and thus there was little threat from above, except for the cracks that lined the space in between the slates—through there long needles could be poked as I walked by, a sudden injection of thorazine into the soft flesh of my skull or a fishing hook to sink into my . . . .

For the most part I found myself steering clear of the walls and knew that if they really wanted to, my killers could probably burst through the ageing stonework. I began walking down the middle of the corridor, placing my feet one in front of the other so as to retain as tight a line as possible.

I stopped to watch Judas crouched at the end of the corridor, picking at the loose brickwork and occasionally feeding himself one of the creatures. I approached him cautiously, careful not to frighten him off, cooing gently to him.

"What have you got there, Judas?" I asked, kneeling beside him, still wary of the walls.

I noticed that he had injured the side of his face, probably from a collision as he dashed around the place after his release. His lip twitched and he sucked on the end of one finger, removing the mushed remains of a winged insect. His eyes were wide and white.

The monkey poked his finger into the crack in the wall again, shoving it in all the way and rummaging around. And as I leaned closer I could hear the scratching coming from beyond the wall, the sound of a hundred little insects rhythmically moving around.

Click. Click. Click

My chest hurt from my swollen heartbeat, my controlled breathing.

Click. Click.

Judas drew his finger back out and with it brought a long stringy insect which he promptly placed between his teeth and began to suck on. Almost immediately he spat it back out, screwing up his face in distaste.

"No good?" I asked him, smiling and reaching for the regurgitated creature.

And when I looked down at it in the palm of my hand, blood rushed through my face, stinging the ravaged surfaces.

It was no insect.


Judas looked on as I examined what he had pulled from the wall as if he were having second thoughts about his interest in the thing. He reached out to take it back but I quickly withdrew and snapped at him.

I raised my hand towards the light.

Electrical wire.

Thin, insulating wiring, the kind used for small electrical appliances.

It was broken at one end from where Judas had torn it out but the other end was intact. There were small indentations and scrapes there, the marks of it having been held in place and then dragged out.

Hesitantly, I leaned towards the hole Judas had burrowed or found and peered in.

I heard the sound of the insects again but this time it was plain to me that it was not the scutter of arthropods, instead the clicks and whirrs of some sort of mechanical system.

But *what* kind?

I stared deep into the hole and noticed something glinting in the very depths of the darkness.

And, as I stared, a light blinked.

A mechanical scraping accompanied it and then the whirr of some parts moving.

My breath caught.

A camera.

I was staring at the lens of a video camera.


My mind began to reel, suddenly aware that the extent of my betrayal went far beyond what even my fevered mind had dreamed up. I had been watched all along. My every move, recorded.

My. Every. Move.

I suddenly jerked back from the hole as if I could somehow undo this event if I rejected it quickly enough but I knew it was not to be. I collapsed back against the opposite wall, Judas returning to his excavations now that I was finished with his find.

There were these sorts of cracks throughout the lab, always had been. Jakobsen had apologised upon my arrival and had offered to have them filled and like the idiot that I was I refused. He was mocking me, even then.

From behind my head, more mechanical noises and I jerked back away from that wall too.

I had been right to fear the walls but not because of the insects.

There were no bugs—at least none of the biological kind—and never had been.

All this time I had been listening to the sounds of a monitoring system and I *hadn't even realised it*!

How *stupid* I have been.

And then a thought occurred to me.

If they have been watching me all along, then they will be watching me now. They will have seen me murdering Jakobsen for certain—and for certain there would be some form of retribution.

I scrambled to my feet and ran towards my main lab, stumbling around in the tight corridor, trying to keep away from the walls and then colliding with the doorframe as I entered the lab.

But that wasn't safe either.

I could hear them, now the cameras. Everywhere.

I ran back down the corridor, past Judas and around the L-shaped bend towards the rear of the building and I wanted to run so much further because with each step I felt the watchful eye of a camera lens. I felt them following me as I ran from room to room, opening door after door and then quickly retreating again as I realised that nowhere was safe.

I turned, turned, turned, each time fully expecting a set of hands to grab me or a blade to bite into me.

I screamed out loud.

Judas hollered back and poked his head around the corner, screeched at me.

I then jumped in the first doorway I could find, a mostly empty room that contained only a battered old desk that I never used and wall-mounted blackboards stacked in one corner, slammed the door shut behind me, reducing the light to the single bulb that hung from the ceiling, casting a dirty, ugly glow.

Still the whirring and clicking!

I threw myself under the desk, squeezing myself into the gap as tightly as I could and pulling the chair back in front of me. I knew I was not safe, I knew this, they would come for me now that I had discovered their surveillance—but I had to escape.

My face was stinging all over, throbbing with the flow of the fresh, bright red blood trickling from behind the healing scabs and I screamed again, rocking myself in that tiny gap, rocking, rocking, rocking.

And still the clicks and whirrs.

I read;

*Zeusophobia*—Fear of God or gods. And I was hiding in a coal bunker alongside the rail tracks that would soon claim the life of my sister, hiding because Dmitri had had another attack and the house was filled with strange men with all sorts of contraptions that they wished to make my brother a part of.

I read;

*Hematophobia*—Fear of blood. And I was amidst a group of children staring down at the corpse of a man beaten to death in a pub brawl by some of our fathers, too scared to touch him and yet utterly rapt by the congealing blood and internal pieces that were leaking out of him.

I read these in the notebook that had been locked in the bottom drawer of the desk, the key to which was, as always, in my pocket. I recited them one by one, and as each turn of the page and new phobia was spoken aloud so too was the dirty, smog-ridden childhood that had bred and taught me. The diary of my own youthful evolution.

I had barely looked at it at all since leaving the asylum, the first time I had been allowed access to personal items since I had been admitted to the first institution all those years ago—but I felt the need to ground myself in a reality of my own choosing while so much of that which was defined by others fell away.

All those times, all those memories, all the fears in the world scribbled down in that book with a scientific explanation for their occurrences neatly written out beside – exact, dissective phrases that peeled away the appendages of the phobias and left nothing but a harmless, dead carcass.

It was the only thing that seemed to help calm me any more in lieu of drugs and that it did. Finally I felt oxygen reaching my lungs as if it were water balming a dried throat and my eyes gradually ceased bulging in their sockets.

I remained under the desk as I had for perhaps several hours now, just waiting for the door to open and Jakobsen's co-conspirators to arrive for me and yet they did not come. I listened for the sounds of their footsteps or of the metal sheets I had secured over the doors and windows being peeled away.

But nothing.

What were they waiting for?

I considered that perhaps they were content with watching me slowly wither away in here, wrapped in my own spiralling panic, just as they had contented themselves with watching me murder Jakobsen without doing anything to stop me. Was my mentor nothing more than a bit-player in this tragedy? Could it be that the man I had believed to have been the master of this conspiracy was nothing more than a lamb sent to the slaughter? A sacrifice?

There was no way to tell how far this struggle for my work reached.

My work.

The Protohuman.

In my panic, I had left it out there—alone, unprotected.

I suddenly felt certain that they had snuck in and already taken the creature, silently while I couldn't hear them with the sound of my own heartbeat in my head.

I crawled out from under the table slowly, the notebook still in my hand.

I stopped before the closed door, holding the book as if it were a weapon. Something was moving out there.

I backed away from the door slightly, the whirrs of the cameras embedded in the walls echoing through my mind.

Something flashed across the gap of light beneath the door, a shadow and I jumped.

Nowhere to go.

They were coming for me after all.

And the door handle started turning.

## Chapter Nine
*Wherein Dziga discovers an awful truth and argues with Judas*

I smiled.

Just beyond the doorway, Judas stood with a piece of frozen meat that he must have stolen from the refrigerator in one hand, tiny drops of red-stained water dripping off of it.

He sidled into the room as if to try and hide his approach, then sat beside me, stinking of the bodily fluids encrusted upon his infectious skin. There was blood all over his snout and I tried not to think about him nosing around at Jakobsen's corpse. He sniffed at me then dropped the meat before me and shuffled backwards.

My smile broadened at this offering and at the strange innocence of this creature—not only that he should help me but that he should think that I would *want* his help.

He ran off down the corridor again, leaving the defrosting piece of meat at my feet. I kicked it to one side and it collided wetly with the door jamb.

Aside from Judas' skittering everything seemed quiet and still.

I moved slowly towards the end of the building's L-shape, placing my feet carefully in front of each other along a tight central line, my attention swinging around from floor to wall to ceiling and back again. I felt as if something had passed, as if an encroaching army had been battling around the lab and had now retreated into the smoggy distance.

As if I was alone once more.

I poked my around the corner before deciding that it really was safe. I still wondered why no one had come for me but was not as threatened by the lack of response as I had been previously. Perhaps Jackobsen *had* acted alone. Perhaps the Engineers had done what they had felt they needed or were asked to do and so no longer had any interest in me. Perhaps it was just an overreaction on my part.

Then I thought again of the cameras.

I stopped by the crack in the wall, only aware that I had been questioning myself when I felt relieved that it was still there. I crouched to one side, taking a moment to prepare myself yet even before I looked into the darkness at the mechanical eye I could hear its workings.

Click snap.

A whirring.

It dilated to focus on me.

I stared back at it defiantly then leaned my head against the wall to listen to it.

"Hello," I whispered.

Click whirr. Click.

I moved my ear to the left and the electronic purring faded. To the right and it grew stronger. I crept along the wall, listening to the concrete, tracing the route of the machine-veins that lay behind it and it went up and to the right, up and to the right.

Another slight crack, a mere fracture.

I removed a pen from my lab coat pocket and pushed it into the gap, scraping away some of the plaster. And there was another one.

Not as deep as the first, more lazily buried, but still there. It blinked at me.

As I listened more closely I felt the noises were branching off in two different directions and followed both for a metre or so before further noises joined it. I stood back from the wall slightly and tilted my head in the opposite direction to try and distinguish the differing sounds but they seemed tangled. I chose a point at random further along the wall and within a few inches of tracing its surface located a source that seemed strong enough to be another camera. I chose another random point, this time on the opposite wall and further down, towards the door, and again within another few inches, more sounds.

How *many*?

Next the storage cupboard from which I had retrieved the old radio and I could *hear* it already! How I not heard that noise before? The camera was in plain sight in the shadows up at the top corner of the cupboard, painted matte black but still the lens glinted at me clearly. I moved slightly to the left but it did not follow me.

Another: behind the microwave oven, next to a set of sockets, sunk into the wall and concealed by what looked like spider webbing.

Another: staring directly down from the main lab's ceiling with a bulging lens that indicated a fish eye view.

Another: in the second step of the set leading up to the front door.

And another. Another.

Everywhere.

They were everywhere.

The noises of their mechanical movements, their dirty little whispers, *everywhere*. Had I been so blind before? Had it taken Jakobsen's death to finally snap me out of my reverie and confront me with the fact of my surveillance? Or had the creatures only just come into operation?

Then another explanation occurred to me—it was my own evolution that was finally letting me see things as they truly were. My senses, now heightened. My intellect sharpened.

My calm quickly faded as I went from camera to camera until it seemed as if the more I looked for them the more I would find until every speck of the lab was an electronic eye peering back at me. My life, detailed in monochromatic hyper-detail.

I considered what to do with the Protohuman, still chained to the wall as it had been prior to my attack on Jakobsen. The man's corpse lay beside it, the spilled blood now thick and dark as I imagined the blood of a betrayed lover would look if you drained them. I stepped over the body without even acknowledging its presence.

I checked my creature's face to make sure there were no signs of infection but the wounds seemed as clean as my own. I felt Judas watching me and turned to see the monkey standing in the wreckage of its cage. I was certain there was some significance in the gesture but my mind was otherwise occupied.

What was on the other end of that camera? Who was watching me?

I stepped up to one of them, concealed in the rim of my chalkboard and peered into it.

"What are you doing?" I asked it. "What do you want?"

If the cameras were all operational, and I assumed they must be, then it would have been impossible for someone to have been watching all their outputs simultaneously—which meant either a large team of observers or recording devices of some sort. I knew little of such devices but reasoned that they would by necessity have to be fairly close by to safely receive the camera signals and so returned to sounding the walls in an attempt to locate the point at which they left the lab.

It didn't take me long to find myself at the very rear of the lab's shorter length and confronted with a dead end. There were a couple more storage cupboards on my right, the room where I had taken Jakobsen to my left and on one side of behind me the room with the desk in it. The mechanical noises seemed to come from everywhere and yet go nowhere and perhaps that was the intention.

I crouched beside a hole I had created while searching for the cameras earlier and pulled on some thicker cabling that protruded. I tugged harder and another small piece of plaster came away as I dragged the cables out. I tugged again, creating a lateral gutter in the brickwork and kept pulling, kept pulling. The gap ran along the wall several inches from the floor and headed for the blank wall straight ahead of me, the dead end. When it reached the junction of both surfaces I had to tug harder still, once, twice, three times, and on the fourth the plaster came away finally and the hole continued into the back wall. And suddenly it came away with almost no effort. I could see just by looking that the debris was of a differing, lighter nature than the rest and kneeled before the gap.

There were no bricks behind the plaster here.

I took out my pen once more, now cracked and bent at the end, and shoved it into the hole.

It went right through with such ease that I jumped a little and dropped the pen.

I heard it clatter to the floor on the other side of the wall.

The other side of the wall.

*What?*

I pushed my fingers into the gap and tore out some more plaster with shocking ease, enough for me to then put my hand into and without pause I jerked my hand back and a half-foot chunk of the wall came away.

I bent over further and with some trepidation looked into the gap.

There are no words to describe the shock at what I saw.

The hole was small but large enough for me to see it was another room that I now stared into. I knew that couldn't be, that there *were* no other rooms in the lab.

And yet there it was.

Not only a room but a room whose only visible wall, directly opposite, was engulfed by a sprawling metal rack from which hung dozens of monitors of varying size and shape bolted onto the framework. Other electronic devices with bright green LCDs were also attached at awkward angles, arranged wherever there was space.

I squinted and could make out the main lab in one of the larger screens. The flash of movement therein matched the skittering of Judas that I heard with my own ears. It was my lab and it was live.

Two lamps with adjustable necks rose out from behind the monitors like curious lizards, both with bare bulbs burning within.

My chest felt as if it was on fire.

There was a worktop at waist level littered with pens and paper and keyboards.

There was a small stack of books, thick enough to be technical manuals.

There was a clipboard hanging from a pin on the rack.

There was a Styrofoam cup with steam rising from it.

And immediately I realised—they were not coming for me because they did not need to.

They were already here.

I felt as if a great shadow had just passed over me like the weight of a morning depression.

They were already here and always had been. Behind the walls. All around me.

All those times I had listened to the insects. Insects that were not insects.

Machines.

Images-thieves and violent observers.

My breath caught in my throat and I began to struggle to find another, falling away from the gap in the wall, from the horrible truth. I pushed myself away on my hands and felt the notebook I had dropped earlier on the ground. I clasped it to my chest, gasping, gasping, continued to back into the room with the desk.

My hands trembled as I flipped it open, unable to look away from the hole in the wall but also unable to remain looking at it, like staring at the creature that has been haunting you in your dreams.

I read aloud to myself.

*Seplophobia*—Fear of decaying matter.

*Phasmophobia*—Fear of ghosts.

I kept turning the pages, pausing every time I heard a sound before returning to the words. I could recall each and every moment of that journal, tracing my life through the fears that defined it.

How long had it been since I had added to it? Not since my mother had confiscated it anyway. And I kept turning pages, I kept turning pages.

Mediated through an infinity of phobias, I grew. I ran away from home and I was dragged back. I began to suffocate in my brother's bubble as if it were me inside it and not him months before the doctors had even dreamed of constructing it for him.

I jumped ahead, recognising the weeks leading up Dmitri's coma, the entries thickening, becoming more frenzied as if they knew this was their last chance—then blank pages.

Somewhere nearby, Judas screeched and I paused involuntarily as if expecting it to be his death-wail. He skipped past the doorway moments later, not even glancing up at me and when I turned back to my notebook I saw more entries. I began reading them without thought, then halted.

This was my mother's handwriting.

I flicked back through the book, eventually reaching my final entries, then retreated back through the empty pages once more until, tucked away into the heart of pages in writing so tiny you could almost miss it, I found the previously undiscovered entries.

About Dmitri. About germs.

Where did she get all the names of these germs from? She noted them like the lists of food she would often send me out with, attaching phrases and afterthoughts with perfectly straight lines that said things like *too weak* and *pulmonary heart failure.*

My own mother had stolen my process.

And yet I continued to read as the story of my own life, my own fears, dissolved and those of my mother's took their place. I began to see how she must have fed Dmitri his terrors piece by piece like carefully assembled segments of aspirin tablets, building up his insecurities at a rapidly increasing rate.

All these years . . .

*Siderodromophobia*—Fear of trains or railroads.

My head was spinning even more than it had been before I had begun reading. From one upturned reality to another. I sought purchase behind me, my hand trembling.

Was everything fake?

Or was this another trick of Jakobsen and the conspirators?

I hadn't noticed the notes until now and although I had rarely looked at the book I surely must have had opportunity to witness my mother's entries before. It would have been the simplest thing for

Jakobsen, as my benefactor, to have gotten access to my personal items while I was still in the asylum and make a duplicate or add to the original. But to go to the extent of being able to precisely replicate my mother's own handwriting? How could he know such a thing? How far would he go to trick me?

I ran my fingers across the scrawls, raised the pages to my face.

I felt certain I could smell her there, in the dust and fragments—all that she now was.

This couldn't be.

I let the book drop and squeezed my eyes beneath my fingers.

Every reality was becoming as unstable as the next. I needed something beyond reality.

I needed to get away from reality.


"That doesn't make sense," Judas said.

"Of course it makes sense. Not only the being as a whole but each part of it can be rationalised. There must be an optimum height, an optimum foot width. An optimum level of scientific competency. Nothing should be safe from the process."

"But how can you rely on the accuracy of what you produce? No system can be perfect if it is created and administered by an imperfect system. The only possible way to produce a flawless system would be to do so *within* a pre-existing flawless system—which is a contradiction in itself, for if such a system already existed, there would be no need to create another, thus the nature of perfection."

Judas paused, adding more weight to his sentiment, but Dziga pressed on regardless.

"Not true, not true," Dziga said. "This is Darwin, v2.0. This is *mechanical Darwinism*. The first generation of beings of course would be flawed but I would expect nothing less. But over time that would be weeded out, diluted. Each subsequent generation would rid itself of more and more unnecessary inaccuracies until finally perfection would be achieved. It would be far beyond my own lifetime of course, but this isn't about me. I am merely the catalyst."

"This isn't about you?" Judas questioned. He adjusted himself on the workbench, still toying with an empty test tube encrusted with something brown-black. "How sure of you are that?"

"What are you implying? Of *course* this isn't about me."

"So what is it about, Dziga?" Judas asked. "What is it you are trying to achieve?"

"I've told you already. A creature free of the torment of irrationality, of imperfection."

"And who are you to judge imperfection? You deign yourself fit to define when something isn't operating as it should? The universe is beyond you, Dziga, beyond all of us. You try to make it fit a pattern that we can understand and you will fail miserably. There are patterns, but they are as far beyond our comprehension as Fermat's Theorem would be to . . . to a proboscis."

Judas smiled a little and Dziga couldn't help but join him.

"Will you play with life, Dziga?"

"I play with nothing." He looked over at the Protohuman, safely protected now by strips of barbed wire wrapped around his feet and onto the frame he was chained to. "He doesn't comprehend what is being done to him."

"And you, Dziga?"

Dziga looked at the monkey hesitantly. "What do you mean?"

"Would you be aware if you were being toyed with as you toy with that? Would you know if you too were the experiment of some other?"

Dziga frowned, struggling to comprehend what Judas meant. Judas merely smiled back, then finally leaned across the bench, across the notes they had been scribbling as evidence during their discussion.

"Would you know if it were *I* who created *you* as you created it? What if you were a little experiment of my own, Dziga? Would you know?"

Dziga stared numbly at the monkey.

"When you sleep, Dziga, do I really sleep too? Or do I open my cage and let myself out to scribble down my notes for the day, my comments on your progress? When you leave at night, I am asleep and when you return in the morning I am asleep—but in between? Who knows, Dziga? And if I in turn are merely the experiment of another? Another link in the Great Assay that the universe has sought to place us in? What of that, Dziga?"

"Preposterous."

Judas pushed a few of the sheets in front of Dziga, turning them to face the man as he did so. Dziga glanced over the scribbled notes of times and places, activities—*his* activities.

"Was Jakobsen another of your pawns?" he asked the monkey. "Which part did he play?"

Judas shrugged, scratching absently at the sores that still littered his body. "That we shall see when the results are written up."

Dziga's speech had begun to slow, his mind thicken. He was vaguely aware of the proboscis climbing down, scrabbling across the floor and into the upturned wreck of metal that had once contained him.

"Judas?"

"A cage within a cage, Dziga," Judas replied from behind the rusted bars. "Who's after you, really? A cage inside a cage—Inside another, inside another, inside another . . . "

## Chapter Ten
*Wherein Dziga summons Dmitri for help*

I came to on the floor of the main lab, the needle I had used to inject myself still in my hand.

Judas remained in the ruins of his cage, asleep or dead, one or the other.

The tatters of my hallucination lay around me like the torn pages of my notebook, little snippets of tragedy and terror. I listened to the sound of the cameras adjusting, dilating, focusing. Beside me, the Protohuman watched me with disinterest, its face wet in places from reopened wounds.

Did it even matter what I did now?

Jakobsen and his co-conspirators obviously had, and always had, complete control over me. The bars to my cage had been revealed and yet here I remained, untouched. I pondered why they remained silent. Were they truly so confident that I was powerless towards them?

Well I would *not* be intimidated any more.

I stood too quickly, blood rushing to my head and my newborn face so suddenly that it unbalanced me and I had to lean against the worktop for support. I worked my way along the counter to the door and out into the corridor.

The walls were chipped and cracked, pieces of plaster and broken wire littering the floor, dark gaps holding darker eyes that were staring back at me. Had I really done all this?

My boots crunched on the debris as I walked to the end of the passage and then around the L's corner and for a moment I thought that perhaps I had hallucinated the hidden room as well but the hole was still there and the glow of the monitors leaked out. I paused before the gap and the machines adjusted to watch me.

I swung my foot back and kicked just above the opening, breaking into it further.

Again.

Again.

Plaster dust sprayed into the air around me, chunks of mortar scattering into the corridor and the observation room and I already knew there would be nobody in there waiting for me. Judas screeched behind me then ran off again. Finally the gap was large enough for me to walk through and I got a better look at what lay within.

Everything was switched on, everything working. The coffee cup was still there but no steam rose from it. It reminded me of the scene from a ghost ship, of sudden, hurried abandonment.

I was out of breath from my efforts as I stepped into the room and it felt like another world. There was a latent heat within, the static buzz of so much electronic equipment and every monitor was filled with the lab. The room was little bigger than the rack of equipment itself and was, as I had suspected, empty. There were no doors or hatches that I could see, no way in or out except for the hole I had battered in the wall.

It didn't make sense.

And yet that in itself made sense.

I wasn't supposed to understand—any of it.

I approached the desk and peered into the Styrofoam cup I had noticed when first peering into the room, still hot enough to be steaming. I sniffed the cup and it gave off the hideous stench of stale coffee and it was cold. Looking closer, I saw a little row of indentions in the cup's rim—teethmarks. There was no kettle or heating device as far as I could see, no pipes to tap into my water supply.

I scanned the notes spilled across the desk and layering the keyboard but the scrawl was so illegible that it almost appeared as if the text was deliberately mangled. Nonsense. Across the bank of monitors, I surveyed my lab's every corner. Little synchronized clocks sat on the top of each screen, counting away the seconds of my surveillance. I stabbed randomly at a few keys on the keyboard but nothing obvious happened. I flicked a few switches and turned some dials on a slim control panel bolted beneath the monitors and the images therein switched to another position, another room, another angle. I turned the dial again—*click*—and I was looking down at myself. I turned it again—*click*—and the camera presented me with a medium close-up of the Protohuman, slumped against the wall, and beneath it, Jackobsen's peacefully decaying corpse.

They knew, of course, they knew, what I had done.

They knew everything that I had done from the moment I came to the lab, monitoring me as intimately as they had back at the asylum. The question wasn't if you were being watch—but by whom.

So why had I not been punished? Again the thought occurred to me that perhaps the man wasn't the central figure to this whole affair, that he was just a bit player. A patsy, a goat they were willing to sacrifice.

What part did everybody else play in this, if Jackobsen was merely a part?

The Engineers? Surely they had no involvement in this prior to my contacting them—unless that had been a deliberate intervention meant to look like serendipity or chaotic guidance. Their dishevelled, ramshackle style didn't suit the grandiose nature of this scheme and also if they had access to the sort of control over me that I was now witness to, what was the necessity of my barbaric mutilation and that of my creature? What did that achieve?

No, not the Engineers.

But there *was* no one else—save perhaps my dear brother.

He had visited me often and had had extensive contact with Jakobsen ever since my leaving the asylum and so might have some insight into what was going on. He had certainly never let on that he had any suspicions . . .

I stopped.

*"You don't owe Jakobsen anything, remember. What he gives you, he gives you of his own choice."*

*"Jakobsen? But it was you who brought me to him."*

*"I know, I just . . . . I only ask one thing of you, brother—just be careful."*

The conversation replayed in my mind verbatim as if I were watching it on one of the surveillance monitors.

That had been only days before I had begun to discover the truth about my situation.

Had Dmitri already developed some of the same suspicions? Had he also realised that Jakobsen, or whoever it was responsible, had something covert planed for me and my work? I went back over the meeting, searching my memories of it for some further sign of his suspicions manifesting themselves. He might have had to have been careful what he had said, might have had to conceal his warnings to me more adequately than his whispered guidance before he left.

But I could think of nothing else and hadn't heard anything from him since. In return I hadn't attempted to contact him either. If he had truly feared for me as he seemed to, wouldn't he have made some effort to contact me, to check on my state?

Then a horrible thought passed over me as the shadow of the chemical factories fell over my lab at sundown—what if they had done something to Dmitri too? He had been the one single person to have helped me throughout my life, the one most likely to be by my side and protect me. What if they had had to deal with him in response to the growing threat he might have posed?

My hands were shaking as I stepped back out of the surveillance room and into the corridor.

It all seemed so different now, the lab, fluctuating from haven to hellhole and back again. The only thing which had kept me safe and secure from the dangers of the outside world now boasted a full repertoire of original dangers for me to contend with. As I walked I was now fully aware of each step I took as if I were studying it on the cameras in slow motion from four different angles. I felt every new facial expression that emerged.

My senses had become heightened, left in a permanent state of readiness.

This is how the Protohuman would operate.

I entered the main lab and everything was still silent. I thought of a lab rat left in its maze at the en of an experiment, running around and around endlessly because it had no concept that nobody cared anymore, that nobody was watching.

Were they still watching?

I crossed to the rear workbench, hovered over the phone. The clicks and whirrs of the cameras were obvious to me now and not just because the things that had concealed and muffled them were now gone. Their presence no longer bothered me—I *challenged* them to watch. Let them see my next step. Let them try and stop hyper-evolution. Let them try and unwind a Chaos spiral.

There was only one way to find out where my brother stood in all of this and if he could help me or not.

Only one way.


When I had contacted Dmitri, I had spoken briefly, avoiding any elaboration even as he had sought it. He knew that something was desperately wrong despite my attempts to alleviate his concerns and I could sense in his voice that his worries had been building for some time even before the call. I think he knew that I had finally discovered Jakobsen's betrayal but I refused to answer his questions about what had happened.

"Nothing has happened," I told him. "Just please come quickly, Dmitri."

After I had hung up the phone rang again and again. I stood and watched it for a time, contemplating what ways they could get at me if it wasn't my brother calling back but instead Jakobsen's agents.

Could high frequency sounds kill you? Or stun you long enough to allow someone to break in? Or was it low frequency sounds?

There was so much, so much.

I backed out of the room as the phone rang again, almost an hour after I had terminated the conversation with Dmitri. I shouted at it to be quiet then suddenly jumped away from the doorway as something ran behind me. I turned and saw Judas lurking in the shadows created by the makeshift barricades across the door. He watched me as he scratched at his raw wounds with curled fingernails.

I should have put the little shit back in his cage, broken or not.

I raised a boot to him and swung out but he must have been recovering his strength for he dodged my attempt and disappeared around the corner. My heart lurched from side to side, playing against my ribcage, and I felt the encroachment of another panic attack.

*Stop it. Stop.*

There was work to be done in preparation for Dmitri's arrival. I could feel the presence of those watching me, just outside of the range of my normal, more human, senses and knew that they would not wait forever. They were a coiled cobra, ready to strike.

The phone had stopped ringing and I didn't know whether that was a good thing or a bad thing. I wanted to pick it up to see if there was anyone still on the line but kept thinking of ways they could get at me through the phoneline. I was creating a miracle here in this research-prison, who was to say other miracles hadn't been created elsewhere, ones that would enable people to travel down phonelines or send poisons via soundwave?

Danger was everywhere, was infinite. Life was too fragile, too easily toppled.

I needed distraction from my own thoughts.

And so I began to tidy up a little, to prepare.

## Chapter Eleven
*Wherein Dmitri arrives and Dziga now suspects him*

Through my lab coat I clenched the hammer I had used to peel back the metal sheeting from the door then slotted into my pocket. I opened the door to the hissing, pneumatic bubble that shared my genes.

Steam burst from the sphere's outlets in angered bursts, an outward manifestation of the stress that had been placed on Dmitri's body by the journey. Plainly, the contraption had become so elaborate as it had developed in its own hurried, oil-smeared evolution that it was as bound to his own body's biology as any of his limbs. Condensation dripped off of it like sweat, the outer skin irritated and reddened as if he had run, or rolled, all the way there. His arrival had interrupted me as I had been carefully arranging test tubes in a rack in the main lab and I suddenly realised I had no idea how long it had been since I had placed the call. Possibly a day or two but maybe it had only been a few hours.

Through the steamed shell Dmitri hadn't gotten a clear look at my new face until I had locked the door shut again and battered the metal plating back into place with several quick blasts of the hammer.

"Dear God . . . Eva was right . . . " the voicebox sputtered before the sounds of his hydraulic lungs kicked in and drowned everything else out.

The bubble tipped backwards, the integrated counter-balances fighting each other for control.

"Dziga . . . "

He rolled into the wall, stumbled back again. I kept my distance, still clutching the hammer. A great burst of steam blasted out at him and just missed scalding my puckered, glistening features.

"I knew you would come, Dmitri. I . . . " I went towards my brother but he was still fighting against his machine-shell to regain his balance. He thudded against one wall, another, asthmatic steam gushing from orifices all around him.

He rolled away from me and as he turned I saw the sheer horror in his eyes. I reached out and tried to steady him but my assistance was answered with an electronic shriek.

"Dziga, I'm taking you out . . . of here . . . " Dmitri gasped, almost recovering his balance. "I spoke . . . with Eva and . . . "

"Dmitri, it's *okay*. I'm *alright*." I manoeuvred myself in front of the bubble, steadying it with my outstretched hands, trying to catch my brother's attention, hold it. "You were right, brother, you were right."

Dmitri continued his struggles but they became quickly laboured and he slouched within the framework of the device like a discarded puppet. I hushed him, holding the bubble still as it calmed with its owner, its twin, its host.

"You were right," I kept saying, over and over, smiling through my nu flesh. "They're watching us."

I looked around and Dmitri followed my nervous gaze, half expecting to see someone standing at the end of the corridor or in one of the doorways. "Dziga . . . brother . . . I think you should come away with me. Away from here. I'm already arranging it."

"But of course," I replied enthusiastically. "But I can't come back to the city with you. It's too dangerous. Jakobsen might have agents there already. We might not be safe."

"Safe from what? What agents?"

Dmitri had recovered somewhat from the initial shock but now studied my mutilation through the steamed plastic coating of the bubble.

I leaned in towards him secretively. "You were right about Jakobsen. He was a betrayer."

"What do you mean? Dziga, you've got it wrong . . . "

I smiled, the exposed muscles of my face working visibly. "I confronted him," I said plainly.

"You've spoken to him? I tried contacting him on my journey but . . . Dziga what's been going on?"

"He did this to me. He lied to me and tricked me, then did this to me."

Dmitri grimaced afresh at the damage that had been done to my face but took seemed to solace in the fact that my behaviour mean it must have been merely surface damage. "I don't believe it. Dziga, Jakobsen was trying to *help* you. We all were."

"Not true. What you said—the last time you were here. You were right. We shouldn't have trusted him. He was exploiting me and my work. He was awaiting the moment that the Protohuman project was almost complete then was set to betray me—steal the credit for himself and dispose of me."

"You're wrong, brother. *I* was wrong. I made an error of judgment. Jakobsen called me only a few days ago to ask me to talk to you. He was worried that you were retrograding, slipping back into psychosis but I didn't realise . . . "

"He *wanted* you to believe that! He wanted to convince you so that you could be coerced into betraying me too! You were right about not trusting him, Dmitri."

"I never said not to trust him, Dziga. He was one of the few that wanted to *help* you."

My flow of argument wavered. "But you said . . . you said to be cautious of him."

"I said no such thing."

"But the last time . . . "

"I said *no such thing.*"

Dmitri was staring hard back at me now, defiant. "You are coming with me, brother. You can't stay here any longer. I won't have it."

"No!"

Dmitri jumped, shocked at the fury that I spoke with, perhaps my new features adding to the effect. Anger that was *efficient* anger, each facial muscle working together to create a perfect and idealised expression.

Anger. Fear. Depression. Confusion.

Everything, more efficient.

"Come with me. I'll prove it to you."

"Prove what, Dziga?"

"The *betrayal*, the *betrayal*. Look!"

I stood to one side, sweeping my arm out to present him with the corridor. I had cleared up the majority of the rubble, the cracked pieces of plaster, the concrete dust but the holes remained. They were scattered across the walls at every level, occasionally spilling across a join with the floor or ceiling. There was still a small smearing of Jakobsen's blood which I had trailed into the corridor after killing him, along the floor just ahead of us but Dmitri didn't seem to take any notice. Perhaps he assumed it was from my face.

"What have you been doing here?" the filtered, mechanical voice of my brother asked.

The bubble kicked into life as he followed me down the corridor and around the corner, the device's caterpillar tracks crunching on the ground, squeaking in protest.

I had widened the gap into the surveillance room, preparing it for Dmitri's bubbles girth, and then nailed a plastic sheet over the opening. I wanted to control the revelations to my brother to make sure they had maximum impact, installing the sheet to allow for a dramatic unveiling that it was now clear I could certainly benefit from.

I stepped in front of Dmitri and pulled the curtain aside.

Inside the bubble I could see little bursts of steam ejaculating from various parts of the mechanism, spraying the inner skin with microscopic droplets of sterile liquid. Dmitri seemed to be in a state of pre-emptive shock, as if he were conversing with a police officer he felt sure was going to tell him that Ana had been murdered. He shifted forwards slightly, cogs grinding against one another, the support struts tilting him forwards to let him have a better view.

"I don't . . . "

"Do you see now what they have been doing?" I asked him, now comfortable that he would realise the extent of the deception.

The bubble hissed, spat.

"What, Dziga? I don't understand."

"Dmitri, see what is in front of you!" I shouted and tugged the sheeting hard enough to pull it out of its moorings, dropped it to the floor.

"There is nothing," Dmitri said.

And I looked.

And there was nothing.

Bare walls. Brickwork like stony arteries, like the map of an inverted Nirvana.

Little chunks of rubble and a cracked floor.

The odour of electricity and nothing more.

"What have they done?" I found myself whispering. "What are they doing?"

I stepped through gap and turned, turned, turned. I swept my hands around in mid-air as if I expected to collide with the rack of equipment, somehow hidden from us optically.

"Dziga, please. Stop all this nonsense."

"It was here!" I snapped, stabbing at the ground. I dropped to my knees and scoured the ground. "Look, look—scratches! These scores in the ground, they've somehow moved it all! It was *right here*!"

How could it have been taken without my knowledge? How could they possibly have done that? "*What* was here?"

"Machines . . . machines . . . " I stammered. "Watching me. All this time, watching me!"

"There *are* no machines," Dmitri replied and I could tell he was having difficulty maintaining his self-control. "There is nothing."

"That is what they will have you believe," I said, and stormed past him back out of the room. Into the air I shouted, "You don't scare me! I know what you are doing! He can see past all of your games! I can see past them! You *will not stop my work*!"

I laughed, already knowing when I leaned into one of the cracks that the little electronic workers there would be gone too.

"They're just trying to undermine me, Dmitri. Don't pay any attention." I turned to Dmitri, composing myself a little more for I realised how odd my behaviour must have seemed to him. "Please, brother, understand what I am telling you. It has all been a conspiracy, a joke. I know all you wanted to do was help me, I know that. But Jakobsen . . . Jakobsen only wanted to steal my work from me. He used us both."

"Dziga, you need *help*," Dmitri said, shaking his weary head. "I can't leave you here like this any longer."

He moved past me, the bubble's motorised underparts sliding him forwards inch by inch, wheels and cogs greasily sliding between one another like elbow joints but I jumped in front of him, blocked his path.

"I have him," I said suddenly and he stopped dead.

"You have . . . whom?"

"Our betrayer. Jakobsen."

Inside the bubble, Dmitri placed a hand slowly over his mouth. A mechanism hooked over his shoulder eased to life, three folds of thin steel like opening like orchid petals and automatically injecting him with a dosage of antibiotics. "He's here?"

I nodded enthusiastically. "In the operating theatre."

I carefully studied my brother, seemingly utterly unsettled by me, by my new appearance or more. Even at the times he had been at his most caring and generous, when I had been consumed by madness and everybody else had rejected me, there had been that uncertainty in Dmitri's eyes, like a warden releasing a prisoner whom he wasn't quite sure was reformed.

"The . . . operating theatre?"

I nodded. I was aware of the impact these revelations might have upon my brother and wondered if perhaps I should have been more demure about sharing them—perhaps worn a mask or waited for longer before mentioning Jakobsen and what he had been doing. And of course I had had days to come to terms with Jakobsen's betrayal—Dmitri would need that time too.

"The Protohuman is *my* project, brother. We mustn't let anyone take it from us. It shall revolutionise humanity, don't forget. We must do everything we can to protect it."

I glanced past Dmitri, down the corridor and towards the operating theatre. There was no light coming from inside, no sound. "I don't hear him," Dmitri asked cautiously.

I shrugged. "He is . . . indisposed."

"I must speak with him."

"But what words would you offer him? He does not deserve the spit from your mouth."

Dmitri cringed noticeably at the mention of bodily fluids, his paranoid mind no doubt dreaming up microscopic imagery of floating, translucent invaders. "Dziga—I must speak with him, please."

I hardened. "Of course. If you so wish."

I held a hand out and motioned for my brother to proceed towards the operating theatre.

We moved slowly, like a funeral procession, and I stared hard at Dmitri, puzzled by the lack of support I had received thus far. When the bubble was parallel with the doorway, Dmitri stopped. Hydraulic hinges hooked underneath the reinforced bottom swivelled him around so that he faced the darkness that lay within the room.

He could only make out vague shapes, the tiny glints of light where it caught the edges of equipment. I moved past him and stepped halfway into the room, dousing part of my wet face in shadow before announcing, "Brother . . . our betrayer . . . "

I grandly threw the circuit switch that controlled power to the room and the sudden blast of light and electronic noise momentarily blinded both of us. Dmitri twitched, his knuckles white upon the support straps inside his bubble.

It looked like a spider or insect at first—an immense cicadian mess that seemed to be constructed of the same substance that my face now was. It was peeled out on the examination table, a dark puddle having collected and congealed on the floor beneath it, what appeared to be limbs but were in fact lengths of skin stretched out on pieces of wire arranged in a starburst from the central shape of Jakobsen's abdominal cavity. The wires were clotted with beads of his blood. His battered face was tipped to one side, the skin on his neck pinched out several inches by a small hook attached to the bed's traction poles.

"I checked him for bugs," I told Dmitri, my breath steaming on his bubble's outer shell mere inches from my face. "Listening devices. I know they're watching us but I'm not so sure they can hear us."

Dmitri wasn't moving. His eyelids flickered involuntarily but aside from that—nothing. Even the bubble had fallen silent as if hushed by the mechanical noise of the devices that Jakobsen had been hooked up to, monitoring his empty life signs.

There was the vague, muffled sound of Judas breathing from somewhere along the corridor.

"We should arrange for transport. Private transport. They'll know that we will be leaving but if we're quick it won't matter. They might be waiting for us—so be it. The scrap metal smugglers will be able to conceal us on a wagon if we pay them enough. I've already plotted the best route for us."

I continued to tell Dmitri the plan I had been assembling as I walked around the splintered remains of my benefactor's corpse, ducking under cables and stretched cartilage and unnecessarily flicking switches on the monitoring equipment from one dead signal to another. I continued to recite my plan until Dmitri finally said, "Stop."

A single, soft emission of steam eased out of the bubble.

We stared back at one another.

I could tell how much he was struggling to control himself, the veins in his temples rising through his skin like subcutaneous insects.

"This has gone too far. You're beyond my help now, Dziga. I'm too weak. I have done my best for you always. Even when everyone else said it was useless to try, I did my best for you." He spoke in slow, measured tones. "There are, perhaps, people who can help you where I cannot—but if you yourself are not willing to get better . . . " He shook his head wearily. "I should have listened to what Jakobsen said."

"Brother what are you saying? Do you not see what is before me?"

"I see it, Dziga. I see that you are a killer. I see you have murdered a man who did as much for you as I have."

"As much as . . . what are you *talking* about? I have tried to explain to you—he *betrayed us*. Just like you said, Dmitri. He was no good. He just wanted to use me to create the Protohuman and then discard me so that he could assume credit for himself. He threatened me by convincing the Engineers to do this to me—it was a sign, a warning! Soon he would kill me, I *know* it! And you would be next, Dmitri—you and Ana both!"

"Don't you *say* that! Don't you threaten my family!"

"It is not *I* who threaten you! Why are you turning on me like this?! You said yourself that Jakobsen could not be trusted and you were right."

"Stop saying that! I said no such thing! Jakobsen only wanted to help you." He drew in a breath sharply like the rasp of a snake and when he spat out his next sentence it was filled with the venom of such a creature. "You are beyond help, Dziga. I shall have nothing more to do with you."

The hydraulic pumps beneath him hissed and spat, swivelling the man back to face the gloomy access corridor as fast as they could manage. I chased after him when he started to roll away.

"Brother, where are you going!? You cannot leave—it is not safe!"

I slammed my foot down on one of the drive motors that powered the bubble's movements to stop it. "What about the Engineers?"

"The who?"

"The ones who did this to me! We were brought together . . . there was a voice on the radio!"

"What radio? What voice?"

"101.6! Remember? 101.6! I placed an advert . . . "

Dmitri seemed stunned into silence, then, "Jakobsen mentioned something about you wanting to place an advert."

"Yes, *yes*. To contact the engineers! But he . . . corrupted it or . . . or maybe not, maybe this was meant to happen."

"*Meant* to happen? You mean your face?"

"Yes. They took me. They came for me and they took me to their studio—a huge building with metal catwalks. I saw all *kinds* of things."

"Dziga, you left the lab? That's not possible. I thought you . . . "

"They came for me and took me—did you not hear me?!"

"Stop it, Dziga! I heard you. I heard you and I believe you need help. I will send someone for you, I promise—but I will have nothing more to do with any of this."

"*Send* someone for me? What do you mean?" I quickly hopped around my brother as he broke free of my hold and manoeuvred down the passageway, the vents beginning to work harder, jumping around as he passed a doorway and then blocking the way. He began to hyper-ventilate. "Send one of *them*? One of his agents? Is that what you mean?"

"Agents? Dziga, there *are* no agents! Jakobsen was merely an aging man who wanted to help you! Let me past! I need to get out!"

There was something new in his eyes, something hidden behind the grey-green irises. I had seen the same thing in Jakobsen's eyes.

"Why, Dmitri—what's out there? *Who's* out there? What do you *know*, brother?"

Dmitri gasped for breath inside the bubble, loosening one hand from its strap and grabbing an oxygen mask clipped onto one of the partitions, slapped it onto his face. His own fear steamed the translu-cent plastic.

"You *knew*!" I shouted suddenly, extending my hands to each side of the corridor to block my brother further. "You knew right from the beginning what Jakobsen planned—you *helped* him didn't you?! I . . . "

I glanced around, my thoughts suddenly very confused and yet utterly clear at the same time. Jakobsen had had Dmitri's help—he'd *had* to have had it.

"*You* were the one that brought Jakobsen to me," I proclaimed. "*You* were the one that convinced me to let him take me from the asylum. *You* led me here, brother."

I looked down to see Judas staring up at us from the doorway of the main laboratory, grinning and displaying his rotten gums. I nodded to him and the monkey nodded back.

"Let me out, Dziga. Please."

When I turned once more to my brother the man had distilled to a pale shade of blue as he rocked back and forth within the straps of his bubble. The contraption attempted over and over to move forwards but I blocked it.

"You were helping him to steal the Protohuman from me," I said plainly. "Was it money? Did he offer you the Final Treatment the doctors always spoke of in exchange for allowing him full control of the Protohuman? Was that it? "

"Dziga, there's no such fucking thing!" Dmitri shrieked, then stumbled backwards inside the shell as the dark gangly shape of Judas suddenly appeared and leapt at him. The monkey cried out madly as it latched onto the outer skin, watery foam stained with blood pouring from his mouth and all Dmitri could see were the millions of viral molecules embedded in the fluid, the ticks that crawled across the bare patches of the animal's fur and the unhealed, seeping wounds. He flailed in a sudden mad panic, pulling blindly at the bindings that held him in place and rocking the bubble unnaturally to one side.

Judas pushed at the skin with one twisted finger and without a moment's hesitation I punched at the bacterial shell. Dmitri abruptly broke free of one leg restraint and tumbled forwards, cracking a number of cylinders of antibiotics and hormones embedded in the metal structural bands. Judas continued to press at the skin, stretching it curiously like bubble gum, the apex losing its transparency and turning a pale yellow.

I grabbed two of the struts and held tight, forcing my fallen brother to look up at me from inside the bubble. He'd cut his hand on the shards from the cylinders, holding the limb as far away from himself as he possibly could and still unable to find breath. Only his eyes screamed now as he watched me pull a scalpel from my lab coat pocket and drive it into and through the bubble's polyfibrous outer layer.

## Chapter Twelve
*Wherein Dziga returns to his work,*
*fearful of further attacks on himself*

Dziga sat at the workbench, his workbooks and sketches sprawled out before him as he calmly went over them. He stopped every now and again to listen for the sounds of the ones who would be coming for him but all he heard was the distant noise of the wrecking machinery in the junk yards.

He unravelled a list of calculations that had become stained by a dark solution at some point, going over them with a pencil. He still had so much work to do on the project but that was fine. He didn't need the approval or support of others. He had always known that trust was a fallacy, even with a brother whom had done everything to help him, supposedly.

There was never truth.

The Protohuman stirred in its shackles. His skin seemed to droop from him now.

No matter.

What was skin but a shell, a covering?

Judas was still loose, still wandering the lab from room to room. Once or twice Dziga had entered a storage closet or back room and the monkey had flown out guiltily, things clattering behind him. Dziga had kept the scrap of paper he had found with badly scrawled equations on it and had studied it, wondering if this was his own work or the monkey's.

He laid the equations next to his own, muttering.

There must surely be a mathematical answer to the question of humanity. It was just a case of rearranging enough digits, ordering enough numbers. Humans liked to believe they were somehow special, something more than merely a biological mechanism but then Dziga hardly expected creatures as egotistical as humans to think any less of themselves.

Everything was clockwork.

Tick tock. Tick tock.

He looked back at the Protohuman. It held the answer to that particular puzzle—beneath its skin, its flesh, beneath even the strands of DNA that lay at its root. There was a simple mathematical representation of the human being and Dziga felt that he was already part of the way to discovering it. Once discovered, it would be nothing more than a case of rearranging the algebraic functions and miscellaneous algorithms, extricating any and all unnecessary functions.

His fingers shook as he scribbled some more, thin smears of blood staining the pencil from hands damaged by another bout of frantic scrabbling at the walls to remove the bugs that would be watching him.

Would they *ever* come for him?

Why hadn't they come?

"Perhaps they finally understand the lengths I am prepared to go to to protect you, yes?" he said to the Protohuman but loud enough so that anyone else listening might here.

Beside the creature was the now-black patch where Jakobsen had fallen and spilled himself onto the lab's floor—another few paces to the left and the doorway hid most of Dmitri's wrecked bubble. The contraption was nothing but a carcass now, a framework, several of the struts fractured and broken from Dziga's attempts to remove his sibling. But it *inspired* the mecha-scientist. He hadn't realised until he had started trying to remove Dmitri from it how close the two mechanisms had become. The plastic tubes that fed nutrients and steroids into his system did not merely slide into his skin but meshed convincingly with his veins and arteries. The breathing equipment was plugged directly into the steel lung that had replaced one of the originals.

There was no distinction between metal and cartilage.

Dziga thought of Nadia after the second suicide attempt, the one that had almost succeeded. She had climbed into a compacting machine that a local refinery used to dispose of old oil drums that were too leaky to patch up or reuse—just laid there as metal splintered and tore around her. After her rescue, she had been sealed in a room in the hospital that was filled with pneumatic chambers and all manner of pipes feeding and extracting chemicals. Another bank of machines had lined the wall, monitoring her recovery.

She had inspired Dziga too, even then when he was so young.

He often wondered if her melancholy, her belief that she should not be a part of the world, was the reason why each of her suicide attempts intimately involved machinery of some sort. Had she truly been trying to kill herself? Or was she trying to become something more, something else, and hoped that technology would be the path to that rebirth?

Even when she tried to poison herself, she had done it alongside the great polluted canal that circled around the train yards.

She had become twitchy at first, he remembered. He had had to explain that later to the doctors for he had followed her from the farm to an abandoned hut and watched her mix the concoction their grandmother had taught her how to make to kill rats and the wild, rabid dogs that roamed the wasteland. He had wondered if that had been how she saw herself, as a rabid dog or rat, as he had sat with their mother at her bedside.

But she hadn't wanted to die quietly in that place—alone and ignored—so he had continued to follow her to the canal where factory workers smoked and laughed and threw things into the sludgy waters. The poison wasn't difficult to mix for it consisted of regular household products, but there was a certain trick to getting the constituents to bind correctly and that was where the skill lay. Nadia had merely upped the dosage levels of the more toxic ingredients and not figured in that it wouldn't bind in the same way which was why it had merely hospitalised her and not killed her. Or maybe she had known it wouldn't be lethal.

He had watched her first seizure from a distance that was more than the mere physical space between them, noting down the progression of her condition in his notepad. She had still been sitting amongst the broken girders and oil drums as the hallucinations had begun.

He wrote *patient shows signs of confusion and distress. Flapping arms around and shouting.*

He wrote *patient has suddenly gone quiet. Patient seems to be studying the ground intently.*

He wrote *patient licks a handful of mud.*

He wrote *patient appears to have lost consciousness.*

And yet despite what everyone had thought Dziga had understood that her sorrow came not from her inability to *belong* to the human race but from her inability to *escape* from it.

Thus he would dedicate the Protohuman project to Nadia, for at least she did not betray him. Though perhaps, he wondered, she was just never given a proper chance.

Things shifted; time passed; or didn't.

Dziga sat hunched over his papers, scribbling randomly across them. The Protohuman project would to continue, of course, of that there was no doubt. Nothing they could do would stop him and what new revelations could be more earth-shattering than those he had already been exposed to? Now here he sat, unshaken by events—determined, brutally focussed. He thought of securing the lab further with whatever he could find but a new passivity lay within him, a sense of certainty that came from somewhere he did not know and swelled him with a simple confidence.

Games, all games.

True men would just kill me if they so desired.

*Let them play* Dziga said aloud.

Eventually, he would have to leave, he knew, even without Dmitri's help.

It would not be easy but it was necessary.

He had begun making a list of the logistics involved, deciding what equipment he would need to take and what he could leave. A lot of it—the operating table, his surgical and monitoring machinery—would be difficult to replace in the near future but the sacrifice would have to be made. There was no way he could take it all with him. His research, in its strictest terms, would grind to a halt, although he was interested to see how the Protohuman would continue to develop outside of the lab environment. He would scavenge his treatment until it had recovered completely, if indeed it would be affected all.

Yes. His priority was the Protohuman itself.

He looked over at Judas, hunched wearily against a workbench, his long arms slumped by his side. Dziga could see the tiny, hurried movements of the ticks and other creatures that infested him. His skin seemed less patchy, a little less dull, but his eyes remained thick and heavy.

"And what about you?" Dziga asked the monkey. "Will I have to leave you too?"

Judas regarded him blankly, tapping rhythmically with one of his fingers on the floor as if counting out his own heartbeat. He grunted weakly, opening his mouth in an almost-yawn.

Dziga's head felt strangely muffled. He watched a cockroach make its way across the workbench, aware that there were more insects of late. Beetles and roaches scuttled behind the walls and in the cracks he had made, amongst the encrusted and broken test tubes that littered the place and the pools of darkening blood.

He had captured one, impaling it on the worktop with a syringe needle as it had idled past him, taking the creature apart bit by bit to make sure that it was genuine. He looked for electronic parts, for tiny transmitters concealed beneath its carapace, didn't find any but that probably just meant that it was a decoy. He wanted to capture more to study them instead but there were other more important things to occupy his time.

The world seemed to be circling him like a great bird of prey, just waiting for him to lose that last drop of energy.

Sometimes Dziga just wanted out of his own head.

But this came later. First, he had returned to the observation room.


After watching Dmitri collapse in unison with his deflating bubble, eyes bulging in their sockets as dirty air and an infinity of biological assassins rushed in around him, smothering him, choking him, Dziga had pushed the remains of the contraption to one side. At least there hadn't been the same amount of blood as their had with Jakobsen but there was still quite a mess, this time of shards of plastic and glass, flaps of bubble-skin and bolts. Judas had run off again when Dmitri had let out a final shriek and so Dziga had walked alone along the corridor, listening to the clicks and whirrs that had returned. He had stopped to allow one of the camera lenses to focus on him, then turned the corner to the observation room.

The equipment was back, of course, but as well as that the hole he had hammered into the wall there was now a perfectly-formed, perfectly natural door. It was ajar just a crack, enough that he could hear the hum of the devious machines inside, their buzz like the chatter of mischievous children.

"Did you see that?" Dziga asked, pushing the door open.

The room glowed with the blue light of the monitors, strobing from the few that seemed to be rewinding past footage automatically as if searching for something. The papers and other miscellany on the worktop had been tidied up since his last visit, neatly arranged in piles and rows but the ringed coffee stains between them were still there.

"Did you see what I did this time?"

And he laughed, just a little.

Pieces of the lab jumped from screen to screen.

"It's all useless," Judas said. "You talk about human arrogance and yet *you* are the arrogant one for thinking you can decode this silly equation of yours."

The monkey swirled a Pyrex test tube between its scraggly fingers thoughtfully. He was wearing one of Dziga's lab coats, the stained garment ridiculously large for him.

"It's all math," Dziga countered.

"Let him speak. I wasn't talking to you."

"Let who . . . "

Judas pointed to the Protohuman. "Let him speak."

"But I am speaking," the Protohuman said, then frowned.

Dziga rubbed his temples. "What did I take?"

"What *didn't* you take?" Judas said. "You're always trying to escape from things, Dziga."

"I'm not."

Dziga stared at his palms, stained with powder from the pills he must have taken.

"Then why chain yourself up?"

"I don't chain myself. I chain the Protohuman."

Judas smiled a horrible smile. "You have no idea do you? Who would want to watch you anyway?"

Dziga ran his tongue across one finger, removing some of the powder. "Jakobsen. His conspiracy . . . to get the Protohuman . . . "

Judas laughed, crossing his legs beneath him as he sat on the worktop. "Listen to yourself! You've been watched all your life, little Dziga. Into one hospital, into another. Another, another." The monkey trailed his fingers across the scored wooden surface beneath him, counting out on it. "You can never leave your cage, Dziga, don't you get that? You just forget that it's there, that's all."

"I . . . "

Dziga pressed the palm of his hand to his head, rubbing the powder across the serrated flesh.

"You're too tired to think just now. Just give it time. It's all behind the walls."

And with that the proboscis removed the lab coat, leapt off the worktop and disappeared into the shadows of the lab.

When Dziga came to, upper body slumped across a treasure trove of gutted pill caplets like jewelled insect wings, he sat up slowly. The white dust scattered around him told its own tale, one he had heard many times before, and he found himself listening for the sound of intruders not with apprehension but with something almost akin to longing.

*Just end this* Nadia had said once when Dziga had been left with her by her bed.

He wrote *patient exhibits an infinite melancholy that is particularly apparent in her eyes and speech.*

He wrote *patient believes oneself to be an enlightened suicidal.*

The Protohuman was staring back at him when he turned and it too was stained with drugs.

On the worktop, atop a pile of rambling equations written out in a descending spiral, was a scrap on which was scrawled words of a conversation.

*You've been watched all your life, little Dziga. Into one hospital, into another. Another, another. You can never leave your cage, Dziga, don't you get that? You just forget that it's there, that's all.*

The handwriting was jagged and weak like a crumbling spider web.

*Just give it time. It's all behind the walls.*

Dziga folded the piece of paper up and slipped it into his breast pocket, walked up the corridor towards the observation room

The entire lab was a mess.

The warped sheets of metal he had stapled across all the openings had come loose in places as if the building was tearing itself apart from the inside out. Smaller patches repaired any gaps and every piece was spattered with rust like dermatitis. The microwave door dangled by a single hinge. The walls were studded with holes and peeling scraps of plaster and the impact points of Dmitri's bubble. Shelves had been dislodged and spilled their contents onto the workbenches below and then to the floor, the storage cupboards emptied. The sinks were filled with broken glass and vials of congealing chemicals; insects crawled amongst it all.

Blood stained the floor next to the Protohuman; the hallway where he had dragged Dmitri away; the operating theatre where Jakobsen was trapped in a spiderweb of his own sinew.

Dziga arrived at the observation room and slumped down wearily into the chair.

He watched the fragmented lab spill across the monitors before his eyes, worked the controls just to see what would happen. Close-ups and wide angles and blurry, shapeless views. If he listened carefully, he could hear the appropriate camera adjusting pitch and focus when he turned controls on the panel before him.

He turned to one of the larger monitors and something new appeared, a corridor unlike his own, so much brighter and a sudden shock jolted through Dziga and the image changed again. Again.

It was a rolling display, waltzing through a series of cameras repeatedly and despite working the controls the images progressed of their own will and so Dziga sat back and waited. Shot after shot came and it was his lab and it was his lab and it was his lab and then it wasn't again. Ready for it this time, he got a better view of what he had seen.

But that couldn't be.

While the monitor cycled he tried some of the other screens, flicking every switch he could find, turning every dial as fully as they would allow, and *there* and *there*, little glimpses of something else.

Somewhere else.

Dziga leaned closer, closer enough to feel the sting of the static and the menacing murmur of the electricity.

*What now?*

He hit a button on the keyboard and the current image froze on the larger monitor, that of a sink in the main lab spilling over with dark liquid and chemical effluent. He hit it again and the images cycled once more. Heart beating, head tumbling, waiting for the shot to . . . *there* . . . and he hit the button, captured the shot.

That was not his lab.

The image was grainer than most as if enlarged beyond what was intended but he could still make out certain telltale features—a dark strip running along the wall just below eye level, a row of small windows at precise intervals and dark nameplates beneath them, a blocky protrusion halfway up the cocaine-white corridor.

Dziga stared hard at the screen.

The dark strip ran throughout the entire asylum to guide partially-blind patients from room to room and to provide psychotics with some sort of focus as they were led in for ECT treatments.

The small windows were so the staff nurses could look in on patients but none of them ever did. Instead it was those trapped behind them who stared back out. The nameplates were labelled not with names but with conditions—*deviant psychosis, delusional stage three* & *primary necrophilia*—and beneath that a code number that matched the one branded into the back of the patient's head.

The blocky protrusion, that was a steel cabinet that housed sprays and weaponry in case of emergency.

His cell had been directly opposite one of those cabinets such that he had once headbanged himself into unconsciousness against the window glass while staring out at the compartment. His eyes drifted to the cell that would have been his.

A face was visible there—disfigured, blurry.

The monitor flicked onto another view, this one an overhead shot of a hospital bed, someone strapped to it with dark restraints and a cap of some sort. The figure tossed and turned, screamed.

Dziga's whole body shook and he collapsed into the chair.

He wrote *patient suffering from lapse of spatial memory.*

He wrote *patient showing signs of extreme terror.*
He wrote *patient will not stop screaming.*
He wrote *this cannot be.*

There was nothing left of the wall now, an entire three metre chunk torn away and lying on the ground. Dust filled the corridor like a dream and yet through it, through this dream, Dziga could see the off-white padding.

Behind the walls, which had come away far too easily, and behind a thin boarding of some kind.

It stank of disinfectant.

He pushed at the stuff and his finger sank in.

You couldn't tear it. He knew this because he had tried it at various times during his incarceration to break through the fabric as if he had believed that was all there was to the wall. He had often fallen asleep to the sounds of other inmates trying to do the same, the squeak-squeak of the coated leather.

This, in the asylum.

This, the padding now exposed behind the fraudulent walls of his lab and embedded in it the machines that would watch him.

Judas sat on top of Dmitri's legs, picking at his own skin.

Seeing the monkey, Dziga strode past and back into the main lab, found the scrap of paper he had awoken to some time earlier. He read from the aggressive handwriting . . .

*Just give it time. It's all behind the walls.*

And he read . . .

*You've been watched all your life, little Dziga. Into one hospital, into another. Another, another. You can never leave your cage, Dziga, don't you get that? You just forget that it's there, that's all.*

The sound of the proboscis crushing microscopic insects between his scabbed fingers echoed in Dziga's skull.

The simplicity of what was now becoming apparent made Dziga smile.

It was a simple, logical supposition which instantly and irrevocably explained everything that had been happening. Such perfect reason could only be indicative of the truth.

Who would want to control him?

The ones who had always sought to control him.

Who would keep watch over him?

The ones who had always kept watch over him.

Who would treat him like a laboratory experiment?

The ones who had always experimented on him.

He randomly chose an area of bare wall in the room and punched at it, denting the plaster and enflaming his fist in a ball of pain. Picked up a chunk of steel piping and slammed it into the dent until the wall broke away and then leaned in to kiss the padding that lay behind it.

Every wall. Every room.

Of course.

He crossed to one of the windows and pulled away the plating that he had hammered across it, letting the great sheet tumble noisily to the floor. The glass was thick with grease that he wiped away with his forearm, clearing it enough to make out the vague shapes of the factories and scrapyards in the near distance, the only view Dziga had had for so long.

But of course, that was fake too.

He looked at the great shadows for a few moments then drew back the pipe and struck it hard against the windows once, twice and it spiderwebbed, and three times and the glass shattered, falling onto him.

The view of the factories broke with it, another illusion falling to the floor.

And where the window had been, the same padding he had uncovered elsewhere.

And then the sound of something like a trolley being pulled along, a sound that triggered horrible memories inside him. Whispers?

"Yes!" he shouted manically, striking the worktop with the end of the pipe. "Perfect!"

Judas had crept back into the lab at the racket of the smashing window, peering out from behind the open door nervously.

"Perfect!" Dziga shouted again. "I never left! Do you see, I never left!"

The monkey swayed, wary of the scientist's excitement as he paced quickly from one side of the lab to the other.

"But what now?" Dziga asked. He looked around at the cracks in the walls in which the little spying machines hid. "What now?"

"Now it ends," a voice said and Dziga turned to its source, to the wall fixed with chains with dark splatters of blood on the floor beneath it.

Where the Protohuman should have been.

"*No.*"

He rushed over to the wall, grabbed the chains and barbed wire and then dropped them limply. The cuffs were unlocked and open.

"What have you done with him!" he shouted. "Give him back!"

He rushed out into the corridor, spinning around and around as he went, spinning to the whirr of the cameras, along past Dmitri's body and the growing stink of Jackobsen's corpse, through the rubble, pushing open doors as he passed them but no sign of the Protohuman. He kicked at the door to the observation room, storming into the electrical glow and seeing himself do it on the blurry monitors facing him in a tenfold reflection.

"Where is he . . . ?" he murmured, tracing the monitors. "*Where*?!"

But what would they take the creature for? Now that he knew where he was and what had been going on? Perhaps they thought that he would attempt to sabotage the Protohuman—were they so arrogant that they thought he would destroy his own work just to spite them?

Dziga randomly hit switches and buttons, turned dials, seeking for a glimpse of the Protohuman somewhere in the lab or even in the corridor that must have laid just outside the construct of the lab but there was *nothing*.

"NO!"

His body fizzed with anger, all the pressure of recent events solidifying inside him, pressing on his chest and stomach, curling around the base of his neck, burning like napalm. He switched views on the main monitor and it was looking down at the outside of the entrance to the observation room from just above eye level on the opposing wall. He could see Judas's diminutive silhouette in the doorway and turned.

The monkey was draped in a lab coat that might or might not have been Dziga's and was coolly watching him back.

"Judas. Where have they taken him?"

Judas scratched at his neck and when he took his fingers away they were patched with blood.

"Judas!" Dziga shouted suddenly and the proboscis jumped. It seemed to shake its head.

"You know what they've done, don't you?" Dziga said, striding towards the monkey, fists clenched, lab coat flapping behind him. Judas backed away awkwardly, always a few paces ahead. "You've known all along. You're a part of this!"

Dziga lashed out with a boot but the creature was too quick. "Judas, come here!"

He chased him around the corner, down the corridor, back past Dmitri's corpse until the monkey came to a halt by the door. It climbed the few steps and sat down calmly, facing Dziga.

The scientist reached down and picked up another piece of piping littering the floor, this one torn at one end, slapped it into the palm of his hand. His face was beginning to sting again with the strain of his blood pumping through his body.

He said, "Judas."

"Can you hear them?" Judas asked him, thumbing the door behind him.

The man has become monkey. The monkey has become man.

"They're always there," Judas said. "How are you feeling today? Any different?"

Dziga's breath was coming in sharp bursts, his vision clogging with sparkling lights like those that would be left over after a shock treatment. He noticed the monkey's name badge pinned to the coat's lapel but it had no name on it.

"Don't ask my how I feel. Don't act like you care."

"Of course we care. We want to help you, Dziga." Then, to thin air, "The patient still believes himself to be a scientist . . . "

"You never wanted to help me. Nobody ever helped me." He glanced back at Dmitri's body, draped within the shattered shell of his bubble. "Nobody."

Judas shook his head. "That's not true, Dziga. Now put the pipe down."

"No."

"*Put it down*, Dziga. And I'll tell you where your creature is."

Dziga's expression hardened. "Tell me."

"*Put it down.*"

"Don't tell me what to do . . . "

Dziga raised the pipe, tightened his grip on it. He could hear noises coming from outside now, the squeak of trolleys and rubber soles on plastic coated floors and perhaps the sounds were real but perhaps not.

"*Dziga* . . . "

"Give it back to me."

Now the smile dropped from Judas' face, now he backed up against the metal sheets beaten into place across the door. From one of the lab coat pockets he took out a surgical knife, its blade snapped halfway up across a rusted fracture.

Without a pause Dziga lashed out with the pipe, striking the monkey's arm and it shrieked, it shrieked but it had nowhere to go, Dziga had it cornered.

"What are you going to do, Dziga? What? They won't tolerate it."

Dziga took another step forward. His face felt as if it were pulsing like a heart. "They've tolerated it so far."

Judas backed up further, pressing himself against the metal, fear on his face for the first time.

"You think I did all this?! You fucking idiot—I'm just a monkey!"

He smiled broadly, perhaps half of his teeth all that was left.

And Dziga brought the pipe down hard in the middle of the creature's head.

## Chapter Thirteen
*Wherein Dziga awakens to find Judas dead*
*and becomes even more confused*

The corridor seemed to be broken, lit erratically by the light bulbs Dziga had smashed, nothing left of the walls. From one hole electrical cabling had been torn out and lay complacently in the darkness like strangled snakes.

Dziga had a hold of Judas' limp arm, dragged him along towards the others.

A corpse. Another corpse. Another.

Who was creating who?

There were spiral patterns of dark and bright blood on the floor from where he had moved what was left of Jakobsen's body and extricated Dmitri's from the bubble. His brother's skin had taken on an odd green tinge to it as if it were overreacting to the sudden exposure to the toxins in the air it had been protected from for so long. Dziga touched the man's forehead and his eyebrow split but no liquids came out. It crossed his mind to pick away at Dmitri's face until all the skin was gone and he should become a member of the Nu-Evolution.

He smiled.

The ranks were growing so quickly.

And as he arranged them against the wall he thought to himself *nothing but puppets.*

"You think you can trick me?" Dziga said to Judas, propping the monkey's emaciated form up a little more. "Turn me against myself?"

He stood, pacing the corridor, twitching at every sound, casting hateful stares at the dead betrayers as he tried to make some sort of order from it all.

"I want to know where my creature is. You," and he stopped before Jakobsen, "you started all of this."

"No." Jakobsen said. His head remained hanging precariously from his neck. "Try looking to your brother for the blame. He was sick and tired of caring for you and getting nothing in return. He asked me to do this. He was in it right from the start. I was only doing what I was told to do."

"Liar." Dmitri now, his fat, purple lips unmoving. "I was the only one who *did* care for my brother. I've only ever wanted to help him. I came to you for help but in the end it was *you* I needed to protect him from! You betrayed both of us, Jakobsen!"

Judas laughed quietly.

"And him!" Dmitri suddenly announced. "The damn monkey's been playing us all as pawns from the start. I've watched him, in that cage. I've seen the way he looks at us all. *He* is a Protohuman, Dziga, don't you see? He is more-than-human, both before and after our own evolution at the same time! You think it is *he* that *you* kept in that cage, *he* that *you* studied but you're wrong."

"It was you that he had caged," Jakobsen concurred.

Judas continued to laugh then stopped abruptly.

Dziga watched the puppets in their momentary silence. "Is this true?"

"We just said . . . " Jakobsen began but I cut him off.

"Shut up! Judas?"

"I'm just a monkey," he murmured.

"So are we!" Dmitri cried out.

"This is getting us nowhere . . . "

Dziga paced, paced, willing them quiet. *Shut up! Shut up!*

He listened to the sounds of the hot water system working away behind the walls, the sounds momentarily taking on new meaning—not the gurgles of heating fluids but test tubes processing samples of his blood and urine that minions would dutifully analyse.

Judas said, "They built you this cage just as they built me mine."

"That's not true, Dziga!" Jakobsen shouted, his head still drooping clumsily to one side. And Dziga thought, *if I was a better puppeteer, I could make his lips move* . . . "Don't fall for his lies. This place is real—I brought you here to help you get better. I knew your work could heal you! You remember your journey here? You remember?"

"Of course I remember," I snapped.

"No you don't!" Judas shouted. "You couldn't! The only journey you took was from one wing to another! You seriously think they would release you, Dziga?"

"I . . ."

"You don't remember Nadia lying her head on her iron pillow and you don't remember coming here. You just woke up here one day. Look at the walls!"

And Dziga did and the padding was still visible beyond the cracks, the padding from the asylum.

"There's nothing *there*, Dziga, he's tricking you!" Dmitri countered. "Look at the walls!"

And Dziga did and the padding had gone, replaced by damp, crumbling plaster.

He stopped pacing, stopped moving altogether, pressed his fingers to his head, juicing the exposed flesh. "I *can* remember . . . "

"You're right, Dziga," Dmitri reassured me. His skin had begun to pucker further in the poisonous air. "Don't listen to them, they're lying to you, trying to confuse you. Jakobsen brought you here, I should never have let him but I *did*. This place isn't a construction, brother—it's *real*. It is Jakobsen who is a fake! They're *lying* to you, Dziga!"

"You're *all* lying to me! Shut up!"

"Dziga, *listen* to me!"

"No!"

"I was only trying to *help* you Dziga!" Jakobsen cried out in defence. "I thought it would make you better, to take you out of the asylum. But your brother wanted the control he had over you while you were inside back! He insisted on installing the monitoring equipment!"

"No! I only insisted that we could keep an eye on him!"

"Spying!" Jakobsen retorted. "The cameras . . . "

Judas laughed again.

"Shut up you fucking monkey!" Dziga screamed.

"*Hush*," another voice said and it was gentle but overpowered all the others. Everything went quiet.

The lights flickered.

Dziga looked up from the corpses towards the end of the corridor. The shadows shivered, parted.

The Protohuman stood in the darkness, bloodied head glistening. He walked towards Dziga, past the inanimate corpses, turned. He pointed to the back of his neck, just above the hairline. Dziga reached out and pulled at the hair and it came away in a small clump and there was something burned into the flesh there.

"Do you see it, Dziga?" the Protohuman said.

"Yes," Dziga replied, and read the numbers described by the brand. "101.6"

"Do you remember, Dziga?" the Protohuman asked, stepping back into the shadows.

Dziga nodded in the silence. "I remember."

## Chapter Fourteen
*Wherein Dziga is left with no other*
*choice than to organise his escape*

I didn't know how long it had been since I'd last had anything to eat or drink.

One by one the lights in the lab had extinguished, the bulbs hissing into darkness or abruptly shattering for no reason, yet somehow the darkness was not complete and I had been unable to find the remaining sources of illumination.

There were smells; and silence.

They were tormenting me now, slowly letting me pull all of my legs off like a demented fly, waiting for the bloodflow to stop. Suddenly I was aware that the world is military.

But nobody was coming. I was alone there with the corpses and the rubble and the fragments of my work.

There's so little left.

My notebooks were all piled up in a cardboard box outside the main lab and I stared at the front door, waiting. Occasionally I listened and sometimes I heard the churning machines of the scrapyards but other times I heard the squeaking of orderlies' rubber soles on the plastic flooring. I didn't know which was real, if either.

And soon enough I realised I had no other choice but to find out.

I sat by door of the lab, staring at the rusted bolts that kept everything safe. I kept expecting a banging to start, someone banging, banging on the thick metal.

I stared and images of the Apocalypse formed in my head. Great cold fires and an endless parade of army vehicles blurred the horizon, the concrete beauty of a mushroom cloud filling the air. A thousand troops marched past my lab without even noticing it, without noticing me, and there I was on the other side, looking out at the repetitive scarring on each of their faces. They felt nothing. There was nothing left there.

They marched because they were soldiers and there was no reason for them to do otherwise. They did not feel fear beyond that which was efficient to their survival.

I could see through the lab's shell as if it were constructed from the same skin as Dmitri's bubble and watched one of the soldiers come to a halt. I looked into his eyes.

He smiled at me because he knew I was there. He knew he had touched God.

Then he raised the barrel of his rifle, adjusting his grip before his red, re-fabricated face, aimed the crosshairs and blew me away. And it happened so slowly that I could see the fragments of bone and brain matter expunge themselves from my head and noticed the flakes of iron and fibrous chrome that nestled there. My corpse fell back to the floor and the Protohuman stared down at me.

"I'm still here," he said.

But this was in my head, or mostly it was.

The Protohuman was gone again, for now, lying on the table in my surgery, breathing softly and as peaceful as a cancer patient awaiting death. The others remained slumped against the wall.

The stink was worse now.

Amongst the notebooks of paper I had gathered from around the lab there were scraps that I didn't recognise as my own. I put them in front of Judas to see if there was any reaction but his head had softened too much and he just lay there limply. I tried to make sense of the equations scribbled upon them but failed, smashing one of the few remaining intact shelves in the laboratory and pouring the broken glass onto the floor. Everywhere there seemed to be broken glass and debris and I knew the lab wasn't going to wait for me to leave. It had begun to force me out of its own accord.

I stared down at the broken glass and an army of me stared back. I couldn't help but think of the soldier I saw. Or hallucinated. Or dreamt.

Or foresaw?

I suddenly panicked and went to the door, listened for the uniform footsteps of a battalion of soldiers, of my children. My breath stung in my sunken chest and I noticed bloody scratches on the door. Had one of the puppets tried to escape me while I let their strings hang by their sides?

Or perhaps the marks were mine because my face had started bleeding again.

I laughed at the metal.

I was moving, we were moving. Everything must go.

I'd lifted the Protohuman that morning and brought him out into the corridor, laid him against the crumbling walls. His eyes fluttered, blinking bloody tears away. It had been an effort that had left me shaking with weakness and I wondered if it would be necessary for me to carry it far once I had left the lab.

Yet I still had no idea what awaited me.

I stuffed the puppets into a storage closet, briefly wishing that I could stand and watch them rot fully. My brother's skin had already begun to blacken in places where his hypersensitive skin bruised at the merest touch. I had racked them up against each other and looking at them, Judas to Dmitri to Jakobsen, was like looking at an illustration detailing evolution. I had to laugh for just down the corridor was the next stage in our biological progress and it would not lock itself inside a bubble, chain up those who would steal genius for capital gain or beat its head again steel bars until it bled.

And neither would it be endlessly affected by the death of those around it.

I locked the closet behind me, and stood before it for a moment.

They would never leave that place, I knew as I looked at it. That would be their eternal resting place, trapped in the hole of their deceit just as Nadia had been trapped on the train tracks all those years ago.

I felt the creatures' eyes upon me as I removed the final few plates from the front door that I had hammered in front of it . . . when . . . when was it I did that? I pressed an ear to the cold metal and listened to the sounds of the factories and machines filter in from outside.

The lab was real, wasn't it? The monkey had been tricking me. He had wanted to scare me into staying here, to study me—not the hospital. Not the hospital.

I disengaged the first lock.

There were no doctors. No ECT.

I disengaged the second lock.

There was no pain. Nothing could hurt the Protohuman.

I disengaged the third lock.

Nothing could hurt me again.

The weight of the door came back off its hinges slightly and a breeze crawled through the millimetre-thick gap that was opened. The Protohuman made an odd noise, perhaps a whimper. I could smell the tarry smoke of the breweries and waste management plants; hear the immense metallic screech of mining pumps having intercourse with the cold, hard ground.

From what had become my prison of near sensory deprivation I found myself subjected to a world that was full of noise and dangerous movements and bacterial armies. But my fear was distant, dislocated. It no longer sat inside my chest but trailed behind me like an IV unit – still feeding my veins and arteries but only in a light trickle, fighting against gravity.

I turned the handle slowly and the mechanism cried out, a true part of the machine-city that lay beyond. And as the door opened and I took my first step outside, my thoughts were no longer of impatient assassins or orderlies ready with sedatives, the lab was no longer a haven but a cage—and everything began to clear.

The air was warmer than I had expected though a good ten degrees less than inside the lab. It was thick with smoke, in such a way that there were no sharp edges—everything blurred into its neighbour, be it chrome, concrete or the night sky. I saw how it was all interconnected and I knew then that the Protohuman project would go on, somehow, because it had a part to play in the organism of evolution.

My spirits lifted, I breathed deeply, tasting the acid in the air at the back of my throat. Of course it was all real. Of course I would be free.

The city went on for as far as I could see, the factories becoming smaller and smaller, intermeshing at the horizon. In the midst of the patchwork of steel that lay there I saw a bright red light, perhaps a warning beacon for the governmental helicopters that occasionally flew overhead.

That would be my star. That would lead to me to the place of safety where the Protohuman could be finalised in peace and safety.

I suddenly wondered why I had waited so long to try and get out of the lab. I hadn't needed Jakobsen or anyone else, at least not for a long time. All my reliance on him and my brother had done was loosen the foundation upon which I balanced precariously.

I began to make plans in my head as I took another few steps from the doorway across the dusty clearing in the front of it. There were bundles of barbed wire and piles of tyres delineating the area from the exposed pipes of the nearest production plants Further ahead, great stacks of oil drums and hazardous waste transporters.

No orderlies. Never again.

I smiled inwardly, already beginning to formulate in my head the design for a contraption which would allow me to transport the Protohuman to the beacon, and our new research base.

But my smile fell when I heard the crash of metal as the lab door swung shut behind me.

My hands sprayed blood onto I began to lose control of my shrieking as I frantically scrabbled at the door. My feeling of comfort had been precarious, the fall from it fast and hard. As soon as I had realised what had happened I had grabbed at the door but there was no handle on the outside, as I had had it removed at my own request upon my arrival all those months ago. There was a little give in the frame but nowhere near enough for me to hope to lever myself in.

My heart raced, my blood filling with the poisons in the air.

The noise of the factories seemed to increase, the whistles of steam shafts piercing my ears and making me dizzy. The acid sting was like nails against my skin. I grabbed a fractured girder from the rubble at the edge of the clearing and struck the door once, twice, three times, barely denting it on each attempt.

I cried out for the Protohuman but I knew already that it was useless. It wasn't capable yet of such a response. And even if it had been . . .

My skin froze as the image of those who would come for me creeping across through the rubble of burnt-out cars and smouldering fires flashed before me and I suddenly knew I would see the glint of their eyes, the glint of their needles, coming towards me.

I should never have let my guard down and become distracted by the outside so quickly.

"No!" I cried into the metal, slamming it with my bare fists helplessly, my head snapping in every direction as I heard new sounds—crunching and breathing and the clack of pistols being cocked. I could almost feel their arms upon me.

I hit the door.

Hit the door.

Hit the door.

I clung to the lab as I would have my mother.

Noises. Movement amongst the electronic trash, whispers.

I closed my ragged eyelids, bleeding over the world, my body shaking from the effort.

I felt like I had to run but had nowhere to run to, a kind of fearful energy building up inside me that I knew would explode at any moment. I could have just run from the lab, away across the wasteland—but not without my creature. My work was the Protohuman and my life was my work. If I didn't have it then I had no need for my own life.

And as I lay slumped against the door the whispers transposed themselves and now they came from inside the lab. They were inside the lab.

Who was inside?

"*No!*"

The Protohuman.

And this time I banged on the door not to escape back into the safety of the lab but in a sudden fury that I had been separated from my work.

"No! What are you doing?!"

Footsteps, lots of them. An army of them.

I peered into the small window but there was still a piece of metal plating hammered across it and what I could see was distorted by grease and dirt. But there were people moving around in there again.

The Engineers?

"Let me in!" I screamed, I screamed, I screamed.

And a voice said "Dziga," and everything went quiet again. I was aware of the great machines in the distance stopping all work, frozen.

I touched the metal of the door and it was scorched from the vicious air and angry hot currents from the nearby smelting plant.

"What . . . ?"

There was a heavy click and the door loosened in its frame. The pressure of the locks had gone and I pushed the door slightly with my forefinger and it moved, it moved, it was opening.

So there was the fear of the world and everything it might contain.

And there was the fear of the lab and everything I already knew it would contain; my cage, my rusted iron sarcophagus, my pneumatic womb.

I breathed once, twice.

Then opened the door.

## Chapter Fifteen

*Wherein Dziga confronts the Protohuman and they become one*

There was no one there.

No lurking figures, no more footsteps.

No squeak of rubber soles against plastic flooring. Nothing.

The piles of paper and chemicals that I had stacked up inside the corridor remained as they were before I had been shut out of the lab. The debris remained but were now joined by the corpses, my puppets.

They lay slumped awkwardly across one another, the storage cupboard open and ransacked. Jakobsen looked like he had been turned inside out but perhaps he had been like that when I had stuffed him in there.

And before them, a message scrawled on the floor.

*You will never get out.*

The words were still wet and running, a dark glutinous red.

*Never. Get. Out.*

Everything was so quiet.

Through the still-open door behind me, the great rusted machines hissed and grated and rumbled in the distance once more, reminding me of their presence.

And at the end of the corridor, the fizzing blue glow that emanated more brightly than ever from the observation room, silhouetting the vague figure of the Protohuman just as it disappeared around the corner. I began towards him then stopped.

My breathing remained laboured but seemed to have shallowed out and I looked down to see that I was standing in the bloody message.

I couldn't swallow. *Just take me.* I felt like I had been lingering on a precipice for so long now that all I wanted was for the wind to sweep me forwards and off into whatever lay below if it meant not having to stare at my death any longer.

I froze where I was, listened.

I gazed down into the blackness below me, wondering what machine-parts, what jagged persecution, lay there. This was the feeling of standing by a roadside and calmly walking into the traffic, of climbing onto a bridge and then stepping off, of holding your head under the water and fighting against your body's every instinct—of not taking your own life but of just letting it go.

"Dziga."

The word, my name, crept through the poisoned air like an arachnid, crunched through the broken Pyrex. I went towards the static light emanating from the observation room and the Protohuman was waiting for me, not so much standing as hanging, as if he were being maintained by an unseen suspension. His hands were crossed before him, his bloodied, guilty hands.

How far he had come.

"Dziga," he said, the first word he had ever spoken.

"What are you doing to me?" I pleaded softly. "What is this?"

He was the only one left, the only one that hadn't betrayed me.

"Dziga." Like a heartbeat, like a heartbeat.

He held up his hands for me then pointed and I looked at my own hands. They were as bloodied as his.

"Dziga."

He motioned for me to sit in the chair and I did so. He loomed over me and took my wrist, slipped it into a leather cuff that was attached to the chair, that was a *part* of the chair. He tightened it, repeated the procedure on the other wrist, then on my ankles.

Images of the lab flickered across the screens before me, and of the factories and drilling machines outside and of the hospital wards, all merging with one another. And then a shot of us in the present and on the screen I watched my creature secure me to the chair solemnly just as the doctors would have when I was due for a treatment.

Electricity filled the air like a swarm of insects.

"Are we safe?" I asked the Protohuman as he finished his work and stood beside me. The restraints were tight enough that I could only sense him there but I watched him on one of the monitors. "They're not coming, are they?"

"There's nobody here, Dziga," the creature said. "Just you."

"So we're safe."

The Protohuman didn't answer. Instead he said, "Watch."

So I did.

Dziga is hunched over his desk, scribbling madly on several pieces of paper spread out before him. In the corner of the shot, Judas circles in his cage, turning, turning, turning. Dziga looks up and says something and the monkey is still. Dziga stands and turns.

Cut.

Dziga washes himself over the sink, staring into a grubby mirror. Scrubs his face, his neck.

Watches his reflection.

Cut.

Jakobsen sits beside Dziga on a ratty, torn sofa chair, holding a steaming mug in one hand. The two talk, then Jakobsen hands the scientist something, rolled up newspapers. In return Dziga gives him a single scrap of paper. A further verbal exchange takes place and they both stand. The camera cuts with them, following them along the corridor and into the main lab.

From the same camera view as before, Judas' cage is sheathed in a black cloth.

The screen flickers, sparked by static.

They both stand before the Protohuman, blocking the camera's view of the creature.

Cut.

From another angle, above their heads, the two men stare at the wall.

At something propped up against the wall.

Cut.


Close-up of Dziga's faced crumpling as he sinks a needle into his arm.

Cut.

Dziga feeding a line of powder into each nostril.

Cut.

Dziga placing two tablets on his tongue, rolling them back.

Cut.

Dziga passed out on the floor, surrounded by broken glass and scalpel blades. Staring up in the camera with a vague smile on his blurry face.

Cut.

Dziga moving through the lab from one desk to another, from one room to another, the film speed double what it should be so that his movements are jerky, comical. He takes a syringe and opens the chest freezer, pulls out all the food, and injects.

Cut.


Dziga spreads out newspapers across his workbenches, pulling pages from them at random, throwing them to the floor, inadvertently blocking the cameras view.

Cut.

Now beside him as he works feverishly with the newsprint.

Stops.

Cut.

101.6.

Cut.

Dziga is moving again, pacing up and down the main lab and his image is somehow reflected behind him. There is a mirror chained to the wall behind him.

Cut.

He is in the corridor, raking through a cupboard, pulling pieces of equipment from the shelves and dropping them to the ground. He takes something out and it drags a cord behind it.

Cut.

He places it on the counter and pressed the cord into an electrical socket next to the microwave.

Cut.

Close-up from behind the counter and the cord is frayed, wires peeling out of their protective coating and Dziga tried to shove these into the plug socket. They drop out limply but Dziga hits the power switch anyway. He adjusts the frequency dial, jumps as if he has been given a shock.

Cut.


Dziga carries something from the main lab into his operating room. It is tall, rectangular, thin.

Light glints within it when it is at certain angles.

He lays it on the operating table and straps it down.

Cut.


The door opens and what lies beyond it is a strange creature cocooned in a bubble-machine. Dziga steps to one side and the creatures rolls into the lab.

Cut.

They are in the main lab, beside Judas' cage. Dziga pokes through the bars and the monkey retreats.

Cut.


And Dziga stands over his operating table, pulls himself up onto it. He swivels, lies down on it. He reaches to each side and puts on leg restraints, then one on his left wrist. With his one free hand he reaches back and takes a metal cap from one of the trays and places it on his head. He grips the table and jerks suddenly.

The camera stares down at him as tears spill from his eyes.

Cut.

Dziga works, Dziga works. A convoluted system of clear glass pipes and test tubes are arranged on the workbench and he moves amongst them. He scribbles notes.

Cut.

He tears through a newspaper.

Cut.

He feeds Judas.

Cut.

He looks up from his work.

Cut.

He enters the corridor, stares at the door, then suddenly turns and runs into one of the storage closets. He presses himself deep inside and closes the door. Inside, he bangs from wall to wall, knocking things from the shelves, crushing them

Cut.

And he bursts from the cupboard, stumbles, flailing at nothing, nothing at all. He collides with the opposite wall and falls to the ground, hiding his face with his hands in sheer terror.

Cut.

Dziga stares into the mirror, grinning.

He is partway through the procedure, half of his face at first what appears to be in shadow but then more clearly visible as being sheathed in blood. He hold a scalpel in one hand, uses the other to tighten his skin before he pushes the blade in and begins to cut more pieces away. He takes a loose flap between thumb and forefinger and pulls. It peels off like rotting wallpaper and he drops it into the sink beneath him, the constant stream of running water chasing these fragments away.

Cut.

Everything froze.

"Do you see?" a voice said, somewhere behind me. This is now, this is live, this is no recording.

"I see," I replied softly.

Then the tapes started playing again.

Cut to a wide-angle view of the lab and Jakobsen standing before Dziga, clutching his briefcase. He is gesticulating wildly and Dziga, face a carpet of frayed red edges, grin back. Suddenly Dziga slaps the briefcase from the man's hands and jumps at him. There is a struggle, the shots cutting quickly, too quickly, and nothing is quiet clear.

Dziga grabs Jakobsen's head and shoves it into the ground until it is a head no longer.

Cut.

Dziga swings, swings a hammer, and the shot pans out to show him attacking the unmoving corpse of his brother, draped in the ruins of his broken bubble. Dziga hits him again and again and again.

Cut.

Dziga is still punching and this time it is the wall he is attacking, chipping at it with a fragment of steel, breaking the plaster away in chunks. He leans in.

Cut.

Dziga stares into the camera, eyes widening.

Cut.

Dziga runs through the lab, hands covering his ears, screaming.

Cut.

Dziga is staring into the object he earlier had laid out on the operating table. He is talking to it, his words numb.

Cut.

He is breaking more pieces of the wall away again, punching through to a storage room, ignoring the door that was slightly to the left and creating his own entrance. He steps inside and the room is empty.

Cut.

He sits on the floor of the empty room, staring at the rear wall.

Cut to close-up.

His eyes move as if he is following something. His bloodied face glows in an non-existent light.

Dziga watches himself.

Cut.


"Do you understand?" a voice said.

My voice said.

I said.

I turned to look at the Protohuman, no longer there. I turned back and the monitors were all gone, everything gone, and I was sitting on the cold, hard floor staring at a blank wall.

"I understand," I told myself.

I understand I am alone. I understand there is no one here.

I got up and walked back down the corridor, past the bodies and into the main lab.

Chained to the wall was a large mirror, five and half feet by two and a half feet, framed with chunky metal, cracked in places around the edges but clear and clean. I knelt before it and the Protohuman stared back at me.

And as everything became clearer, as it does when you are faced by your own demise, I smiled a little.

The Protohuman smiled a little.

And I realised I had built a god.

There was only a small part of me left now, the only thing that linked us to the human race, the final strand of DNA to be unravelled. After this what? Would there be a place for the Protohuman out there, amidst the dunes of static and wrecking yards? In that instant I pictured us wandering majestically through the wastescape, a

Chromosomic Prince that continued what I had begun, discarding the irrelevancies, inconsistencies and irrationalities of *Homo Sapiens.*

The creature moved as I moved, my reflection.

It was my duty as the progenitor of the Protohuman to step aside when we had reached a point where I myself was too full of irrationalities to be of use to our development. How many painters can leave their portraits to complete the rendering themselves? How proud would a sculptor be as he observed his finest work cleave itself from the raw block it started as, shaping and toning itself by the very hand the sculptor gave it?

And yet I could not deny my own instincts. That final human part of me was not ready to be discarded.

I stared back at it from within the glass, mocking the arrogance that allowed it to think that it had not outgrown me and that it was through a mistake of my own making that I had made this error in the Protohuman's maturation.

"Let me go," Dziga said to me as firmly as he could manage. "I want to take you away from here. It doesn't matter if you're responsible for all this, none of that matters. I forgive you."

But the pact he was trying to make was a desperate one, the pact of a convict trying to buy his way out of his execution when he had nothing of value for his executioner.

"I don't want to have to harm you, but I will if you leave me no other choice."

I could see myself so clearly and my expression was as unreadable as I had intended—anger or deceit or happiness, which? I was so proud.

"Dziga," the human said again. "Would you kill me?"

But I was no longer a part of that name, of that creature.

I raised my hand and showed him the scalpel.

There was fear on Dziga's face. There would never be fear on my face again. Never.

*Automatonophobia*—Fear of anything that falsely represents a sentient being.

"Don't . . . " he said weakly.

But he knew what would happen.

And he looked down again at my bloodied hands and the blade.

I told him, "*You will never get out.*"

And I shoved the knife into his face, cutting and thrusting , punching him with it, hard, harder, again and again and there was the sound of glass shattering and more and I grew wet with blood and it was beautiful.

When I finished I looked down and there were a thousand fragments of me staring back instead of just one.

An army.

I stood, walked into the corridor and then wrote on the floor with my bloodied hands.

*Never get out.*


The Protohuman is that which sustains me, the concept, the hallucination. The dream and nightmare. I watch myself stoop over the mirror, telling it I am going to draw blood, then sink the needle into my own arm. I take notes. I draw up further procedures. I try to escape myself. I try to escape everything that I am.

Over. And over. And over.

But I can't escape myself.

I can't escape.

I will never get out.

*Never. Get. Out.*

It all goes around. Everything is cycles, a production line. I build myself then that new construction builds another. There is no purpose to it. Its creation. There is no reason.

And I will never get out.

# DEVASTATION

The thing was immense and skeletal, rising out of the spray of the rain, one hundred feet and more, jagged and painfully incomplete. She stared up at a length of girders towards the very top of it through the grimy window of the bus as they left the construction site. It looked like a finger, pointing.

She sat towards the back of the bus, away from the other workers, although nobody really spoke anyway. The rain made it sound as if they were driving through a war zone, water machine gunning against the rusted metal of the vehicle. She played with the dressing that was wrapped around her wrist, prodding the soft flesh beneath just to feel it sting.

The bus arrived at the drop-off point and the workers began to unload, gathering their bags and belongings from the storage area underneath the seating. She took her own backpack and left without exchanging a word with anyone.

It was a simple three block walk to the squat but she procrastinated, meandering through alleys and across the loading bay of a storage warehouse, down through an underground tunnel that passed beneath the main road. Around. Around. She was already soaked through but the rain didn't bother her.

Eventually she ran out of diversions to take and approached the old house she had been squatting in for . . . for how long? She couldn't remember. It was three stories high, around twenty rooms but most of them were completely unliveable. She produced a key and unlocked the padlock holding together the chain link perimeter fencing around the back then climbed in the kitchen window. The doors had all been nailed shut.

The sudden softening of the noise of the wind and rain made the place seem even more desolate than she remembered it.

*Keep going* she whispered to herself.

She breathed in. Dumped her bag on the ground and slowly walked out and into the narrow main corridor. The tag art of previous tenants covered the walls, covered the once-expensive wallpaper, the once-glorious decorations. There were scorch marks where fires had been set. Chunks of plaster missing to reveal the support beams beyond.

The building a corpse, slowly rotting.

"This is my home," she said aloud, because it didn't feel like it and she needed that reassurance.

She listened to the sounds of the house, the plumbing, the floor-boards, the click and hum of a defunct heating system. She listened within these noises, between them.

Her heart rate was steadily rising, she fought to control it.

He'd told her that she wasn't ready to return but she hadn't taken any notice. What reason was there not to?

She stood at the foot of the staircase, looking up. It looked like the entrance to another plane of reality, or a dream. Slowly she climbed, staring at her feet because she couldn't bare to think of something waiting for her up there, in the shadows.

One by one by one by one.

Past two rooms nailed shut with biohazard flowers stencilled across them alongside lovers names.

Fourth door on the left.

Inside—the bare mattress, the tossed sheets. Empty bottles of water. Some CDs.

An upturned television, face down amongst the glittering frag-ments of its own screen.

She entered the room, tried to suppress the sensation of something behind her.

Perhaps it *was* too soon.

"There's nothing wrong," she said to herself. She was rubbing her wrist subconsciously, suddenly aware of the stinging there.

She lay down on the mattress, her muscles sighing with relief. She had to lie on one side because of the rods in her back that were all that was left of the spinal brace. Stared out towards the window.

At first the noise seemed like nothing more than the splatter of rain against the windowsill or the tree branches outside but it quickly became more than that. She tried to control her breathing, to soften it.

There was a sudden flare of light and the upturned television began to glow.

"No . . . "

She heard the desperate whine in her voice and hated it but couldn't help it.

The static hiss grew louder as if someone was turning the volume up steadily on the dead TV.

She wanted to sit up. She wanted to move or cover her ears or *something*.

Another flicker, this one filling the room like a quick explosion.

Something moved across the window, a shape.

She looked away suddenly. Told herself it wasn't real.

She looked back and it was still there, a reflection lingering in the cold glass and panic swept through her in one guttural tremor. A figure, a man, grainy and broken like a bad television signal.

She got up and ran.


Everything in the medical suite was a bright headache-white as if to give the illusion of approaching Heaven.

Luca pressed the needle into her arm quickly and gently, prepped another one.

She looked over his shoulder, focusing her attention elsewhere. At the row of three beds, two empty, the other with the privacy curtain pulled halfway around it. At the glistening pieces of equipment that lined the walls and the small windows that looked out of the temporary structure to the construction site beyond. At this man, Luca, who touched her so softly.

"Have the rods been giving you any trouble?"

She had her arms crossed over her bare breasts as he lightly touched her lower back. "They ache a little sometimes."

"The areas around them look a little swollen. We'll have to watch that. But apart from that you've almost made a full recovery. How do you feel working again?"

"I couldn't lie in that bed any longer."

"I understand," Luca said, touched her arm. "I'm lucky if I can get most of my patients to stay in for a few hours. Having you here for those weeks . . . well, it was company if nothing else."

She didn't say anything, just stared along to the closed curtain.

"How about otherwise, Ylena? Any other problems?"

She had already made up her mind not to say anything. The night had been long and hard, small snatches of sleep on park benches and doorways because she had been unable to go back to the squat. As the sun had risen, however, her apprehension had lifted. She had panicked, that was all. The painkillers were distorting everything . . .

"None."

"That's a good sign. For a fall of that size you've made a surprisingly quick recovery."

"I can't remember it," she said. "Any of it. That night."

"That's normal," Luca assured her. "You sustained a massive blow to the head along with everything else. Memory loss is expected."

It looked to her like he was peeling his skin off as he removed his surgical gloves. She blinked the image away.

"I want to remember, though. I want to know what happened."

She looked at him then, her greenish eyes wide and wet, brow furrowed as it always was. "I need to know."

Luca nodded. "You're due on in five minutes. How about you come back here after your shift, we can talk further. Maybe get a drink or something."

The machines beeped and hummed over his shoulder and the patient behind the screen stirred.

"I don't know," she said. "Maybe."

Another three floors had been started on since she had fallen, one of them almost finished. She had manoeuvred to the top floor which was still just steel girders and support beams. Plastic sheeting had been pulled over the area to protect it from the rain, creating a deafening drone of noise that filled her head.

She used a nailgun to bolt into place a strip of iron then finished the work with a few deft blows of a hammer. There were a half dozen other workers that she could see, some attached to suspension cords, others relying on their own experience and balance. She had never worn a cord.

She left the nailgun and made her way to the outer edges of the framework. She pushed aside the plastic and was immediately battered by a strong blast of wind but instinctively she grabbed a pole for support. The only reason she could tell where the ground was far below was because of the red cross painted across the top of Luca's portable hospital ward.

She closed her eyes and listened to the wind, imagined falling through it.

And she realised she didn't even know where it was she fell from.

Once the shift was over she knocked on the door to Luca's building and he smiled when he saw her.

"I could use some coffee," she said.

"You'd become caught up in some of the weatherproof sheeting as you had fallen and it must have acted in part like a parachute to slow you down enough that you were still alive when I found you. I thought a bomb had gone off from the sound of the impact and then there you were, wrapped up in all that plastic."

She stirred her coffee endlessly, watched her reflection swirl in the darkness.

"The wind carried you away from the building too. I've had a few that have been thrown into the construction rather than away from it and believe me, what's left is no pretty sight."

"How far did I fall?"

"About thirteen stories. You were on the top floor. Or, what *was* the top floor."

"I've never fallen before. I never use suspension cords."

"Maybe now's a good time to start," Luca said, smiled.

A waitress arrived with his order of soup. Her hair was teased into several foot-long Mohawk spikes, each one dyed a different colour, a punk statue of liberty. She tongued her lip ring as she asked them, "Anything else?"

Luca waved her away and she sidled back to her previous position, slumped across the serving counter.

"I can't remember any of it."

Luca reached across towards Ylena's hands, wrapped around the coffee cup.

"You said memory loss was expected, " she said softly, not looking up. "What else?"

"What do you mean?"

"A blow to the head . . . what other side effects can it cause?"

Luca frowned, leaned forwards. "What do you mean? Have you had any other symptoms?"

In the cold coffee, Ylena's face rippled as if her very being was becoming distorted. "I . . . can't sleep."

"Insomnia?"

She shook her head. "No."

She withdrew her hands abruptly but Luca reached out to her again, pulled her back. "I've . . . seen things. And I'm not sure if they are real."

"Hallucinations," Luca said, not a question this time.

"I don't . . . I guess so . . . They feel real."

"Most do. Have you been having many headaches? Maybe I should take another look at you."

"No . . . please. You've done enough already. I just . . . I feel . . . "

"*What*?" Luca urged softly.

"Dread," she said suddenly and looked him in the eyes for the first time. "I feel as if something awful is about to happen and there's nothing I can do to stop it."

"What do you think is about to happen?"

"That's just it, I don't know. It doesn't seem related to anything, except perhaps the squat. But this feeling, it follows me."

"You slept rough last night didn't you?"

Ylena looked a little unnerved by the observation. Luca smiled. "I could smell the oil on your clothes. It just sits in the air down by the factories but you don't stink that bad by just walking past them."

"Oh . . . " She wrapped the workshirt she wore around herself tighter as if suddenly self conscious.

"It's okay," Luca reassured her, still smiling. "But maybe you could do with a bath."

Ylena seemed to soften. "There's no running water in the squat."

"There's a tub in my apartment."

Ylena held his gaze.

"I don't think you should be alone tonight," Luca said.

Washing her slowly, the candlelight reflected in each drop that sat like a pearl upon her skin. Nursing her scars, caressing them. Unravelling her limbs, unravelling her tension, reminding her that the blood still flowed. Gentle, sweet, the dread begins to fade, spilling into the bathwater, left behind when he lifts her out. The towel soft like his lips, then the heat of their bodies.

In the night, in the dull heat of Luca's apartment, in the tangle of moist sheets.

She stared at a dreamcatcher hanging from the ceiling, mottled feathers swaying gently in the updraft as if the thing was currently working its way through Luca's dream. She could almost see fragments of his subconscious mingling there amongst the shells and stones and bones.

His touch had been distantly familiar, her foggy memories of the time after the accident filled with it and that feeling had brought her some security, as if it attached her once more to that from which she felt had come loose. Yet now she lay apart from him, having slipped out from between his arms, a gutter of two inches of space between them.

Outside a storm festered, raising the temperature degree by degree, pressing itself against the window. Lightning flashed and Ylena sat up with a start, her breath coming quick.

Something had moved.

Most of the room was in shadow, sparsely furnished, shapes inventing themselves.

She gripped the bed sheets to her breasts, holding her breath so that she could listen into the silence.

Something there.

Another crackle of lighting and she jumped.

She had seen a figure in the corner. Gone now.

Her breath began to come in quick, sharp blasts. The air sparkled on her tongue.

A sound, a whisper.

She pleaded.

"No . . . ."

Luca stirred beside her.

Goosebumps patterned her skin. She had stopped breathing.

"Ylena . . . "

She turned, looked down at Luca's prone form next to her. His mouth was still yet her name slid from between his lips.

"Ylena . . . "

She felt the primitive urge to close her eyes, to shut her senses down and escape the fear but there was no escape. She reached out towards him, hand shaking. His chest rose and fell with each breath.

"Ylena . . . "

The word drifted from him again and she hesitated, her fingertips an inch from his arm. He lay on one side, curled foetally, sweat trickling from his brow.

"Luca."

She touched him and it felt like she had been bitten, snapped her hand away and Luca shot awake suddenly. The room was lit by a lightning strike and he gasped for breath, something shifted across his face, blurred, static grain.

Not Luca's face.

A scream escaped Ylena's lips before she could stop it. She threw herself backwards away from him, off the bed, hitting the ground hard.

Another flash of lighting and there was someone standing in the corner of the room, hands crossed before them. The image jerked and spat as if distorted with interference. A radio on a table near the bathroom blared suddenly, screaming noise for one terrible moment before falling silent again.

"Stop it!" she cried out, and buried her face in her hands.

She felt someone grab her and screamed again but it was Luca's voice she heard and when she looked up this time, his thin dark Soviet eyes were staring back at her.

"It's okay," he said. "It's okay."

A mantra, soothing her towards calm again . . .

She let him embrace her, couldn't help the tears that leaked out and down his back.

Her fingers found a rough patch and Luca hissed in pain when she touched it. He drew away from her and turned.

"What the . . . "?

He moved into the light coming in through the window.

On his back, just beneath his left shoulder blade—a slim, inch long wound that he instantly diagnosed for he had seen it so many times on-site.

An electrical burn.

The low-level workers, the grunts and welders like Ylena, worked on a per-day basis, their knowledge of the building's shape and size and structure limited to the next type of join they had to make or the positioning of a beam. Nothing more.

Builds such as the one she was currently assigned to often seemed infinite with more and more levels being piled on top of the existing ones as each week passed. There was now seventeen floors and the skeleton of more were being added above her. The sky beyond it seemed iron clad as if it were part of the same structure, ready to be joined onto. Ylena could almost see the rivets holding it together.

"Careful," one of the others said as they passed her by. He held a heavy steel plate in his gloved hands, an oxygen filter dangling from his neck for use if he got out of breath at the high altitudes.

He was gone before Ylena could acknowledge him, a little stunned at the comment because it would normally be deemed offensive. Had he seen her lingering on the edges of the skyscraper, contemplating the fall? She had found herself uncontrollably drawn there repeatedly over the days following that first night at Luca's, tantalised by the whisper's breath between security and death.

She edged further along the girder, the high winds buffeting her. She held both arms out a little to steady herself. Luca's building was a blur now, the red cross smeared with rainwater and mud. She closed her eyes as she had each time before and instantly her balance shifted. Arms raised. Heartbeat increased.

She thought that perhaps the fear that was still lodged inside her was left over from the fall for as she leaned over the very edge of the girder she felt nothing but peace. The first few times she had been drawn to the edge she had considered that the fall had been so fast that she hadn't had time to become scared but now she thought differently. Now she wondered if she hadn't been scared because it had been what she had wanted.

What if it hadn't been an accident?

She caressed the fresh dressing on her wrist, working the wound that was refusing to heal despite Luca's attempts.

A sudden noise made her jump and it took all her years of experience to catch her balance once more with nothing to hold onto. Behind her the radio of one of the workers had blared to life. Out on the horizon, an electrical storm was gathering, great spikes of blue light ricocheting around in a field of pylons.

One step, she thought. One step.

Ylena raised one foot and took it off the girder.


"I think I jumped," she said suddenly, in the post-coital silence. Her sweat had cooled to a freezing sheen on her body as she paced from one end of the room to the other.

"*Jumped*? Why would you do that?"

"I don't know. Why does anybody?"

"What kind of question is that? Lots of reasons."

"So why is it so unreasonable to assume I couldn't have had such a reason?"

"Okay, it's *possible*," Luca said, turning and sitting on the edge of the bed, his back now to her. "But I just don't think . . . "

"Well how would *you* know! *I* don't even know!"

"Will you sit fucking down!" Luca snapped. "I can't concentrate."

"I want to go out," Ylena said, still moving. Her arms were wrapped tight around herself as she had gotten into the habit of doing, securing herself as if parts of her might float away. "I want to go for a walk."

"I've told you already, I don't think that's a good idea."

"You can't fucking *keep* me here!" Her pacing became more frantic. "I want to go back to the squat. I'm ready to go back to the squat."

"Don't be ridiculous—remember what happened the last time."

"That was weeks ago!"

"And you're even jumpier now than you were then!"

"Only because you keep me locked up in here," Ylena muttered under her breath. She stopped by the window, stared out.

Luca went to her and touched her arm but she snatched it away. "Locked up, bullshit. You're free to go whenever you want, Ylena".

"Fine. Then I will."

She began to dress herself, pulling on her work boiler suit because it was still piled on the floor by the bed. Luca grabbed her wrist and she cried out in pain. Blood began to soak through the dressing.

"Oh God, I'm sorry, Ylena. I didn't mean to . . . "

She backed away from him, gripping her arm.

"I only want to help you. That's all I ever wanted."

"I'm going out," Ylena said flatly. Slammed the door behind her.

The storms, like the skyscraper, would go on forever,—she knew that now.

Dark clouds choked the sky, unloading themselves in a heavy and constant stream of silvery rain. The air crackled with energy as she ran through the streets, just ran.

She kept her head down, quickening her pace as the sensation of somebody just behind her returned, a feeling of lurking intent, a weight. Her tears were lost amidst the rain.

Lightning flashed and she stopped suddenly as a figure was revealed ahead of her. The shape was described in flickering static, a TV ghost.

"Stop it . . . "

She pressed at her head, turning and running off to her left and now wet footsteps chasing her, she screamed, legs burning with the exertion, stumbling into a dumpster that she recognised instantly. She looked up and saw the squat at the end of the block.

"*Ylena* . . . "

She jumped, turned.

Nothing.

Running again, through the vicious rain falling like scalpel blades.

She pulled the key from the sole of her boots where she had kept it since moving in with Luca and unlocked the padlock on the fence. She jumped at the open window and felt something brush against her ankle as she pulled herself through as if something had tried to grab her. Then inside and the noise of the storm faded.

She lay on the floor for almost a minute, looking back up at the window and expecting to see someone climb through, before getting to her feet. She was soaked through, trailing water behind her as she made her way along the corridor.

The squat felt different this time, protective rather than threatening.

She climbed the stairs slowly, past the doors with the biohazard flowers and into the room beyond. Stopped and turned back.

The stencilled flowers were rough and had been scraped away in places, beneath them names etched into the woodwork.

YD+VN.

She traced the letters with her forefinger and it felt as if she were following a path she had taken many times before. There was familiarity there but nothing more. Her own breathing echoed in her ears.

She traced the letters over and over as if she were stroking a reluctant animal into trusting her, encouraging the marks to reveal themselves. Her hands began to shake, repeating the manoeuvre more frantically, again, again.

"Ylena."

A crack of fierce lighting exploded outside, visible through the hall windows and she jumped.

A figure climbed the stairs and this time it didn't shimmer, didn't disappear.

"What are you doing here?" she asked it.

"I followed you. I knew you'd come back here."

"Where else is there for me?"

"You know where," the figure said.

"These initials . . . " Ylena stroked them as she spoke. "I remember them."

"They're just initials."

"*My* initials."

"This is a squat—do you know how many people have been in here?"

"These are *mine*," she insisted as the man climbed another few steps. "I remember knifing it into the door."

"No you don't. You *think* you remember. You *want* to remember. But the fall . . . "

"*Fuck* the fall, Luca," she snapped at the medic. "I remember."

Luca hesitated at the top of the staircase, blocking it.

"Let me past."

Luca held still, hands on balustrades on either side. "Please, Ylena, come back to my apartment. You're not well enough for this yet. You need to calm down."

"Let me past," she repeated more insistently this time.

Luca didn't move. "You're still sick. Let me help you. You trust me don't you?"

Another lightning strike cracked near the window, searing the rubble outside.

"Okay," Ylena said, softening her stance, dropping her head. "Okay, I'll come back with you."

"Good. Good."

As Luca reached to take her arm Ylena lashed out suddenly at him, striking him firmly across the temple with her elbow, knocking him backwards. He struggled for balance, grasping for the banister rail and just before he could grasp it Ylena struck him again, this time with one of her steel toe-capped workboots under his chin and he fell, fell, fell.


The thing was immense and skeletal, rising out of the spray of the rain, one hundred feet and more, jagged and painfully incomplete. She stared up at a length of girders towards the very top of it through the grimy window of the bus as they left the construction site. It looked like a finger, pointing.

The electrical storm had guided her once more, away from the squat and all the dregs of memories lingering there, untouched. Away from Luca and his bondage. Back to the start.

Static blurs had followed her all the way but she felt no threat from them anymore.

She climbed over the temporary fencing that had been erected around the building site, avoiding the places she knew the security guards would be patrolling and over to where Luca's prefab treatment ward sat. It seemed to be sinking into the mud, its steel legs lost amongst grey murk. There were no lights on and the door was locked. She went around the side to the window she had once stared out of for hours at a time. The lock was still busted, just as she remembered it.

Pushed her way into the antiseptic prison.

Luca grunted as he got to his feet. His left leg sparkled with pain but it wasn't broken.

Blood flowed from his forehead where Ylena had kicked him and he had to blink several times to clear his vision. He broke open the front door and chased her into the rain.

Across to Luca's desk and the filing cabinets behind it.

The air was full of heavy crackling energy. Every hair on her body was standing on end.

The cabinets were locked but again from those wasted hours spent staring at nothing she knew the keys were in a secret drawer in the middle of the desk. She opened the cabinet drawer marked A-E.

Dudjekovic, Ylena.

YD+VN.

He sprinted up the access ramp that lead up towards the building site, glimpsing one of the night watchmen's flashlights scanning an area to his left. Hauled himself over the boarding, landed in the soft, cold mud on the other side.

The folder was well-thumbed and had an odd scent to it. She opened it on the desk, flicked through the stack of medical notes and scan results. A photo of her wrist, flesh ribboned and bleeding. X-rays of her spine, arms and legs. Several of her naked torso as she lay unconscious on the gurney.

She scanned the handwritten pages, reading the list of her injuries, past them to the initial report on where she fell and how she was found.

She turned suddenly as she heard a noise behind her.

There was a light on in the medical suite as he approached it, his footsteps slopping in the mud. He reached for the door handle carefully and jerked his hand back as a small shock ran through him as if he had been bitten. Looked at his finger in the stormlight and there was a puncture mark with blood leaking out of it so he pulled his sleeve down over his hand and tried the handle again.

Locked.

He took out his key and opened the door, ready to see Ylena charging towards him but instead glimpsing first his case notes scattered out on his desk and secondly her legs disappearing out through one of the rear windows.

"Wait!"

The sound of plastic sheeting flapping in the strong winds. The air tasting of iron shavings. The cold sting of the rain and the godlike rumble of the storm.

She used one of the temporary ladders to climb up onto the outer scaffolding that surrounded the lower few floors. She moved deftly, expertly.

Something blurred ahead of her as she ran towards another ladder and she slowed, her breath tumbling from her in blasts that were visible in the freezing air. The movement of a figure, static-distorted, flickering. Inside her chest, a warmth began to expand.

She walked slowly towards the figure and held out her hand. The figure took it.

Then climbing again, floor by floor, across gaping holes and pulling herself up poles and struts, through access tunnels and along safety ramps secured with nothing more than electrical tape.

This was how it was meant to be, Ylena realised, as she made the journey she had taken once already. Up and up and up. The feel of his hand around hers came and went as if reality couldn't decide whether he was there or not. She did not look at his face because she knew there wasn't really anything there—but she didn't need to see it anyway.

She heard shouting as she hauled herself onto a platform that stuck out from the scaffolding, ignored it. He helped her up and there was warmth in that hand now.

Memories interlaced with each other and with the present like the lines on a TV screen, joining to finally bring into focus the images she had been unable to see clearly since the accident.

"Two more floors," he said and so they climbed.

It had been raining that night too and Ylena wondered if that part was memory or reality or both or neither. How much was actually happening now? How deeply had she fallen into this replication?

The whole building seemed to shake as they reached the top floor. The sheeting that acted as a temporary roof had come partially loose in the angry winds, peeling away in one corner so that the planks that floored the area were soaked through.

His arms went around her as they stood at the edge, looking out over the city and its fractured silhouettes. Electricity crackled amongst the great shapes of the pylons, giving the impression of a battle between great gods taking place.

He squeezed her tight and she closed her eyes, wanting that feeling to go with her into whatever came next. That was how it had been. That was how it was.

The only thing that felt good amongst all the trash.

"Tighter," she told him and he squeezed. Her breasts flattened, a sweet spike of pain shooting through her chest.

She was numb from the storm and more.

"I love you."

The words, whispered into her ear as if the storm itself had spoken.

"I love you too," she said.

And he began to fade, his arms, his warmth, fading again.

Ylena stayed calm however, for she knew where he had gone to.

She looked out over the edge of the skyscraper, down to the muddy ground far below. She could see his outline there, waiting for her.

She took one step forwards.

"NO!"

Luca, running towards her, stumbling across the unfinished flooring, almost falling through at one point. "Ylena, no!"

She ignored him, retaining her focus on the ground far below.

He grabbed her arm but she pulled it away, balance momentarily lost and she had to snatch at a scaffold pole to steady herself. It was only then that she realised how loud the wind was because she couldn't hear herself when she said, "Leave me."

"No. I won't let you do this."

"I have to."

"You don't!"

He looked ready to grab her again but seemed unsure of sending her over the edge. "I'm sorry, I should have told you. I know I should have but . . . "

"We had said we would do it together. That was the pact."

"I was only doing my job. I had to help you."

"You didn't help *him*," she said flatly.

"There was nothing I could do! He was already dead when I found you both! When you awakened and couldn't remember anything I delayed telling you because it thought it would be too much of a shock but then the more time that passed the more difficult it became to say anything. I wanted to tell you!"

"Bullshit. You didn't say a thing because you wanted me to yourself and you knew that what he and I had you could never come close to."

Luca said nothing, instead reaching into his pocket for something.

"Leave me alone, Luca. I have to be with him again."

"I'm not leaving you," he said.

A bolt of electricity lashed across the rooftop, stinging the air with hot energy.

In his hand, a small length of barbed wire.

And as she had stood on the very edge of the skyscraper, he had stood next to her and taken her hand. Their palms clutched together and he had begun to wind the wire around their wrists, binding them. This was what he had done and this was what Luca now did because that's the way things were meant to happen.

"This is the wire you used," Luca said, and then, "I don't care if you don't want me."

The spikes of the wire pierced her dressing, then her skin, matching her existing wounds perfectly like a plug in a socket.

The wind buffeted them, pressing them towards the drop, urging them on.

Luca tugged on the wire, sinking it further into their flesh, binding them tighter, locking them together.

The air was fused with energy, sparkling with it.

One step each.

Now.


The ward wasn't his but it was similar. If he was out of action the chances were that the on-site facility had shut down and he had been taken to one of the general hospitals in the city.

He was in a private room, the walls once white but now grey, the traction device that he was a part of gleaming in the glare of the striplights. He studied the pins in his legs and arms as he had for several days already, these new little pieces of himself.

His neck was fixed in a brace that bit into his skin like an aggressive lover.

Vertebral fractures, spinal lesions, shattered tibias and fibulas, broken ribs, fractured jaw, more, more.

Broken heart.

He almost smiled.

When he closed his eyes he saw Ylena's face blurring beside him as they fell, remembered the angry slicing of the barbed wire across his wrist. He remembered it all.

He listened to the electronic chatter of the machines that kept him alive and pain-free and thought *none of this matters*. He would sometimes seek out Ylena's voice amongst it all although he had heard nothing so far.

She was there, however, between the grooves, inside it all. In the space between the raindrops, lingering. Waiting.

The doctors had given him three months to recover but he knew it would only take half that. Enough that he could stand and walk and climb. How many floors would have been added to the building by then? How far to fall?

All the way, was the answer.

All the way.

# PRETTY

I pan out across the gathering before me, revealing around twenty people, a better turn-out than most of late I have been told. We're in a scrapyard, dead automobiles walling us in between the crushing machines and splinters of metal. A stage has been constructed of aluminium sheets with bare light bulbs bolted to the sides, a strand of old wire connecting them and powering their weak yellow illumination. Music plays on a battered old CD player plugged into the lighter socket of one of the flatbed trucks parked to the side.

The girl I am here for, she thinks she has been here before, she forgets. Everything has begun to blur at the edges for her.

She stands awkwardly on the stage as if uncertain as to what she is supposed to do up there and the men watch her. Raoul, the man funding this job, barks for her to turn so she turns—awkwardly because of the heel of her left shoe that snapped a week or two back, repaired by hammering a six-inch nail through the sole thus leaving it free to spin around as she moved.

The men cheer, some of them moving around the stage to stare at her from different angles. "Dance," Raoul tells her. She dances. I move around to the opposite side of the stage to stop one of the lights glaring behind her.

The temperature has dropped drastically since we arrived at the junkyard, the sky greying as if colours were being drained from the world and injected into the neon decorations the Splendour Collective had assembled.

**XXX. Triple D's Guaranteed. Come fuck your fantasy.**

Torn from the strip joints and porn-barns they spent the rest of their time in.

Two of them, they move around the woman with black-market Sony digital cameras on their shoulders. I recognise some of them from jobs I've done in the past, rogues that have gone rogue, filling their time with either shitty exploitative gigs or big-time hardcore that most people couldn't stomach. I listen to the whirr of their cameras, ten generations more advanced than mine, as they zoom in for close-ups on the woman's hips, her breasts, her calves; her scars pixellating beneath their gaze.

The other contestants stand behind the men or lie in the back of the trucks. I'd assembled my collage shots of them earlier when I first arrived, planning to inter-cut them throughout the piece. There's the African Queen, painted and wrapped in shiny see-through fabrics, heroin-eyes staring out across the rusted shells of old Cadillacs and people carriers imploded from the rear in freeway pile-ups. There's the lobotomy blondes, standing stock still against each other like shapes cut out of an unfolding piece of paper, sharing a cigarette.

My girl, she steps down, waits for a few minutes as the men decide a winner. They huddle together, exchanging notes and money and drugs, joking with one another. Then she steps back up minutes later.

They've put a chair up there for her that has been ripped out of a police riot van, wrapped a sash around her that's torn and stained with every conceivable bodily fluid. The men cheer and she breathes a sigh of relief that they are not too feisty this time, probably due to the worsening weather.

This is one of many times I will witness one of these events.

Since I had gone freelance most of my time had been split between Russ and his little anarchist regime, creating propaganda docu's and shooting reels of buildings falling apart and other forms of the natural chaos they wish to achieve, and the rest of it with the Media Virus guys downtown. But this job came out of the blue from Den Perry whom I hadn't seen or heard from in a long time. It was a blank note shoved under my door with the words "Fall" scrawled across it. *Fall*, short for Fuck All, short for "How many of you are up for this job? Fuck All".

It was high pay and I knew from experience that it would only have been sent to those who were more into the documentary scene than simple filmmaking—meaning it could be a nasty one because it would require a certain level of professional distance

Things had been dry for a while and I was behind on just about everything I could be behind on—editing for past projects, rent on the apartment and my truck. If it wasn't for the fact that one of Russ's buddies had hooked me up with illegal cable and electricity I'd have been in deep shit.

The contact was Raoul, the manager of the girl I was to film. She was a contestant in one of the unsupervised Beauty Pageants that I'd heard rumours about in the past and this Raoul thought she was destined for the Big Time, wanted to capture it all on film. I don't know what Big Time he was thinking of exactly because all I knew about this world was that all there was were Small Times and even Smaller Times.

The square framing of the mechanical zoom captures her as she huddles into the side of the truck. We are speeding across a concrete desert, Raoul in a place where it seems like he is screaming when in fact he is not making a sound as he sits behind the wheel. His eyes are wide, focused entirely on the animal bounding ahead of them. Clarity, her make-up artist, is in the back seat with me, as powerless as the Beauty Queen is, struggling for grip as we are all thrown around inside the car.

Raoul swerves as the animal, some sort of wild dog, suddenly changes direction and heads towards dunes of old tyres and oil drums that have been dumped.

"Look at it go!" Raoul shouts, bouncing up and down in his seat.

The Beauty Queen can't look and can't not look. She watches the creature run with the terrible knowledge of what Raoul will do to it if or when he catches it but also with the acid sting of the hope that it might escape, as a few have done.

Cut to later, in the cool midnight air, where the Beauty Queen and I stand outside a gas station waiting for Raoul. Clarity is in the back of the truck, his head hung low, occasionally glancing up at us through the dirty glass.

"It was my own fault," she tells me, and I have to remind her to look into the camera and not at me. "I should have known better."

"He's done this before?" I ask her, watching her through the camera's viewfinder.

She nods. "He says that beauty deserves beauty. He caught me playing with a lizard once and stuck it with a stick before I could do anything. Clarity made it into a wristband for me. I haven't worn it recently, though. Clarity can make anything pretty."

Cut back to the truck racing between patches of rocky mounds and dried-up cacti, right over a small crater that looks somewhat like a shallow grave.

I keep the camera on the Beauty Queen because this is about her reaction to what is going on not just what is going on. Yet I can see out of the corner of my eye the wild dog still running but visibly tiring as Raoul herds it in with the giant flatbed. The camera is almost thrown from my hands as we come suddenly to a grinding halt and it's the Beauty Queen's terrified eyes I see first, before I realise that Raoul has a shotgun out. The man stands, sliding open the sunroof and taking aim. The framing becomes blurred as an arm flashes in front of the camera and causes the autofocus to go wild and you can hear the Beauty Queen whining.

"Clarity . . . "

I swivel the viewfinder, instinctively following my subject's line of sight. The man looks up, eyes circled with black rings and splintered by crow's feet, the line of facial piercings running across his eyebrow ridge glittering. He shakes his head even as she grabs Raoul's legs and pulls weakly on them. There is a blast as Raoul takes his first shot and the Beauty Queen screams, pounding his knees and pleading with him. Another shot, another, then a yelp then one more shot and silence.

Raoul slides back down into the truck, grinning widely.

"I got it for you, Precious," he says, stroking the Beauty Queen's face. "I got it."

Cut back to the gas station and the Beauty Queen is framed by a pump that is lined with peeling rust. In the background you can see Raoul in the store picking up some snacks and paying for the gas.

"Step back for me," I tell her and she immediately responds by leaning back into the light cast by the dirt-encrusted sign advertising the latest special offers to any drivers that might pass by.

I feel strange in that moment, realising that it was now I who was positioning her.

I bring the camera down across her scraggly form, across the blood that was drying on the tops of her breasts and across her shoulders. You can see the skin beginning to curl there as if it were her own, like the dark petals of a dying rose. There aren't as many flies as there had been earlier.

Cut again and we are in the middle of the concrete plains. Raoul is holding out his hands as the Beauty Queen stands before him proudly, the dog's fresh blood trickling down her back. I pan down to Clarity, hunched in the shadow of the truck, the knife in his bloodied hands but before I can zoom in Raoul shouts at me, reminds me what I am meant to be filming here.

Cut once more, a few minutes earlier.

You see Raoul's blurry face as he leans across in the front seat and kisses the Beauty Queen. You see him flinch momentarily as he tastes her bile on those cracked lips.

"Come on, we'll go see it," he says and grabs the Beauty Queen's wrist harder than necessary, tugging her across the gear stick and out his side of the car. Clarity gets out and follows a few paces behind them and it takes me a few moments to catch up and come out after them. I only realise as I step out how fast my heart is beating. You watch an amateur with a camera and when something noteworthy happens they remove themselves from the viewfinder and watch it with their own eyes. But me, and others like me, we can't help but stare through the mechanical eye because its somehow become our only way of seeing.

In Clarity's hand is Raoul's flaying knife which he grips tightly as debris blows across him and the heat of the smog cover scorches his shaven head, watching the two of them ahead, mere shadows in the rising dust storm.

The dog is still twitching as Raoul raises the butt of his shotgun and drives it down onto the thing's tiny skull. I miss the killing blow as I hurry towards them and quickly move to the Beauty Queen's reaction but there is none. She stares off at the distant pyres of infected farm animals being torched, black smoke crawling across the darkening sky, trying not to listen as Clarity begins to expertly remove the creature's skin below her, out of shot. Raoul comes up behind her, wrap his arms around her waist, one finger brushing against the scar tissue of her gunshot wound, making her tense suddenly.

"You're the most beautiful thing in this world, you know that?" he whispers through her strangled, clumpy hair. "More beautiful than anything I have ever seen."

He looks straight at the camera and there is one of those little moments where you jump because it's as close as someone looking at *you*. I stay on them, shooting them like newlyweds that have just stumbled out of church.

There are wet sounds from beneath them as Clarity works then the thud of the knife hitting the soft ground as he finishes. Raoul turns, taking the Beauty Queen with him, as they behold Clarity, smeared in the animal's fresh blood, holding aloft the dripping skin.

Raoul draws her towards Clarity and turns her back to him. His eyes are wide with delight and he nods. "Let me see my fairy princess," he says.

"It's not ready yet," Clarity tells him. "We must dry it out properly first—and I need to bathe it."

Raoul shakes his head. "Let me see."

Clarity looks at the Beauty Queen and there is recognition that she is back in that vacant place she seems to spend so much of her time in. He spreads out the skin as Raoul slips off her sash and removes the flimsy gown she had been wearing, pooling on the ground at her feet as if it were a part of her. Then the flesh is draped across her, cold and wet on her bare skin, she shudders as it touches her. Raoul replaces the sash, not wanting to let her forget that she won the latest contest, and stands back to admire her.

The Beauty Queen stares back numbly as the dog's blood trickles across her breasts and down her back.


Cut to later that day and a diner sandwiched in between aged iron ore plants.

Before they had entered the place, Clarity had managed to convince Raoul to let him clean the Beauty Queen up and remove the dog skin.

*Overlay audio from earlier shots as the viewfinder pans across a half-full café populated by fat truckers and teenage runaways, stale coffee steam and Perspex barrels of donuts –*

"We must save it for the next contest," Clarity argues, his breath uneven as he hurries across the parking lot. "Give me one day to alter it here and there."

""We don't need to alter it. Her beauty is raw, therefore everything else about her should be too."

"Fine—but at least let's not spoil the surprise."

So while Raoul pays for a room for the night and goes to the diner to make his calls to the rest of the Collective, I go with Clarity and the Beauty Queen. I load a new cassette and hesitantly film what follows.

*A collage –*

Clarity showering her, rolling a bar of orange soap across her to remove the smell. Caresses that are somewhat maternal. Neither seem bothered by my presence.

He is helping her into a black leather dress but she insists on wearing the sash for Raoul over it, arguing with him long enough to cause the makeup he has applied on her to begin to run in the mist of the shower room.

Her face, reflected in the bathroom mirror, smudged with black mascara tears.

Then a sudden jump to the noise of the diner as we see her shuffle through to meet Raoul, seated in a booth with another man. Some of the diners glance up at the camera as it passes but most take no notice.

"My, my," the man next to Raoul says and I hurriedly frame his ugly face." So beautiful—and I'll bet even more so close up."

Cut to the Beauty Queen, wrapped in a bathrobe, sitting hunched up on the sink counter, pellets of water frozen on the glass behind her. She holds the razor blade Clarity used to shave her earlier in the palm of one hand as if it were an insect she had found. I am standing at an angle to her to avoid showing up in the mirror.

"So you'd seen him before?" I asked her.

"At some contests. I know it's a terrible thing to say but . . . sometimes they all look the same."

"Is he a manager like Raoul?"

"No," she says, her voice wavering. "He always hangs around the guys with the cameras."

"And what do they do?" My question is hesitant as I become aware of the direction of the conversation.

"They film us girls."

"On stage?"

"Yeah."

"Anywhere else?"

She shrugs. "Sometimes."

"Where did they take you earlier? Did they film you?"

The razor blade flares in the camera's view for a second. She won't look at me any more.

"Of course they filmed me. Someone had to, right? I mean, how will people know that's you've done something if they don't film it?"

She smiles nervously and looks down at the blade; it flashes as she turns it, catching the glare of the strip lights above us. "Do you think I'm pretty, Miss Afterlife?"

I begin to look away from the eyepiece, catch myself. In the harsh light you can see the white keloids of her older scars even more clearly.

"Elisabeth," I correct her. "And yes I do."

She nods vaguely, frowning down at the razor blade as she plays it across her palms and I don't think she really hears my answer.

Cut back to the diner once more.

A waitress arrives with plates of breakfast food, lays them down randomly on the booth's table and blushes at the way Raoul and his friend stare up at her, then hurriedly makes her exit. She ignores me sitting at a booth across the way.

"Eat," Raoul tells everyone, slotting a piece of crisp bacon into his mouth. He pushes a plate towards the Beauty Queen with her runny black tears and tells her she will need her strength.

"Why do you watch?" I ask Clarity.

This is back in the hotel room, later that night. You can see the corner of the TV in the shot but I train the camera firmly on the waif-like figure slumped in the chair. There's a half-empty bottle of pills on the bedside table nearby and he has the wild dog's dried out skin draped across his knees, a needle and thread abandoned in it. I feel a tendency to avoid what is on-screen but he's been playing the tape over and over for an hour now ever since Raoul gave it to him.

"I have to. Have you ever noticed how shows about murderers always have reconstructions from the murderer's point of view? Like their sole purpose is to the let the viewer fantasise about committing the crime themselves. Why do people watch things over and over again if it disgusts them so much?"

"So are fantasising about yourself in this video?"

He points to the TV screen. "Shoot it. You know you want to see it properly. Voyeurism is nothing to be ashamed of—it's what we're all being brought up to be. I'll keep talking, if you want. Just shoot it."

I hesitantly swivel the TV screen into view. The tape has come to an end and he is rewinding it again. It's a strange image, someone squeezed into a toilet cubicle getting fucked from behind in reverse by the man holding the camera.

"She told me nothing was going to happen this time."

Clarity shakes her head. "But it always does. These contests don't take place just so they can give out sashes, she knows that."

"You knew what was going to happen when they took her out of the diner?"

"I had an idea. There's only one reason that Raoul separates her from me."

"Do you ever do anything to stop them?"

He pauses before answering. "If I truly thought she wanted me to, I would."

As her clothes are peeled onto her and as she is bent over the toilet seat and as a small crowd of eager and slightly bewildered truckers are visible gathered around her and as they are invited to show her how beautiful they thought she was.

Cut back suddenly to the diner and Raoul's friend leaning across the table. "So beautiful," he tells her. "And I'm sure even more so close up."

And back to the video in time to see vomit fly into the Beauty Queen's mouth as she leans over a sink, then Raoul removes his fingers from her throat and take his hand from her head.

"I don't think her body knows what a calorie is anymore," Clarity says and he hits PLAY once more.

The tape is the first of the hundred or so copies currently being made in the portable setup that Raoul's friend has had ready in his own motel room while awaiting their arrival.

The Beauty Queen's features are blurred because the camera is held so close, every now and again crashing into her face and at one point near the end smearing with a spot of blood from her lip where it splits it. Clarity watches it, over and over.

"What are you feeling when you watch this?" I ask him.

"Nothing."

"Lust? Anger?"

"Nothing."

"Frustration? Sadness?"

"Nothing."

He just watches, as many more will once the Filmmaker has begun sending the film out via the Splendour Collectives' many distribution branches.

Clarity suddenly turns and I pan around to follow his line of sight.

The Beauty Queen watches us from the bathroom doorway, her lip still bruised and a little swollen, her dressing gown open and sloping off her bony shoulders, one finger brushing against the scar of a gunshot wound in her belly.

Clarity turns back to the TV and hits the rewind switch as the screen goes blank then the video starts again.

"Turn around for me," an off-camera voice says on the video, barely heard because of a lack of microphone.

Clarity hits pause then looks back and sees that she is now gone, the bathroom door shut. I'm muddled. I've lost my train of thought, what I was shooting.

Without saying a word, Clarity hits PLAY again to the muffled sound of vomiting.

She is wiping her mouth when I enter, leaning over the sink. She throws a tissue into the toilet bowl, then rinses out with a glass of water to get rid of the bitter aftertaste of her own stomach acids. Her gown hangs open as if it were an outer skin that had been partially flayed away, revealing the innards of her scarred breasts and stomach.

She watches herself in the mirror that is almost a TV screen, ignoring me for the meantime and she is a young starlet. Her hands cross the keloids that she is collecting along the way on this never-ending journey. Raoul says the circuit ends at The Shore, underneath the piers late at night after the bare-fisted boxing matches have finished, but they have never gotten that far before, caught in some intangible hurricane-spiral that kept them away from that mythical ending.

The camera frames her hand caressing the left-hand side of her stomach, fingers spread around the puckered scar tissue where the bullet had entered.

"Where did you get that?" I ask instinctively. It's like as long as the camera is rolling I have to be asking questions, discovering.

"I can't remember the name of the town. Some little place back east," she says.

She is either unaware or unconcerned that she is standing before me practically naked as she traces the leathery edges of the wound.

"I meant how did it happen?"

"It was an accident."

"Raoul?" I'm slowly moving in on the wound.

"He took me to a doctor straight afterwards. Not a real doctor—well, not anymore. But he fixed me up."

She draws the gown away from her hip and turns, exposing her buttocks to me. "Look," she says, her hand sweeping across the small of her back. "No exit wound. It never came out. The bullet is still inside me."

She is whispering to it, her little metal child, telling it not to be afraid, when Raoul opens the door and enters.

"Come on, we're leaving," he says.

It never ends, from one city to the next to the next to the same again and never, never ends. I ask her how long this has been going on, when the glittery, champagne-fuelled parades became broken and distorted as they were now. But she just watches the world flash past the windscreen, reflections of birds, an eagle, a wild rabbit sliding across the glass.

We are somewhere into the third week I've been with them and we've been driving all night across bumpy roads that have taken us further and further from the skylines of cities and the lifeline of the main highways. I feel drained from the events of the past week or so, beginning to regret taking the job.

Trailer parks litter the sides of dirt tracks, ragged little children playing chicken in front of the trucks and Raoul not bothering to slow down as they come within an inch of their tiny lives.

Now he pulls the truck in between two burnt-out mobile homes that have been tilted back and leaned against each other by some vandal-artist so that they form the gated entrance to this new venue. The scab-kneed children chase after the truck, howling at it as they scramble across garbage bags and discarded satellite dishes then suddenly vanishing as the truck skids to a halt and spews dust back at them.

They get out and are greeted by a woman in a threadbare dressing gown and military boots three sizes too big for her. She wears her straggly hair in a pony tail and a T-shirt that says *John Lennon Died For Me* and her arms are crossed tight. She speaks to Raoul who heads off to another trailer.

"You look thirsty, honey," the woman says to the Beauty Queen through the open window of the back seat. The Queen doesn't move, doesn't speak. The woman looks at me as if in search of an explanation as to the silence. I feel the Queen waiting for Clarity to speak for her but he was left behind at the last stop and I desperately want to tell her that was she thinks happened didn't. The woman holds out a hand until the Beauty Queen gets out of the car, unsteady on legs slowly wasting away.

She regards me warily as I climb out after them, eight-millimetre in hand, but she doesn't say anything. I assume Raoul has explained the situation to her beforehand.

We follow the woman into a trailer choked with trinkets and stained clothing, the walls adorned with torn old movie posters, discoloured Polaroids and sashes. She sits the Beauty Queen down and returns moments later with a glass of the kind of water that should come with a label just to reassure you of what it was.

"You rest here just now," the woman says, then flinches at the rising sound of dogs barking. "You'll be okay. I know you got the strength cause you sure as hell got the looks. My name's Cheryl".

I begin shooting as the Queen takes a sip of the water, keeping her pinkie finger extended as Clarity had taught her to. She fights back the grimace of pain that shoots through her mouth as the cold liquid passes over her worn enamel.

Cheryl lights a cigarette and places it in a holder. Her eyes narrow as she takes a drag. "So how far along are you? Only a couple of months, I think?"

The Beauty Queen looks worriedly at her, then at me, but doesn't say anything. She doesn't realise I already know. She doesn't realise just how much I know.

"It's okay, honey, I won't tell anyone."

Some of the guys who have been doing this for a while told me that long ago people didn't know how to act in front of a camera. They'd become shy or outgoing or adopt strange accents as if there was a set way a TV person should be. But all I'd ever seen is people so used to the sight of a lens that it failed to even register most of the time. People that see no difference between telling a camera something and telling a person something—see their own faces reflected in the lens and think they are talking to themselves as they reveal things they never normally would to even their closest friends.

"I can just sense these things. It wasn't long after my last title that my first came along. That one didn't make it but I kept the ultrasound they took before it died." She takes another drag. "You want to see?"

The Beauty Queen shakes her head. The dogs' barking is getting louder, meaner, more frenzied. I know she is wishing Clarity was back with her and I have to fight to keep filming. The smoke from the woman's cigarette peels upwards, scattering like the jagged pain of a knife wound.

"Well you make sure you take care of that little thing inside you cause it might one day be all you have."

"It's going to save me," the Beauty Queen says, her voice soft and raspy from lack of use. She glances at the camera and I think she is telling me, not Cheryl. "That's why it's here."

The woman laughs a little, takes a final drag on the cigarette. "I think it might take more than that to save girls like us . . . but it's a start, right?"

The Beauty Queen nods as the sound of the dogs fills her ears, rises, overlaid on three audio tracks, rises again and we cut to another stage, this time in a barn with chickens running loose around her and the men behind a chalk line that has been drawn on the concrete flooring as they cheer for her.

Poise.

Elegance.

The dogs are snapping at her and the other girls, their spittle slapping against her calves and she stares straight ahead, breathing calmly, a wide smile on her face. The books they all had tried to keep on their heads have fallen but it doesn't stop them. They huddle together somewhat, backs to each other protectively as the dogs strain their leashes to the maximum. She can hear the leather stretching to breaking point.

Raoul shouts at her angrily, then laughs with one of the men just as one of the other women shrieks. The girls instinctively jump away from the sound and are immediately cat-called, the Beauty Queen turning just enough to see that one of the lobotomy blondes has been caught by a dog that has her by the ankle.

Someone turns the music that is playing up louder, a crackly old 45 rattling out 20s show tunes. One of the girls struggles for a moment as she almost slips off the stage, her smile carved on her face even as she dangles before the dogs, but no one helps her because it would be unladylike to bend to grab her. She manages to struggle back up again and it is then that the Beauty Queen sees the other lobotomy blonde pinned to one corner of the stage, blankly watching as her sister/partner/doppelganger is mauled by the dogs.

"POISE!" Raoul shouts at the Queen and she feels the pressure of tears behind her eyes, flinching as the spotlights of one of the other cameras focuses on her face in agony from smiling for so long, her legs weak and her mouth stinging from stomach acids.

There's the music and the dogs and the screams and laughter and it all swirls together like a nosebleed into a stream of water and away from her, away . . .

She tells me that she has a fantasy of her skin being like that of a panther.

She tells me that she imagines herself standing beneath the moon-light, turning for Clarity who smiles admiringly at the way she gleams as she moves, her black fur revealing patterns of halos for a split-second before they vanish once more.

She tells me how the new skin wraps around the back of her neck and behind her ears, leaving her face and hair free, replacing all the scars and bruises with a clean, smooth makeover. And the skin is *hers,* not stolen from some other creature.

She says that now when she imagines this scene she fantasises about running a hand over her delicately swollen belly. Clouds cross the sky, illuminated by the moon.

"Pretty," Clarity says as she stalks towards her, runs his hand across her skin.

Raoul is on top of him, standing over him and pulling him by the hair upwards, exposing his neck. There are two others, both armed with knives. Everything is blurry, the colours bleeding into one another because I haven't bothered to switch the auto-focus on.

The shot wobbles furiously as the men shout but Clarity, Clarity is silent.

"You fucking dirty *cunt*," Raoul shouts at him, tugging on his hair and you can see all the bruises, even without focus.

It's a men's room, it's dark. Every shout echoes across the cracked porcelain.

"I didn't . . . " Clarity says once more. It's all he says in this take.

One of the men slam an elbow down onto Clarity's neck and he collapses, choking.

The camera suddenly moves from him to the ground and you can see my feet.

"I told you not to fucking move!" Raoul shouts. "Keep filming! I'm paying you to film!"

I re-frame instinctively but its no easier to look at what's happening through a lens than it is my naked eyes.

They just keep hitting him.

"I told you never to *touch* her!" he screams and the sentence is punctuated by another blow.

Why doesn't he fight back?

I'm aching to turn and leave.

The sequence continues but it will never make it into the final cut.


It's 4am according to the digital clock next to her bed. She's been watching it count forwards, endlessly performing that single task, all night. The swellings have gone down thanks to the cold water Cheryl applied after the parade had finished but the noise still rings in the Beauty Queen's ears. She touches her neck where Raoul had been strangling her with her sash. Nothing less than first place was acceptable, she knew that. She had known that as her legs had finally given way and she had fallen to the ground, crumpling like a flower, and she had known that as Raoul had helped her to her feet and away from the stage.

There was no such thing as the second most beautiful person in the world—only yet another ugly one.

She is hurting and she is cold but she is less dejected than she has been in a long time.

There are the sounds of Cheryl snoring in the trailer's only bedroom as she looks to the window again, to the electronic waste and old tyres. Every now and again people will pass, mostly men laughing and drinking or scraggly children wandering aimlessly by themselves. A light rain falls.

The low light means the shot is grainy, constantly adjusting itself.

"I'll do better next time," she says softly, more to herself than to me. "There's no such thing as second most beautiful, you know."

I'm too tired to ask her any questions but I know I must.

"Whose is it?"

She frowns. "It's mine."

"I mean, who's the father?"

She seems to struggle with the question, eventually reverting to, "It's mine."

The way she looks, so lost and tiny, I feel a maternal pull towards her. I wonder how many men there have been and imagine the Moreau type of creation that could be nestling inside her, the combination of a hundred types of sperm and distantly think about what Raoul is currently organising for her. Maybe it will be better this way.

Regardless, I am certain that none of the sperm would be Clarity's as Raoul suspected.

"Thank you for what you did tonight," she says suddenly.

It surprises me because I didn't think she would be aware of me having done anything to help her, so drowned in her own terrible world was she. It makes me wonder what else she is aware of.

The cassette, if it is ever to be played back, will end just as they bring the dog up behind her. It will show the same scene as previously, the barn, the makeshift lighting equipment, the boom box, but the crowds have fallen to the exclusive numbers allowed access to this very special performance.

Previously, she has won and in return received her prize.

And, like that night, she has been defeated and subsequently punished.

I see no difference.

If that cassette is ever viewed, you will see how my hand shakes as it grips the camera and as I fight myself. There's another side to these kind of jobs and that's not that you can handle the extremity of them but that you have the lack of morals necessary to go through with them.

If that cassette is ever viewed, you will be all too aware of what is going to happen as the stage is cleared and the women chosen as winners or losers or whatever are quickly washed of blood and dirt and then put up on the platform again. The dogs have calmed again by this point, thankfully, their temperaments now required for a wholly different reason. You can hear my gasp if you listen closely, as the men rub the undersides of the dogs.

The remaining lobotomy blondes have already been and gone, played their part before I was quickly retrieved by Raoul, excited at being able to work up this deal even though the Queen lost.

The Beauty Queen is curled almost into a ball on the stage, dress raised, and it is then that the camera swings to the ground and everything goes blank as the lens cap clicks shut. You can hear me, if this tape were to be viewed, tell Raoul to stop because there's something wrong with the camera. You can hear him argue with me but I tell him, plainly, it's not working. As he shouts, the event organisers grow impatient with him, reminding him they were only letting him do this as a favour, the winners had already had their glory.

"Goddammit, woman, *shoot it.*"

I tell him again, the camera isn't working, must be dirt or sand in the mechanisms. I can get it working again but not tonight.

It's then I flicked the power switch off just in case and this particular little segment ends.

Give it ten seconds of silence, fading out the sounds of the dogs low growls and yelps, then back in with the squeaking of the bed that the Queen lies on.

"Do you think he'll come back?" she asks me, still watching the clock count onwards.

"I don't know," I say.

"I hope he'll be okay. Do you think he'll be okay, Elisabeth?"

I say nothing this time.

"I think he'll be fine. He can go anywhere he wants, whenever he wants, now." A pause. "I'll miss him, though."

I feel as if someone has shoved a bowling ball into my chest I'm so heavy and choked. There's no reason to tell her. As much as it might hurt her to think he has abandoned her I couldn't bring her the truth.

I manage to say, "He said he would miss you too."

Let him continue in her mind.

"Really? He said that?" It amazes me she seems surprised.

"Anyway, now I have someone else in my life," she says and touches her stomach.

And the bowling ball has just caught fire.


It is a little before seven am and I've turned the camera on myself.

The Queen is asleep, having finally drifted off a couple of hours ago. I've plugged up AV cables to the black and white TV set in the corner of the trailer and watch myself in it.

I want to tell her to run. Fuck *I* want to run.

This is going to have to end soon. I can feel myself crumbling from the inside out.

I have four days editing time when this is done but I don't think I'll be able to look at the footage again.

In the TV, I look haggard and utterly exhausted. My eye make-up is smeared, strands of my hair hanging out of the pins they're supposed to be held back by. I must have lost fifteen pounds. And there, in that moment, having spent almost a month being dragged along by Raoul, feeling utterly devoid inside, I realise why Clarity didn't fight back as he was beaten to death and why the Beauty Queen lets this go on and on.

"Can't sleep?" a voice says and I look up to see Cheryl, cigarette in hand.

I shake my head, flick the camera off. She comes and sits next to me quietly, tilting her head and smiling as she looks at the Queen. "He's going to take it away from her, isn't he?" she whispers.

"Yes."

"He told you that?

"It's what his type do."

I can see in Cheryl's eyes the Queen's pain, compressed over the years into a piece of cold stone.

"There'll be others," she says. "And one day he'll let her keep one."

"Maybe she'd be better off without it," I offer. I can hear people beginning to move around outside, the kids kicking beer bottles from the night before between each other. "Maybe *it* would be better off."

I wait for a response then look at Cheryl after a few moments and hesitate.

There are tears running down her cheeks.


Cut to noon, the sun blazing overhead, and it's an ugly day, I can just feel it.

Supplies are being packed into the truck and the Beauty Queen stands politely to one side as the men load it. She is wearing the wristband Clarity made for her and a light dress that is frayed at the edges. She has done her best to apply her makeup to cover the bruising but she does not have Clarity's talent.

I watch as Raoul comes out of the trailer he has been in, smiling broadly, rolling a coin between his teeth as he stalks over to the Beauty Queen. I watch them for a few moments then suddenly she jumps into the air and hugs the man, her arms barely long enough to wrap around him and I feel sick seeing her so close to him, knowing that she has probably been a lot closer. When she finally lets go she seems lighter than air, the sun now radiating off of her as she hurries around the truck.

Raoul is left smiling in the desert breeze. He motions to me with one finger and I move forwards in my own time, refusing to be summoned.

"You better make sure that camera of yours is working again," he says, voice like the burnt remnants of a nailbomb.

"It's working," I say hesitantly. I look around at the bustling activity. "Why? What's going on?"

His grin almost splits his face.

"The Shore, Ms. Afterlife. We're going to The Shore."

It take about three days in total to reach the seaside motel that Raoul has booked us into and that entire time I sit silently as the Beauty Queen tells me about The Shore.

She tells me that there were no men there, only other Beauty Queens from the past, as pretty as they always have been and ever will be.

She tells me that the sand is fine and golden, like glitter, and that it all takes place under starlight with the sound of the ocean filling your head.

She tells me that after the contest at The Shore you can have anything you want.

When we get out of the truck the Beauty Queen stands by the railings that look out onto the beach and lets the ocean winds blow through the clumps of her hair. She looks back at me, waving with one hand and gripping her increasingly swollen belly with the other.

"Look at her," Raoul says, abruptly behind me and making me jump slightly. "What has she done to herself?"

I exhale the cigarette smoke, the taste something I hadn't experienced for six years until Cheryl had handed me one the morning we left the trailer park.

"Stupid, stupid, stupid," Raoul says.

The Queen's dress flutters in the breeze and I can feel myself urging her to take off.

"I told her to keep her weight down to stop her from ovulating for her own good. I know she sneaks food when I'm not there. But then, we all make mistakes, don't we?"

I don't look at him.

"I should have known better than to trust Clarity to look after her. You would think, though, that a faggot would keep his hands off of her at least, right?"

I take a drag on the cigarette.

"But *you're* not going to make any mistakes are you, Ms. After-life?" He stands in front of me, blocking the light. "You just do your job and I'll do mine and everything will be fine."

"That's what I'm here for," I say, then stamp out the cigarette and walk away.

I feel like I'm watching someone falling from a cliff, unable to do anything but stare into their eyes as they tumble towards the ground at a hundred and fifty miles an hour.

I want to tell her that it will never end, that The Shore isn't real, that *this will never end*.

I don't know if there will be a contest here or not—I don't know what Raoul is up to, though I have strong suspicions. He said he would take the child from her and I knew that sooner or later it would happen.

But he stays close to her the entire time, knowing full well that I might interfere as Clarity might once have tried to do, before the endless nights and neon signs, the whirr of cameras and crowds cheering, sucked everything out of him.

I shoot a full cassette of the ocean lapping the beach because it's all I can do.

They both spent the whole day inside the motel room together and finally Raoul emerges after twilight. He notices me, then crosses to the payphone in the car park and doesn't take his eyes from me the whole time. He hangs up thirty seconds later then goes back into the room.

The Beauty Queen emerges ahead of him when they come back out, wearing a glittering evening gown of dark red sequins with a slit up one leg and matching choker. Around her waist is wrapped the skin of the dog, only half-sewn by Clarity. It bulges over her belly which seems to have almost doubled in size since this morning.

She is beaming a she walks across to me. I flick on the camera and frame her.

"Are the others here yet? Have you seen them?"

"There are no others," Raoul says from behind her. "This contest is a special one, just for you."

My gut turns but I keep filming.

"Come on," he says, then takes her hand and leads her towards the steps that descend onto the beach. I follow a few paces behind.

The stars are out but the beach only glitters because of the discarded junky needles embedded in the grey sand. It's even darker down on the shore, the lurking form of the boardwalk above us blocking out most of the artificial light.

My heart rate is picking up. I struggle to keep my footing on the sliding ground beneath me and we all search the shadows. I have a knife in my pocket but I have no idea why I might need it.

"Is it here?" the Beauty Queen asks, her voice light with excitement. She has removed her heels to walk across the sand and I don't think she even sees the garbage all around her.

"Up ahead," Raoul says and I swing the camera onto him flicking on the clip-on light, making both of them jump at the sudden illumination.

"It's too dark," I say, both an explanation and also somehow a warning to him.

"Not dark enough," another voice says from somewhere amongst the rotting wooden beams. "Turn it the fuck off."

We all look towards the direction of the voice and see a figure to the right.

"Turn it *off*," he repeats.

"She's with me, Kline," Raoul said. "I told you she'd be here."

"Fine, she can stay. But not with the light on."

I flicked the light off once again, bathing us in darkness as I fumbled for the night-vision lens in one of my pockets. I found it and hurriedly attached it.

Cut to Cheryl's trailer and she is crying softly as we talk about the Beauty Queen's pregnancy.

"They just kept taking them away from me," she says, struggling with the words. "They kept giving them to me then hiring that bastard Kline to take them away again."

Her head in her hands and her tears falling through the gaps in her fingers.

Cut back to the beach, wherever it was.

"Raoul?" the Queen asked, perhaps wary for the first time that this was not the dream she was expecting.

"It's okay," he assures her, easing her towards the man. "He's going to help you."

She takes a few more steps, then begins to lean backwards into Raoul as he encourages her forwards. "I . . . don't . . . "

My grip is knuckle-tight on the camera. Everything is lit with green light, eyes and teeth a bright, bright white and glowing like jewels. The light catches on the needles and piece of scrap metal from boats that has washed up on the shore.

No stage.

No girls.

No beauty.

I see the blade in Kline's hands before they do, hidden in the shadows.

Is this what Clarity felt as he watched the videos of what they did to her? This numbness, this separation? I was hiding behind the lens, lost in it. This wasn't real—this was TV.

The Beauty Queen doesn't scream when they grab her, maintaining the poise Clarity has taught her, trying to remain upright, fixing the smile on her face. I think she believes this is some kind of test. I start forwards, feeling some part of myself want to reach out to her but instead it is the camera that reaches out, zooming in on her as she is dragged to the ground.

"Hold her," Kline instructs calmly as he must have done so many times before for the Collective, opening her legs and clamping some sort of metal rod with cuffs on either end onto her ankles and still she isn't screaming, still she smiles.

He has the knife in his hand as it disappears under her dress and *now* she screams, now she breaks The Shore's spell and shrieks as the blade is aimed inside her.

My whole body shakes with helpless rage and I just keep filming until her screams become too much and then suddenly it happens—the night explodes in a gunshot.

Cut to that first night and the Beauty Queen, immaculate in between the healing bruises and a small patch over her wrist tied on with a miniature leather buckle as she sits on a stool in the garage that was the only place I could find for me to interview her. There are tools hanging from the walls behind her, a Playboy calendar and some overalls. It's after hours and the only lighting is from the camera.

"Are you happy?" I ask her.

"Of course," she tells me. "But not only that, Raoul has shown me how I can make those around me happy too. And that's even more important."

"More important than your own happiness?"

"Uh huh."

"Where do you want to be in a few years time? Where do you see yourself?"

She pauses long enough to make me wonder if it's a question she's ever posed herself then finally answers, "At The Shore."

I'm in my apartment , in front of the bank of rusted old TV's and frayed cabling that act as my sorry excuse for an editing suite. I've been editing for five days straight, going over and over even though there's no need anymore. I thought I wouldn't be able to look at the footage again but I was wrong. I can't stop looking at it.

Everything is there, captured on those tapes.

I roll the player dial around with my forefinger, then hit play.

It's the beach and everything has finally gone quiet.

I'm on the ground—I'm not sure if it's because I fell or because I was knocked over. The camera is beside me, half embedded in the sand, still recording. You can see my hand in the frame until I get up and then you see the heap of figures.

In this scene, I crawl across to the bodies of Kline and Raoul. The bullet went straight through them; there's a tiny perfect hole in Kline's chest and Raoul's head. But it's nothing compared to the wasteland that the Queen's stomach has become.

She lies on her back a few feet away, her legs still clamped open, her dress torn and spattered with blood. She's still alive as I go to her, my eyes still adjusting from the explosion of the bullet that burst from her pregnant belly. I'm dazed but I know before I look that there is no gun in her hand. I sweep her hair from her face as she coughs blood and stares back up at me.

There's nothing to say.

She looks down at her belly, half open and glistening, and she smiles.

And as she lays her head back down onto the sand and the last few remnants of her sorry life abandon her I think she might finally have reached The Shore.

# FUCKPUNKTOWN

The sixth time she has come to me, this is the sixth time.

One. Two. Three. Four. Five. Six.

Six times.

She has one head, two arms, two legs, seven bodily orifices.

Eighteen tattoos in all, nine of which she has shown me.

Thirteen body piercings, of which I have seen eleven.

Twenty six years.

Six separate spikes on her Mohican, three colours.

One hundred and sixty-four centimetres tall.

"How often do you wash, per day?" I ask her.

Maybe she would take offence but she doesn't. I have asked her stranger things as she has worked on me.

"It varies, I guess. Dozens if I'm here at the Perforation Gallery. Otherwise . . . three times? Just hand and face washing, though. Showers, maybe one a day or every other day."

I nod, mentally noting the numbers in my head.

Three washes. One to one-point-five showers.

I ponder how many times she rubs her hands as she washes them, how many times she strokes each side of her face. How many times she replenishes the lather. How many minutes she spends under the hot spray of the shower, how long she takes on each part of her body.

The world is just digits, just binary.

Paxton is just a collection of equations, that's all.

Meaghan presents me with a lump of tough spongy material, black and slightly reflective. "Bite down. This will probably hurt."

I stare at the lump for a few moments, contemplating it.

"Take it," Meaghan insists.

I open my lips and she presses the sponge into my mouth, far enough it for it to nestle between my upper and lower sets of teeth. It tastes like latex smells.

She doesn't ask me if I am ready or prepare me before she triggers the little gun she has and shoots a bolt through the plate of stainless steel she holds against my shoulder.

Something overcomes me, a sudden rush of heat and energy, a starburst of nerve activity ballooning from the penetration point.

It makes sense—my body has no need or use for the fragments of metal she is bonding to me and so will alert me to their presence and the damage they may be doing. But even then it is inefficient for my mind now clouds with fizzing neurons screaming at me what I already know, that my body has been invaded, and I am less able to do anything about. Perhaps there are reactions there that are lying dormant—I don't pull away, I just feel the pain.

"Two more," Meaghan says and quickly punches me again with the weapon's deviant bullets, panelling me with the metal as she has elsewhere on my body.

Now done, she draws the sponge from my mouth, indentations clearly visible in the material, and wipes the blood trickling down my back.

"All done for now," she says, stands back to admire her work. "How do you feel?"

"Static. I feel static."

"Static? What, you mean like buzzing?"

"Yes, like buzzing."

"You're probably just weak from the blood loss. Have you been eating?"

"I forget sometimes."

"Then I'll bring you some food," she says. This is what she says.

The room is no more than 12 feet by 12, the walls covered with yellowing tiles and shaky electrical sockets. Her equipment is all attached to the various limbs of the chair I am lying back on, the trays moving jerkily around me on pneumatic hinges to appropriate her needs. The ceiling is mesh and through this and the walls I listen to the sounds of other procedures taking place throughout the building.

I wonder how many of the dozens of people who enter this place leave the same person as when they came in. This is a place of redesign, Meaghan once told me. *Everything* can be changed.

So that was the sixth time I saw Meaghan.

The first was not long after I had come to after I had escaped whilst I was hiding in an auto wrecking yard. I had stumbled there, drawn by the stench of engine oil and the ferric atmosphere of the decaying metal, slotting myself amongst the vehicular carcasses and burnt-out hovercars but *just not fitting*. And I had known even then how wrong everything was.

A fat Choom ran the place with a small collective of workers who wore oxygen packs and trawled around the yard plucking pieces of machinery to order. They way they moved, the way they acted, I was pretty certain they were Verios—Version 2.0's, modified humans. Part clone, part machine. I managed to stay hidden within the collective wreckage for those first few days while everything was still dysfunctional, moving from place to place without ever going beyond the confines the chainlink fencing that delineated the yard.

I didn't dare move from there, imagining each noise to be that of my attackers coming back for me to finish what they had started but soon the sensations that had been building in me were getting too much for me to bear. I didn't know what was wrong with me until one night I saw the Choom shoving a bowl of hot noodles down his throat and I wondered if I might have to eat now instead of inject, I wondered how much they had taken from me.

Wait.

Is that the order that it happened in? Was that the first time?
I . . .

Yes. That was it. That was the first time. When Meaghan came to
the yard and handed the Choom a list of parts which he then passed on
to the workers and let them scuttle off like insects to find. She went
looking too and at first I thought it was just that she was impatient but
as I watched her from the rusted trunk of a haulage truck I realised
there was something else to it. She seemed to caress the disembodied
pieces of machinery rather than examine them, running her small
hands across their parts as if it were a sexual act. When a Verio came
near at one point she quickly dropped what she held but he didn't care,
of course. He had his duties and he followed them, no more, no less.

A signature of perfection.

She saw me of course—at least I assume she did.

Glimpsed me through a bullet hole that had rusted to the size of a
fist and I had held still, utterly still and she moved on as if nothing had
happened but she saw me. I know this because she returned later that
night when the Choom was passed out in his office-shack and his
workers had been put to rest and came straight back to the truck. Sat
next to me and said nothing for 1283 seconds, then;

"It's okay. I won't hurt you."

The room is no more than 12 feet by 12, the walls covered with
yellowing tiles and shaky electrical sockets. Her equipment is all
attached to the various limbs of the chair I am lying back on, the trays
moving jerkily around me on pneumatic hinges to appropriate her
needs. The ceiling is mesh and through this and the walls I listen to the
sounds of other procedures taking place throughout the building.

I wonder how many of the dozens of people who enter this place
leave the same person as when they came in. This is a place of redesign,
Meaghan tells me. *Everything* can be changed.

Heads, hearts and heels.

Bones, breasts and brows.

"I just want . . . some of the damage repaired," I tell her.

"I think I can manage that. We get people wanting modded to be more like Verio's all the time. I guess with you it's a little different but that should only make things easier."

She examines me, walks around and around me, uses an instrument like a large compasses to measure me.

"Let's see what we can do," she says.

And this is when she has taken me to the Perforation Gallery for the first time, having convinced me to leave the squat so that she could work properly. 10,134 minutes after she came back for me in the scrapyard.

"Let's see what we can do."

Drill bits and solder, metal shavings and trickles of deep red, protein-rich blood.


Huddled beneath the tarp alongside the disembodied engines and loose, jangling chunks of metalwork that she had bought from the Choom earlier before she smuggled me out. The truck stops and I listen and wait until she lifts the tarp and helps me out.

"Are they here? Wait. Wait. Are they coming for me? Do you see them?"

"It's okay. There's nobody around. Come on."

"Wait. Wait."

She pulls me along as I repeat the mantra.

Beneath immense brickwork behemoths tinged yellow by sodium lights, we go up a wrought-iron external staircase to the second floor of a crumbling warehouse and she opens the padlock on a four-inch-thick door and helps me inside.

Dusty, dark, cobwebbed. Spray painted names and pictures on the untreated walls.

"You can stay here. It's safe. There's a tap at the back though use it at your own discretion. Do you need water?"

I haven't spoken since she came back for me and I wonder why I hadn't felt the same sense of panic that I was being abducted again as I had when the Choom and his men had gotten close.

"Yes, thank you," I say, at that time not even realising the implications of the question—that it indicated that already she knew, or suspected, what I was.

Had been.

If someone removed your stomach would the rest of you still be hungry?

Cautiously, I walk across the room, a single expanse of grey light punctuated only by a series of support beams that stretch from floor to ceiling and random piles of pneumatic junk. A row of small windows runs along the far wall but the grease and dirt that covers them makes it impossible to see anything beyond, however I can vaguely make out the collective clouds of toxic vapour that signal the field of factories from which I was taken.

"I've got to go just now but I'll be back later. Will you be okay here? Can I get you anything?"

I don't know. I just don't know.

"Okay," she says to the silence. "Stay here, don't go anywhere. I'll be back soon."

And she locks the door behind her again and when she returns 18,234 seconds later she stares at my work, at the equations I have scrawled all over the concrete floor using a chunk of white plaster. It's dark outside and so she flicks a switch and a string of bare bulbs are illuminated along the middle of the room, dousing us in harsh white light.

Guiltily, I lay down the piece of plaster, now worn down to a stub, hang my head.

But she says nothing.

She is carrying a backpack that rattles when she moves, unloads a brown bottle from it. "Antiseptic," she tells me. "We need to clean some of those wounds."

I let her dab me with a rag soaked in the solution, jumping back suddenly at the rush of fiery sensation that shoots through my arm as she applies it there. The feeling spreads, thinning out across my shoulders and chest and I scrub at the offending flesh to try and get rid of the prickling heat.

"It's okay," she soothes. "It'll hurt for a few moments to begin with but if we don't do this it'll hurt a hell of a lot more later."

I acquiesce because it feels natural.

She doesn't ask any questions while she works as to the nature of my wounds or where I received them but she examines me in such a way that I can tell she is investigating me silently. When she is done she removes some tools from her back and holds them before me.

They glitter like stainless steel shin bones.

"I can help you," she says.

Later. This is later.

They came for me post-shift as I made my way along one of the long, narrow corridors that led to the massive block of sleeping quarters at the rear of the factory. The passageways were lined with dark, leaking pipes and sodium bulbs, staggering the light all the way along. They must have emerged silently from one of the anonymous doors because all at once I was aware of soft-soled footsteps behind me that certainly did not belong to Verios.

I had stopped, presuming it to be one or more supervisors and announced my batch and ID number.

"100-VC-755, bloc 5. 109098883."

And something dropped from my tool belt, clattering to ground, the sound echoing through the length of the corridor like a murderous scream.

I turned and they had been wearing plastic masks that covered their entire heads so that all that was discernable was a mass of blurry textures before they jumped on me and then I don't know what.

"Then when I next came to I was in a studio of some kind, like a workshop. I couldn't move because of the pain. I was on a hospital gurney, some sort of traction device suspended above me. And they were watching me."

A warmth spreads across my skin as Meaghan's finger traces my back, a delicate heat like cooling solder. I keep thinking she is holding a match to me. "What had they done?"

"Removed most of my machinery, internal and external, save for a few intricate mechanisms. Run a few transplants, reawakened the dormant areas of my cerebral cortex."

I lean to one side and indicate the ugly gash that Meaghan has recently stitched up. She presses her lips to it momentarily. I rub a piece of fractured metal in my hands as we talk—two strokes north, two south, two east, one north, one west, one south, two west. Over. And over.

The squat glows red from the portable gas heater she has brought with her.

"How long were you there?"

I shake my head. "I don't know. The figures were there, in my head. But I think they took them too. I can't remember things any more."

"You had perfect recall, before?"

"Only as much as it was needed."

"I don't know if I'd want to be able to remember anything."

"Forgetting something doesn't mean it never happened."

"No, but it means you don't have to relive it."

"What about things you want to remember but can't? Good experiences?"

And Meaghan says, "I'll let you know when I have one."


I got the job at the factory, once again thanks to Meaghan.

She took me from the scrapyard, took me to the squat, then took me to the factory and I began to see her as the tracks to my own locomotive anxieties. Slowly the obsessive compulsive tendencies began to drop away, particularly once I was back on the production line. They wouldn't let me back into my old job, of course—and if they knew I was the freak-creature that I was I wouldn't have gotten a job at all.

They don't let humans do the real work anymore—too slow, too inaccurate. The Verio's do the bulk of the manufacturing and assembly in another part of the building adjacent to the great towers that house them when they are between shifts.

My job is to check that the machine parts that are brought to us in a large plastic-lined cart by another worker have been securely and correctly assembled. It's a redundant task because the Verios never make mistakes, this I know only too well, but the human labour forces are still powerful enough to make sure that their members aren't done away with completely.

I find comfort in the work, the repetitiveness calming me, though I react as I should when the others complain and agree with them. They know there is something not quite right about me but I am able to keep to myself most of the time, enough so that they cannot realise what.

And I know they must never find out.

They laugh and joke about the Verios as we stand outside one morning, our breaths steaming before us in the freezing air.

"Look at them—useless fucks. Sure they can solder sixteen components per second but what else? If this place goes bust like they say it might what the fuck use are they going to be to anyone? They'll end up on the fucking scrapheap where they belong."

The others laugh and drop their cigarette butts as the shift horn goes and they all shuffle inside. I remain behind for a few moments, watching the Verios march with military precision along the path that has been prescribed for them to go to work on the shore where the products are loaded onto rusted trawlers. There is a sudden break in the flow as they all stop simultaneously and look back—right back at me—then they face forwards again and continue with their journey.

I pull my beanie hat down to my eyebrows, stick my hands in my pockets and quickly catch up with the others.

"Let me see," Meaghan says and turns me towards the light of the squat's bare bulbs. She wipes my forehead clear of blood with a rag and checks her handwork. "You know, you're healing incredibly well."

I say nothing.

She stands back to get a good look at me. The metal pieces stapled to my body glitter like fine art.

"Your wounds . . . they're very clean. Almost surgical. What did they do to you?"

"I'm not sure."

"There seems to be . . . a purpose."

And I say nothing.

"Do you remember?"

"Not any more".

She stands behind me, traces the line of a wide, curving keloids around my bare hip. "It's okay," she whispers to me. "I know."

I remain where I am, staring out the bleary window at the glow of the smelting plants in the distance.

"It's okay." She continues to trace the keloid. "Your ID and batch numbers went here, didn't they? Just beneath the skin. And your injection points, here and here—your feeding sockets. This bruising was probably at attempt to corrupt the nutrient veins that bypassed your stomach. But I don't see too much damage around your head. I take it you escaped before they could finish the job?"

"I had to get out," I say. "They said they were going to free me from 'my pneumatic restraints'. Make me human."

"But?"

"But they assumed that would have improved things for me. They assumed that I would *want* to become human. Now things . . . things are getting so complicated and I don't want them to find me to finish the job. Maybe we can reverse what they've done so far?"

"I'm afraid that might be a little beyond me."

"But you could try?"

"Look, you're talking serious surgical procedures here. I know some people though . . . "

"No. It has to be you. I can't trust anyone else."

"I don't think I can do what you are asking."

"You have to at least try. This isn't fair, this isn't how I am meant to be. I need you to help me. But I'll understand if you don't want to be around me."

"Why would I want that?" She takes a step closer to me so that there is less than an inch between our bodies at all points.

"Because of what I am. I'm not . . . like you."

"Maybe there isn't as much difference as you might think," she says and leans towards me, places her lips across mine

And she leads me once more—to the bare mattress under one of the windows, to the buttons and zips of her clothing, to her warm skin and damp openings. I let her control me, falling away into the orderly replication of movements and gestures, feeling some sense of structure beginning to reform from the chaos my existence had become.

When the procedure is complete she curls herself into me, the spikes on her Mohican flaccid, her skin bathed in a fine glittering sweat.

She says, "I can understand how you feel about not wanting to become fully human. People can't seem to make up their minds whether replication is a good thing. They revile Verios for being production-line beings but spend most of their lives trying to find a clique they can become a part of by acting and dressing like others. They idolise individuality and ignore the fact that we're all just variations on the same group of amino acids. Fuck, what's so great about us anyway?"

"The ones that took me seemed to think there was something."

"Hey, I wouldn't trust a human's judgement as far as I could throw it."

"They seemed fairly sure they were right, considering the lengths they went to. Sure enough to try and finish the job."

"You're safe here, I've already told you. Where was it they took you from before? The factory?"

"Yes. They jumped me as I was heading back to my quarters. When I next came to I was in a studio of some kind, like a workshop. I couldn't move because of the pain. I was on a hospital gurney, some sort of traction device suspended above me. And they were watching me."

A warmth spreads across my skin as Meaghan's finger traces my back, a delicate heat like cooling solder. I keep thinking she is holding a match to me. "What had they done?"

"Removed most of my machinery, internal and external, save for a few intricate mechanisms. Run a few transplants, reawakened the dormant areas of my cerebral cortex."

I lean to one side and indicate the ugly gash that Meaghan has recently stitched up. She presses her lips to it momentarily. I rub a piece of fractured metal in my hands as we talk—two strokes north, two south, two east, one north, one west, one south, two west. Over. And over.

The squat glows red from the portable gas heater she has brought with her.

She works. I work.

We repeat the procedures and it helps me find peace.

She begins to carefully ask around to see if there is anyone who can help us, mindful that my abductors might still be out there, listening for such whispers. Meanwhile she continues to do what she can with me cosmetically.

I clock on.

Clock off.

On. Off.

I meet her outside the factory and she drives us back to the squat. She feeds me.

We fuck, once a night, just as the area's power grid surges in response to the infestation of night clubs and strip joints business hours commencing, three thousand miles of neon signage causing the squat's bulbs to flicker and almost die. It lasts for forty minutes.

She gives me pills to make me sleep but they don't always work.

She works. I work.

We repeat the procedures and it helps me find peace.

One of the others brings the cart full of machine parts into the workshop and docks it into a set of metal joints. The joints hoist the cart upwards and tip the machine parts onto a conveyor belt.

The conveyor belt starts automatically and drags the little pieces along its length. We each take a piece in turn.

I am seventh. I take the seventh piece.

I rotate it once, twice, twisting it as I rotate so that I can see each side clearly. I trace my fingers along the joints to make sure they are properly soldered. They always are.

I place the machine part onto a pseudo connector fitted onto the conveyor belt's rim and check that the part screws on properly, that the thread has been correctly carved. It always has.

I tilt a hinge on its underside to check that it operates properly. It does.

I hit a switch next to the screw joint to allow a blast of highly compressed hot air to flow through and the machine part guides the gas and dissipates it. The function is irrelevant.

I snap the hinge back into place then unscrew the joint. I lay it back down on the belt and let it drift off.

I reach down and there is another part before me. The procedure takes one minute and thirty four seconds, the loading of the parts timed so that it arrives just as I finish. This is the fourteenth piece. The fourteenth.

I rotate it once, twice, twisting it as I rotate so that I can see each side clearly. I trace my fingers along the joints to make sure they are properly soldered. They always are.

I place the machine part onto a pseudo connector fitted onto the conveyor belt's rim and check that the part screws on properly, that the thread has been correctly carved. It always has.

I tilt a hinge on its underside to check that it operates properly. It does.

I hit a switch next to the screw joint to allow a blast of highly compressed hot air to flow through and the machine part guides the gas and dissipates it. The function is irrelevant.

I snap the hinge back into place then unscrew the joint. I lay it back down on the belt and let it drift off.

I reach down and there is another part before me. The procedure takes one minute and thirty four seconds, the loading of the parts timed so that it arrives just as I finish. This is the fifteenth piece. The fifteenth.

I rotate it once, twice, twisting it as I rotate so that I can see each side clearly. I trace my fingers along the joints to make sure they are properly soldered. They always are.

I place the machine part onto a pseudo connector fitted onto the conveyor belt's rim and check that the part screws on properly, that the thread has been correctly carved. It always has.

I tilt a hinge on its underside to check that it operates properly. It does.

I hit a switch next to the screw joint to allow a blast of highly compressed hot air to flow through and the machine part should guide the gas and dissipate it but it is not secured properly to the screw joint and the blast of air shoots sideways and into the face of the worker standing next to me.

I snap the hinge back into place then unscrew the joint. I lay it back down on the belt and let it drift off. But my task is not complete. There is an error

The man next to me screams, staggering away from his position, clutching his face and others are going to him, shouting, shouting for the supervisor.

One of them shoves me.

I reach down for the next part but it slides past me as I am batted away from the conveyor belt. I make another grab but somebody is holding onto me. Tight.

This isn't right. Out of sync. *Idiot! Idiot!* They shout.

This isn't right. *Help us!* I turn or am pushed, or both.

I see EXIT, above a door with a horizontal bar across it. EXIT, it says. Pushed again.

I turn back to the conveyor belt and take the next piece. This is what I do. *Leave it! Help us!*

The door says EXIT.

I push the bar and run.


There is a pattern to everything.

1, 5, 9, 13, 17.

Every other consecutive odd number. The next would be 21. Then 25.

10, 16, 23, 31, 40, 32, 25, 19, 26.

The numbers rising along a bell curve, starting at 6, rising by one and peaking at nine then falling again by one until they hit 6 once more. The next would be 34. Then 43.

34, 456, 654, 23, 0, 1, 1, 45.

There will be a pattern in there too, whether you are aware of it or not. The universe does not need your permission to sustain order.

These patterns are everywhere.

And yet I am finding it increasingly hard to find them.

I run from the factory, run from the hooded figures and their van, back towards the squat. I count my footsteps, each swing of my arms. Across a plateau of demolished housing, through gangs of children huddled amongst satellite trash and I lose my count, the numbers fragmenting like a nail bomb I've stepped on. This secret terrorist device steals the patterns from me and I almost lose my way, finding myself amongst the narrow corridors that run between the network of old chemist labs neighbouring the squat. I recognise them only via the jagged tag art that has marked their reclamation by pirate radio broadcasters and aerosol punks which I have looked out onto over the past few weeks.

I use the more recognisable pieces to navigate through to the alley which leads towards the building where we squat and that is when I hear her voice. I stop, the rates of bodily systems ballooning within me, utterly out of control and so dysfunctional, but beyond them I listen and yes, I hear her voice.

Meaghan.

Her voice, but not lucid and distinctly described words—slurred verbs, groans. Like I have heard before, each night just as the area's power grid surges in response to the infestation of night clubs and strip joints business hours commencing, three thousand miles of neon signage causing the squat's bulbs to flicker and almost die. It lasts for forty minutes.

There is movement and I go towards it, around the back of a lab and away from the squat. Back through the low, grotty maze and brightly coloured skate scenes, stopping when I hear and glimpse movement.

*Meaghan.*

My mouth opens to vocalise the word but doesn't get that far.

It is not Meaghan but a man.

I can see in the reflections of puddles on the ground ahead of me a light coming from one of the other buildings and in that reflection, figures. The man has come around from the other side of the building and opens the door and for a brief instant the groans get louder. Still Meaghan's voice. Door closes.

I edge closer, now able to keep a hold of the digits as I count my steps.

And now I can see a van parked across the way and I know I have seen that van before.

Twelve. Thirteen. Fourteen. Fift . . .

Now at the window, smeared with grease and partially covered by spray paint but with movement and light inside.

Meaghan.

On the bare floor in the bare room with harsh light pouring onto her. Three shelves lining the length of the rear wall, stacked full of glass containers and flasks, each labelled on brown paper with their chemical contents. A free-standing sink swathed in crusted mould, an elongated tap with a plastic cap over its opening.

And a hospital gurney shoved to one side, almost hidden in the shadows.

One two three four men around Meaghan. On her knees. One behind her, one directly in front. Two on either side, her arms outreached to them. Another one underneath her I realise. Five. Naked. All naked.

Moving like a disjointed mechanism.

Flesh-covered machinery.

Fucking Meaghan.

Group-fucking her with exactly the same rhythm as we use and the other man, the one I followed to the shack, enters the room and begins to remove his clothing. Everything but the plastic mask. That is last.

Tumble from the emergency exit of the factory just as a siren begins to sound and I don't know whether it's triggered by my opening the door or whether it's to summon medical help for the injured worker.

Stagger through a meshwork of hot pipes doused in slimy condensation where everything smells of burnt metal and alkaline. I know the cold dead streets that lead me back to the squat, know how to avoid the main walkways but as I cross the parking lot a vehicle moves out of its slot at the corner of my vision.

I push my hands into my pockets and quicken my pace, weaving through the stationary cars and trucks but it's following me. I begin to run and look back as I leave the parking lot, see a black, unmarked van crawling along on the far side. The sliding door that takes up one entire side is wide open and there are a number of figures inside. One steps out as I stand staring at them, desperate for breath.

His face is distorted by the plastic mask he wears.

This time I don't look back when I run.

And I run.

I run to the squat and loose my numbers in a nailbomb of confusion and spiralling panic and before I can get to the security of the building I hear Meaghan and I see Meaghan and she is naked and surrounded by three men.

Four men.

Five men.

Joined by one more as he removes everything but his mask.

Cheating on me.

Without thinking I slam a fist against the window and the Verio's look at me, so does Meaghan. I see her mouthing the words . . . *oh shit.*

It seems this night was built for running.

I awaken and water is tipped into my mouth.

I awaken to the sting of an injection in my upper arm.

I awaken and am vaguely aware of being paralysed, a flat surgical light bearing down on me, blinding me. There is the sensation of cutting without the damage indicators that would normally accompany it. I wonder if I have a wiring problem or if I have been brought to the Engineers for repairs.

Recall error.

I awaken and someone speaks to me in soft, low tones. *Lynch the landlord. Our knees are there to help us to jump higher, not to have us bow down. Freedom is the purest form of energy in the universe and there is no way to inhibit it. Oppression is merely an illusion—you can't cage somebody. Your bars—these microchips, these pneumatics—don't exist. All we are doing is destroying the illusion that you have no self-control. You aren't a Verio.*

I awaken and at first I think my leg is on fire, and my stomach. I look down and find myself swathed in dirty bandages. I am aware of figures around me, four masculine and one feminine. *10 ccs* a voice says, then I am asleep again.

Soon my conscious moments begin to sustain themselves over longer and longer periods of time and I watch my captors coming and going. They tell me they want to free me and yet they tie me to the gurney. Their faces are distorted by translucent plastic masks, turning their features to a watery putty.

*Don't worry, you'll be as human as we can possibly make you.*

And I consider, what makes them think I would want to be human?

Why would I want to be human?

I find it more and more difficult to run, my limbs burning, my chest feeling as if someone has shoved a hot rod through it. I hear the screech of tires as some or all of my captors bundle into it and chase me, Meaghan probably with them.

I stick to the smallest passageways, to zones polluted with trash and piping that the van couldn't possibly fit through and emerge onto the walkway that leads down towards the docks. I can see fat, heavy tug boats docked into the loading bays and scarred fork lift trucks feeding them cartons and boxes like drugs. Great balled nets of suffocating fish are suspended from poles next to the boats.

I've lost the van for now. All I have is a displaced agony that flares when I think of Meaghan. Meaghan, my bullet in the head. I begin to see her in my memories of my time of incarceration and can't tell if I am rewriting things or seeing them as they actually are. I see her standing by my side, holding my hand as one of the others fiddles with the exposed circuitry in my forearm. And wiping blood and sweat from me. And watching me carefully from the shadows, a cracked test tube between her fingers, the outline of her Mohican like the visualisation of a heart attack.

*I don't know where I'm going!* This is so inefficient, I have no route, I am wasting energy, there is no *structure*.

Then headlights are suddenly upon me and the van thuds over the old tram tracks that line the docks, swinging around to face me. The rear tyres burn out and take off past the tugs and the tattooed workers, their protective oxygen masks throwing little spikes of memory at me as I pass them—their distorted faces, their handheld oxyacetylene torches. Up ahead a narrow bridge sprouts from the chunks of concrete that make up the loading bays and into the dark sea mists but there is something not quite right about it.

Behind me, the van clatters across the tram tracks, battering its undercarriage and showering sparks around it. The side door is open and shouts are coming from inside but they are lost to the winds rushing through me.

I jump over a small railing that runs alongside me, putting it between myself and my kidnappers and I am on the path that leads towards the bridge. Up and along, my boots hammering against the corrugated metal beneath my feet, leaping over another fence and a sudden rush of pain in my legs as I land. When I stand, more pain and I think I have done something to it.

The van screeches to a halt beside me, lining itself up with the access road to the bridge.

I turn and scramble to my feet, gritting my teeth at the pain that travels up my leg with each step, I can't run as fast, can't run.

"Wait!" The first discernable word from the van. I think it's Meaghan's voice.

The bridge seems unfinished, exposed pieces of scaffold and internal structures emerging from between the concrete mouldings. Curved iron rods like the vertebrae of some twisted spinal column, flapping pieces of plastic sheeting and dead hazard lights. Battered construction signs.

The van starts after me again and I don't even know where this bridge leads to but that doesn't matter because when you've got nowhere to go each place is as good as the next. Then I see why the structure looked odd as I had run towards it—it really was unfinished.

Up ahead, the tarmac and metal walkways suddenly stopped dead, ribs of wrought iron poking out a few extra yards ahead but nothing more. Just the blackness of a sheer drop into the poisoned waters below. I came to a sudden halt a few feet from the edge and through the mists I could see a twin structure, as well unfinished and no doubt intended to meet with this one over the bay. There is a hundred metre gap between them.

Behind me the van grinds to a halt, skidding around so that it faces me side-on.

Nowhere to go.

I back up another couple of paces towards the edge.

"Stop!"

Unmistakeably Meghan as she scrambles from the van.

Every muscle in my body burns, aches. My head is warping.

I begin to count the rivets beneath my feet.

"This isn't what you think!" she shouts. Two of the masked men flank her.

"What did you do to me?!"

"Let me explain!"

Another bolt of pain shoots through my leg but it is nothing compared to that I feel upon seeing her. "I trusted you. But you were there . . . I remember now."

"I know," she says. "but please . . . let me explain."

"You helped them do this to me. I don't want to be fucking human! I never asked for this."

"But you did! You did ask for it! That's the whole point!"

"No! Fuck you! Fuck the factory! Fuck Punktown! Leave me alone!"

A strong gust of wind rocked me where I stood and I felt my heel rolling against one of the exposed splints of iron.

"Goddammit I'm getting tired of this! I can't do this anymore!"

"Do what any more?" I ask.

Meaghan takes a breath and motions to one of the men beside her. He steps forward and for a second I think he is going to come for me but he holds up his arms to show that he is no threat.

"Take it off," I hear Meaghan say, but only just audible above the winds.

The man reaches back and unclips the band that holds his mask on.

He takes it off and then I lose any and all numbers I have ever possessed.

"What . . . ?"

The man let his mask drop to the ground—this man with my own face.

The others emerged from the van, all of them there, each holding their masks in their hands and each with my own face.

"Meaghan . . . "

My head feels weighted, my neck sloppy and weak.

"It's okay," she says, stepping towards me. Only a foot or two away now. Her piercings glitter in the yellow fog lights. "Don't be scared. I won't hurt you."

"Don't hurt me. Don't hurt me."

"I won't." And she reaches out and touches my arm.

"What are you *doing?*"

"Only what you ask. What you always ask—to be human."

"I keep telling you, I *don't.*"

"I know. It's part of the pattern. You don't know *what* you want."

"Meaghan . . . "

"You asked me to help you become human, to lose your Verio status. Every time you ask me and every time it doesn't work because I don't think it's really what you want and every time we have to start again with a new clone. Six times already we've done this, for fuck's sake."

"Who are those men? Why do they look like me?"

"I told you already—they're part of the same batch you came from. Each time we try and each time we fail."

"I kidnapped myself?"

"In a manner of speaking. And I have no doubt we'll do it again—because that is the pattern. That is the routine."

"The routine."

"It's what we do. I don't know why the fuck we have to go through it again and again but we do. We just do."

The routine. My thoughts begin to fall back into place. There *was* an order. There always is an order if you just look deep enough.

"Are you going to operate on me again?"

"There's no point. It won't work. That's what I'm telling you—it'll fail. It always fails. But we keep trying."

"Because that is the routine."

"Exactly."

"Why do you help me, Meaghan?"

She shrugs. "I guess even humans can find comfort in repetition."

I look back at the men gathered behind her, my fellow batch-members. Our botched attempts at humanity—or humanity's botched attempts at machines.

"I don't trust you," I tell her. "I don't believe you."

"You never do," she says.

She reached out towards me with one hand, offering it palm up. Instinctively I backed off, onto the metal rod that all was that kept me from the black waters a hundred metres below.

"Don't . . . " she says.

I look down, my head still spinning, watching the lyrical pattern of the foam on the water.

And I step off.

Step One: Retrieve subject from workplace.

Step Two: Remove majority of non-human, Verio functions and devices from subject.

Step Three: Allow subject to engage with its own uncertainty and indecision and escape mid-procedure.

Step Four: Track subject to breaker's yard and socialise.

Step Five: Integrate into human environment and test procedure's success.

Step Six: Attempt to recover subject after procedure's failure determined. Prevent any attempts at destruction or suicide.

Step Seven: Repeat steps one through seven.

"Here," she says and hands me a mask.

I stare at it, this plastic configuration of my own face, then at the others with me, my brothers. I pull it on and we get out of the van.

"Good luck," she says.

We all know where we are going, our paces match, our breathing in sync. We all turn back in unison to look at Meaghan as she slides the door to the van shut and we all reach the back entrance to the factory at the same moment.

The timing is perfect of course, as the end of shift siren sounds. We use our tools and bypass the simple locking mechanism, enter a long tunnel with strip lighting illuminating its length.

It looks like the air vents in a pyramid.

We follow the predetermined route, heading through doorways, down slimmer tunnels, through wider ones until we reach a long corridor lined with dark, leaking pipes and sodium bulbs. The light is staggered all the way along. We step into one of the many doorways that line the passageway and close the door behind us. It is a storage cupboard and we each begin the count.

We can hear him coming but it is the count that we listen to.

1297 . . . 1298 . . . 1299 . . . 1300 . . . 1301 . . . 1302

And then we open the door silently and there he is up ahead. He stops after a few paces, hearing our soft-soled footsteps and says, without turning.

"100-VC-755, bloc 5. 109098883."

He thinks we were one of his supervisors because that is the pattern.

And we grab him suddenly and something drops from his tool belt, clatters to the ground, echoes the length of the corridor like a murderous scream.

In the struggle he turns and looks up and I stare right back down at him, my face reflected back at me just as it is when we fuck Meaghan and all he sees are a set of masked men looming over him.

Only there are seven this time.

One.

Two.

Three.

Four.

Five.

Six.

Seven.

# HER LOVE FOR ME IS
# OXYACETYLENE

Every time I open my eyes it's a disappointment. Disappointment that I'm still here, that I haven't been sucked from the world yet. I open my eyes and there is the cold, clinical ceiling of a hospital above me and I wonder how many people have died with that image burned into their retinas. I open my eyes and there are the stars and I don't move as people walk past me, taking me for a bum or a dope fiend. I open my eyes and there are hateful faces staring down at me and I think *maybe this time* but soon enough I open my eyes again.

This time a woman stood over me, arms crossed. My vision was blurred, I could only see her outline.

"Which hospital am I in?"

I realised it was sore to speak, my throat feeling bruised.

"You're not in hospital," she replied. Her voice was hard like concrete. I knew she'd be staring at my forehead, like they all did.

And I dared to dream that she might be the one to kill me.

Later I am aware of her in the room again. She stays outwith my line of sight, my neck too sore to move to see her. I can smell soup and notice a steaming bowl lying on the table next to the bed I am on. There are no restraints, as there have been in the past.

"It's homemade," she says.

I consider if this is a threat, that she might have laced it with poison and be daring me to take it. So I reach over and take a few spoonfuls.

"Do you remember what happened to you?"

I shake my head, little spikes of pain screaming their way down my spine. I think I do but all the attacks have blurred into one.

"Some of the workers from the smelting plant a few blocks down jumped you, looks like. I'm amazed they didn't kill you. You're just lucky I found you before someone else did".

Lucky like I've been found all the times before. So lucky that I'm still alive.

"But I guess it can't come as a big surprise considering . . . "

She let her words drift off.

*Say it.*

"I'm assuming they didn't do that to you. It doesn't look fresh," she said, nodding at the scarring on my forehead. When I didn't say anything, she continued. "Look, I'm going to be honest with you here—I don't know exactly why I brought you in, if it was the right thing to do or not. I still might call the cops. Are they looking for you? Have you escaped from somewhere? Because if you have I want to know right now."

"Nobody wants me," I told her. "Nobody's after me."

"Good. Because I'm going to work soon and I don't care if you are here when I come back or not but I don't want to find my apartment busted apart by the PD or Psych. Services."

Still she stood away from me, out of my line of sight. I stared down into the soup's steam. And then finally she asked the question I knew she had been dying to ask ever since she had found me.

"Is it true? What it . . . says?"

I dropped the spoon back into the bowl, swallowed. "Yes."

"Still here," she says when she returns.

When you didn't belong anywhere, each place was as good as the next.

"If you want me to leave . . . "

"No. At least not until you're in better shape. How are you feeling?"

"Fine. Thank you."

Her footsteps, surprisingly heavy-sounding, moved around me and finally I saw her in the room's half-light, this woman who would rescue a fiend like me. She was wearing a set of baggy, stained overalls peeled back at the waist and a tight long-sleeved t-shirt with the name of one of the smelting plants stamped across it.

I didn't mean to show my shock when I saw her face but it's a natural thing to see something different and be surprised by it. This is something I know so well.

She stood defiantly, her arms crossed as if daring me to say something. This was obviously a deliberate revelation, made when she was good and ready. She'd probably learned to take control of other people's shock from years of the same look I had given her in that instant.

"I can take you to a hospital if that's what you'd prefer. But what with all the gang victims and viruses that have been hitting the A&E's lately there'd be no certainty that you'd be better off."

"I don't want to go to hospital."

She clumped towards me, her industrial boots comically large on her, sat on a chair that had been positioned beside the bed. I could feel her hostility bristling now that she was closer to me.

"Who did that to you?"

Normally they weren't that direct. In fact, most of the time, it didn't even occur to people whom might have scarred my forehead in such a destructive manner, they were so busy hating me for what it said.

"Concerned citizens," I said flatly.

"What did you do?"

Of course. The details. They despise you for what you've done but they always want the details.

"What do you think I did?"

She took offence at my tone, her strange face suddenly hardening as it stared back at me. "Then you deserved it."

I shrugged a little. "Most people seem to think so. Did you deserve yours?"

I don't know why I said it, it was cruel and I didn't mean it. And immediately we were engaged in something. A game, a fight, some form of deformed intercourse—I don't know.

Her hands were trembling in her oil-stained lap. I noticed they were littered with dozens of tiny cuts, probably from whatever machinery she worked with each day, some crusted and old, some fresh and weeping from her rubbing them against each other.

She looked like she was going to say something, then her features relaxed again. She stood up, walked over to the bedroom door with those massive footsteps of hers, and left me in the silence.

And so it began.

I would listen to her in the morning as she prepared for work with the sun still not fully risen, bleeding hot reds into the sky like the molten steel that surrounded her in the smelting plant. Then I would be alone all day with my wounds, listening to the water and heating systems bubble and pop in the crumbling walls of the bedroom as I assembled in my head various scenarios of how she gained her own disfigurement.

It was an industrial accident, some errant machine part grabbing her as she walked past.

It was a spray of metal lava.

It was a gang of rowdy bikers that had jumped her as she walked alone one night.

And then the evening would settle in and she would return, trampling from room to room for a while before she would come into the bedroom and sit beside me and we would both have all the questions in the world about each other.

"It doesn't bother you, having me here? Considering . . . what I've done?" I asked her one night.

"Some people believe things happen because that is the only way they could happen. We think we have control but we don't. If we just accept that then everything become a lot easier."

"Is that what you believe?"

She doesn't answer.

"I have a feeling the parents wouldn't agree with you."

"Was it one of them?"

I told her, no. I told it was a group of retired policemen whose friends on the force had their hands tied and weren't able to touch me. I told her they kept me hidden in an old garage for two days before dumping me in on the street in front of an A&E ward.

She unwrapped the bandage she had placed around my left arm, very probably broken, and began to apply a fresh one.

"How many?" she asked, then tensed as if I were about to inject her.

It didn't matter. All it took was that one time when things got out of control and you became defined by that act. I made a figure up because I think it really didn't matter to her either.

"What are you going to do with me?"

She shrugged, tugging on the bandage unnecessarily. "I haven't figured it out yet. If you were being actively hunted then they probably would have found you by now, or at least been at the door asking. Are you on some sort of register or something? Do they keep track of where you are?"

"I'm supposed to report in once a week to my parole officer then call them an hour later to prove I'm still staying at the same address."

She considered this for a few moments. "You've been here almost a week now. What will happen if you don't report in?"

"Not much. It's happened before when I've been in hospital or . . . "

"Or what?" When I didn't answer she shifted forwards on her chair, leaned towards me on her elbow. "What have people done to you?"

I shook my head, growing tired quickly. My strength didn't seem to be coming back to me at all and it crossed my mind once more that this woman wasn't the Samaritan she made herself out to be, that for all I knew she could be slowly poisoning me and filming it on hidden cameras to sell to the families whom my actions destroyed. Was I her plaything?

"What have people done to *you*?" I countered.

Again she seemed to try and hide the flinch that resulted from my words but failed. "Most people have done nothing to me."

"Someone has," I said. "Someone's made a mess of you too."

She didn't look at me, instead concentrating her attention on unnecessarily tightening my bandage. I knew I was pushing her. I knew she might snap and turn on me like so many had, whatever had been holding her back so far suddenly breaking under the strain of my inferences. It was the very reason I pushed her.

Then she raised her head and her features were shivering, eyes shining as if filled with lightning. "Fuck you," the words sliding from her mouth, and she stood and stalked back out the room.

I was left alone long enough to consider leaving.

This hadn't been what I had expected, it was taking too long. I just wanted it over with.

If she was going to turn on me then what was she waiting for?

By that point I was well enough to stand, as long as I had the support of a wall nearby. I stared out of the room's single, tiny window that framed the massive insect-corpses of the smelting plants.

When she finally came back she charged into the room, her hair out of the pony tail she usually kept it in and flying wildly behind her. She pulled the chair into place and sat on it back to front.

"*This*," she snapped, pointing to the white keloid that doused her right eye and cheek, "is where he got me first. Almost took out my eye. *This* is where my nose bone came through my eyebrow ridge. *This*," she turned, lifting her hair away from her neck, spitting with the fury of her words, "is where he slashed me when I turned and tried to get away, and here and here. And *this* . . . "

She turned once more lifting her T-shirt away from her stomach and revealing the puckered fleshy ridge of another scar that ran across is it. "*This* . . . "

Her words were torn apart by her anger and she pulled the T-shirt back down again, leaning onto the bed and in that moment I felt almost certain she was going to attack me after all. Her hands had clenched into fists and I wasn't sure if she was even aware of it.

I felt the familiar calm begin to wash over me, ready to close my eyes and let her begin the assault but she was hesitant. When she spoke it was in strained, but measured, tones.

"You're fucking pathetic. You think I'm going to pity you any more? Well, *fuck* that."

That was better. Her anger poured over me, Jesus, that was better.

"Christ, I can't believe I didn't just start in on you the like the others did. You're just a piece of shit that deserves all the beatings I'm sure you've had."

I felt myself grow lighter as whatever bond that had formed between us began to burn away like the fuse on a bomb.

She jumped onto the bed suddenly, straddling my bruised legs, pressing down on them, her boots crushing my feet.

"Do you still think about fucking them? Pushing yourself into them as they screamed for you to stop? *Do you*?!"

No. Not like that.

Don't mention them.

"You do, don't you? Is that what you've been doing while I'm away?"

*Stop.* I'm not even sure if the word came out of me. I hissed as she moved slightly upon me, grinding my legs together at the damaged knees.

"Oh you don't like me mentioning it do you? I suppose your scars up there remind you enough already? Well maybe you need reminding a little more."

"No," I murmured, reaching out for her but she slapped my hands away and I didn't have the strength for another attempt. "Please ... "

She pushed me down then pulled off her t-shirt, exposing her breasts to me.

"So this does nothing for you, right? You wouldn't touch me, would you?"

She grabbed my hands and put them to her breasts, rubbed them against the soft flesh, grimacing down at me. "No, not a damn thing."

"Get . . . off . . . "

She kneaded herself harder to the point that it must have been painful, forcing my nails into her nipples, squeezing them blue. "You wouldn't . . . fucking . . . *touch* me . . . you wouldn't . . . " She murmured through gritted teeth, moving against my hips as if to gauge any reaction then suddenly shouted, "well at least *he* fucking touched me!"

And everything went still.

She was struggling for breath, dropped my hands and lifted her weight from my legs. Her hair hung in sweat-clotted strands over her disfigurements, re-describing her face in shadow as drops of perspiration fell from it.

She reached down and placed a hand on my face, stroked it with a strange tenderness and her expression changed as she looked down at me. Her brow furrowed.

"Why did it bother you so much for me to mention what you did?"

I couldn't answer, just stared back at her. I saw in the spirals of her scars, the puncture marks where the stitches had been, and the canals of dried skin where tears must constantly have trailed down. I hadn't had a chance to look at her properly thus far and took the opportunity to see her, really *see* her. And there was beauty there.

Her big green eyes sparkled. She seemed to be considering something very carefully, traced the words on my forehead with her forefinger.

*Paedo.*

"I don't believe you're capable of it," she said softly.

"We're all capable of much more than we like to imagine," I countered.

"Not that much."

I took her wrist in my hand, stopping her from touching the words any more. "Don't let yourself think that you know me. You don't."

"I know that you flinch when I even mention raping those children."

"I'm not proud of what I am," I told her. "They found their bodies, hidden amongst the husks of cars from road traffic accidents in the scrapyard. Decomposing. Of course the parents would want revenge, who could blame them? They roamed the neighbourhood for days."

"You said it was policemen."

"Yes. They were there too. They needed to find him. Me."

She tilted her head. "Which is it? Him—or you?"

My head hung, suddenly very heavy. Why did things always get so complicated?

"They got it wrong, didn't they? You didn't do those things."

"No. I deserved what they did to me."

She turned her head slightly, almost shaking it.

"I shouldn't have been in the scrapyard anyway. I just wanted to look. To see—where they found them."

"Shit. You didn't do it."

Now I was shaking my head, my entire body feeling like it was filling with lead. "No. They . . . I deserved what they did to me."

"Shit. Shit. Oh, shit."

She just kept saying it, over and over as she leaned forwards and cradled my head in her arms, her warm breasts pressing against my face. *Shit. Shit. Shit.* I think she was seeing all the attacks that I had told her about, all the things that had been done to me because of the scarring.

I faded into a curious mixture of sleep and unconsciousness there, in her arms, as she stroked my hair and kissed my face.


And her affection instantly became the greatest pain that I had suffered for it threw into disarray everything that I thought I had felt certain of.

She lay next to me at night after that, naked in the bed beside me. We listened to the sounds of steam being released from pneumatic vents and crunching of metal being chewed in huge compaction units. I studied her face as she slept, ran my fingers along the contours of her markings as she had mine, learned each and every one of them.

I thought about the man who had done this to her, I fantasised each and every cut being made, inscribing upon her the new identity that she suffered from. I wondered about which point she became a pariah such as I was.

This scar? Before or after?

This scar? Before or after?

When did she become an unacceptable member of society?

"Maybe we were born that way," she said softly without opening her eyes. I hadn't realised I had been talking aloud.

I moved closer to her, inhaling the scent of engine oil that seemed infused into her pores.

"Everything happens for a reason," she said. "What he did to me didn't change anything. The scars were already there. Don't hate him."

"I don't," I told her.

She paused, as if trying to decide how to take that. "Well I hate the ones who scarred you. They've made you into something you're not."

Her eyes were open now but I kept staring straight at the scars, indulging in the way her eye slanted sharply about two-thirds of the way along. I wanted to tell her.

I *knew* I should tell her the truth.

It was time.

"I should have left him long before he did this to me," she whispered. "That was my own failing. I shouldn't have kept pushing him like I did. Some of us aren't meant to spend our lives with others. But you . . . "

I had stopped caressing her, my hand going numb.

"I did it to myself," I said, stopping her from saying any more. And then there was silence.

The dead, glassy flesh of her markings seemed to twitch minutely as she considered me.

"I did it to myself."

She had said that the men who had attacked me the night she found me had been talking in the mess hall at the smelting plant. One of them had found an article about my supposed crimes and they had decided that they weren't finished with me yet. They had been checking the hospitals and any squats or shelters I might have hidden in and even asked her if she had seen someone like me around lately, as if I would somehow gravitate to a fellow Disfigured.

She held my hand as we walked, rain like shards of glass tumbling down upon us.

I felt how hard she was gripping me, could almost hear her teeth grinding against each other, as we moved between the massive concrete walls of the surrounding buildings. Old garbage bags littered the streets, spilling their guttermelt into streams of water tinged orange by rust.

"Are you sure about this?" I asked her.

She gripped me harder, wrapped her arm around me.

"Just look out for them. I want to have my eyes open when it happens."

She was still wearing her work gloves as she removed all my dressings, the fat fingers singed at their edges, black pock marks where chemicals had begun to burn through.

My recent wounds had finally healed, though we both knew they had been that way for several days already. My injuries had somehow come to encapsulate what we had and as they disappeared, so would we.

We had talked about it in that way we had, a communication of silence and filtered remarks. She had been listening to the men who had attacked me each lunchtime and knew that their interest in me was waning. They still prowled but had resorted to picking random fights in lieu of their proper prey, their wandering hostility eager for satiation.

She said they were like a binary liquid explosive just waiting for their partner fluid to set them off. I said that maybe we were the same. She smiled as best she could with that crooked face.

The rain began to fall more heavily, hissing as it hit the ground because of the high acid content in the area. We saw them at the end of an alleyway, stumbling along with bottles of alcohol and weapons stuffed in their pockets, then out of sight behind a building.

She led me along the street parallel to the theirs which then began to curve inwards, inevitably meeting few hundred yards ahead. Their voices echoed through the smog.

After I had told her my secret, it was like a switch was thrown in both of us.

She didn't ask why. She didn't need to.

But even if she had I wouldn't have had an answer up until that moment.

When you are born pariah, that knowledge is inscribed upon you, etched onto your muscle and sinew, your heart and your very being. To mark yourself externally is no different.

What I had done to myself hadn't made me what I was.

And what her lover had done to her hadn't made her what she was.

"Born pariah," she said and I nodded.

She told me about the cuts she had made growing up, the things she had done to try and understand that feeling of detachment, as if the world was taking place behind a foggy screen.

"He caught me one night, not long after we met. Wanted to know what I was doing. But I couldn't answer. There was no answer. I think he knew I still did it after that but I did my best to hide it from him and he seemed to do his best to hide it from himself. But I guess I just kept pushing him. How could I make him understand what I didn't under-stand myself? He said that if I liked it that much—he would help me. I think maybe he was trying to cure me."

She told me this as we sat on the roof of her apartment building, wearing oxygen packs because the smog was too thick around us, a smog turned electric orange by the sun falling somewhere in the distance.

"There's no way out of it," I murmured.

Her breath steamed in the oxygen mask, the pupils in her thin, green eyes suddenly dilating.

"Except one."

We saw them before they saw us.

We just kept walking, our footsteps stilted as if we were fitted with leg braces, our hands locked and then recognition began to set in.

My heart started to beat faster because I still wasn't sure if we should be doing this. Maybe there was a cure. Maybe there was another way out.

One of them shouted at us and I think at that point they still hadn't realised who I was, they just knew it was a bit of fun. We got closer and they had spread out in the street, their eyes narrowing as they saw our deformities.

"It's him," one of them said.

She squeezed my hand and I felt how much she was shaking.

*Let's turn back.*

The words only occurred in my head. I was unable to voice them.

We were driftwood.

"Miss, are you okay?"

One second behind the rest of the world, forever out of sync.

"Step away from him, Miss."

Discarded electrons. A number 2 in the binary code.

"We told you once already. *Step away.*"

Chromosome 24.

"I'm with him," she said as they encircled us.

They laughed amongst themselves, partly in disbelief.

"You must be more desperate than you look," one of them said and I suddenly felt a blow to the back of my head. I fell forwards, hitting the cobblestones of the road hard and a foot was on my back, stamped.

I heard her cry out and saw out of the corner of my eye one of them grab her by the hair, tugging her around. She had promised she wouldn't scream or beg and she didn't. Not as they threw her to the ground beside me, not as they began kicking her. Not when they brought a piece of lead piping down across her beautifully damaged face.

"Don't you know what he is?!"

They were pulling her around as they dragged me to my knees, holding me up so that the others could get a better swing at me. Blood was pouring from both of us but the whole time we were watching each other because at least if there was nothing else that was meant for us there was that.

"I'm with him," she repeated.

And they hit her again.

They hit me again.

"Worthless piece of shit, you don't belong here!" another said and shoved the ragged end of the pipe into my chest.

*Don't belong anywhere*, I thought to myself.

There was the sound of the factory machines churning and the little noises she made as they broke her body.

"There's no way out of it," I had murmured through the oxygen mask.

And she had told me—"Except one."

# ELISABETH AFTERLIFE IS DEAD

It's no great secret that everything is for sale, that everything has a price—because everything is desired. We are consumers and therefore it's our purpose to seek possession. Of land. Objects.

People.

Emma Larson is worth $50. It says so on the sign that sits next to her under the old bridge downtown, the one that she painted herself.

I bring my camera's lens to bear on it, resting the crosshairs on the wooden placard that so devastatingly reduces life to dollars.

"I've made us something to eat," she tells me and I turn, retaining the camera to my eye. The lighting under the bridge is minimal but she has candles burning in little pots and wine bottles she has scavenged so it almost looks like an altar and the steaming bowl she holds some sort of religious offering. There are fly posters for Bill Hicks gigs pasted and pinned to most of the walls and a pirated CD of his plays in the background.

She has the build of a swan, beneath the rumpled combats and hooded top.

It's been six days now since I first met Emma Larson.

The man takes off his jacket and tie, rolls up his sleeves. The air seems full of static as if one of the giant broadcasting pylons that straddle the land above the underpass has collapsed and bleeds electricity. A few have gathered to watch but Emma tells me this is a weeknight and that things will get much livelier at the weekend.

She has removed her hoodie and stripped down to an athletic vest and martial arts trousers, her small, broad feet bare. I've brought in some extra lighting borrowed from Russ who had taken his little anarchist mob to Prague for one reason or another and pan down the patchwork of reds, yellows, blues and blacks that cover her skin. I want to see her training. I want to see her contorting herself, the shape of her muscles as they move beneath her skin, the ripple of cartilage and tissue that I know would be so exquisite on her.

She limbers up and the man stares straight at her, cracks his knuckles. He's about one hundred and fifty pounds heavier than her and from the looks of it most of it sits around his waist but I know from experience that it doesn't take skill to cause damage. The pair of them stand within a loose chalk square that has been marked on the ground, Emma taking in several deep breaths as the man unclips his watch strap, slips the device up to his knuckles, then clasps it again. The gold band glitters across the broad side of his hand and he tells her, "Okay."

And suddenly they are moving like boxers, circling each other in an uneven spiral that brings then closer then draws them away and Emma's raised hands go to her side as she straightens, muscles taught, and the man delivers the first blow. He cracks her across the face cleanly with his makeshift knuckleduster and Emma stumbles backwards, abruptly wrong-footed. Before she can right herself the man has kicked away one of her legs, bringing her to one knee, then delivers another blow to her head with the watch, and another.

She has already told me what would happen here, what they were paying their money for, but seeing her being beaten into the ground like that was something I could never have prepared myself for. She doesn't raise a hand to defend herself, instead using them to scramble away from him along with whatever other parts of her body she can call into order to complete the manoeuvre—elbow, shoulder, hip.

The crowd surges around me and the two fighters as if subconsciously contemplating, as a single entity, joining the fray. I have to fight against them to retain the clear view I have had of her and feel strangely naked without my camera. I know that if I had it I would be afforded an opening by the crowd as they bowed to the authority of the mechanical eye but she wasn't going to let me film one of the events, not yet. I felt insanely anxious at letting all this slip by without recording it, my fingers twitching for the curve of the camera's body and the sound of its inner workings next to my head like a second pulse.

By this point Emma has managed to get to her feet again and the crowd shout at the fighters—not words of encouragement, for there was no question as to whose efforts were being supported in the battle, but instead instructions on where to attack her next and how. With their increasingly loud and frenzied cries Emma seems to be growing smaller and smaller. Everyone is against her.

I pointlessly urge her in my mind to fight back.

But I knew that that wasn't what the man had paid fifty bucks for.

"His name is McLaren," she tells me and this is later that night, or early the next morning depending on your point of view and body clock. Whichever, the sky is grey with the first attempts at sunlight, watery beams penetrating the smog clouds at irregular intervals. My mind is still on the night's events, framing what is happening over and over from different angles, different distances. I couldn't film it as it happened so this was the closest I had.

"Pierce McLaren. He was a client of mine back when I was on the game. He started off like a lot of the others, wanting a little rough but soon I realised it was more than that with him. Soon enough we were wrestling and fucking at the same time, then not longer after that we were just wrestling. It was around about the time . . . oh—wait . . . "

In my head I am watching her tumble backwards into one of the bridge's slimy walls, bouncing off of it in slow-mo and back into McLaren's bloodied fist. It takes me a moment to realise she has interrupted herself.

"What?"

She raises a finger to her swollen lips, the disinfectant-soaked rag hanging limply in her other hand. "Wait."

"*The House of Senate says that pornography is anything of no artistic merit that causes sexual thought*," the tape player says. The speakers were rusted and semi-fused but Hicks' southern drawl was clear. "No artistic merit, causes sexual thought? Sounds like every fucking commercial on TV . . . ."

Emma smiles to herself, shakes her head lightly. "Anyway, you were asking about the people that come to me. McLaren, he's a classic. Don't know how much he must have given me by now between this and hooking."

"What do you mean, a classic?"

She glances briefly at the camera sitting on its tripod between and behind us, suddenly reminded of its presence by the whirr of the auto focus. I think it was one of the things that attracted me to her those first few times we spoke, her reticence to be put in front of the camera. It was a rare thing now, to find that in a person, and it intrigued me as to just what it was that made her nervous. I had managed to get her to agree to me setting it up and running it remotely for now in the hope that she would get used to it.

"I mean he's realised what I've realised—that violence is the new sex. We're all so fucking saturated with dicks and pussies in every possible combination that nothing stimulates us any more. There's nothing left. People are beginning to look elsewhere."

"Beating the shit out of you turns them on?" I ask. It's almost painful for me to look at her face all puffed up and oil-coloured as it is. At this point I'm obviously not one of Emma's *classics*.

"No, no. It's not like that. This isn't about sex—you have to get away from the idea that the only true stimulus is sexual. This is different. There are all these holes inside us and if you can't fill one of them, then maybe you just have to move on and try filling another."

"Sounds sexual to me," I say, then smile to try and soften the atmosphere. It takes a moment but then she smiles too, pressing a stone to her face in lieu of an ice pack to stem the swelling.

And as I watch her I realise that already she has forgotten about the camera.

"What about the rest?" I ask quickly, before her mood can stiffen again.

She shrugs and inhales the joint she has rolled, hands it to me. "Frustrated husbands fantasising about assaulting their wives or secretaries. Young guys that still can't comprehend what they've paid fifty bucks for even as they land the first blow. Executives looking for a new toy, a new stimulus that doesn't lie between the legs of some teenage office junior."

"They're all men? You never get any women?"

She shakes her head, takes another toke on the spliff. "Not so far. Just guys. You'd be amazed how much aggression men have inside them towards women."

"You're never scared it might go too far? That they might beat you too hard, rape you?"

She lets out a small laugh. "Hah. Look, I already told you this isn't about sex. Guys looking for a fuck don't get this far. Plus I can sense them a mile off. And I can handle myself if need be. I wouldn't do this if I weren't in full control."

"But how can you be sure of that control? There was two dozen guys there tonight. If they had turned on you, what would you have done?"

She throws the rag to the ground and stands up stiffly, dusting herself off. "You don't believe me? Fine. If you're that concerned you can come with me later, see for yourself."

"Come where?"

Her back is turned to me as she opens up a small tin and begins to roll another joint. "You'll see," she says. "And turn that fucking camera off."

I won't deny the fact that the first time I saw her the thought crossed my mind about what it would be like to fuck her. My introduction was to her legs, draped over the low concrete wall she sat on near the underpass she called home, and my eyes had followed the tiny dancer's feet up the muscled calves, rounded knees and sturdy, pale thighs.

I thought of all the wonderful shapes she could put herself into and that's why I stopped and watched her on the rare occasions I was downtown.

X. and I had broken up in that way we had which was more just a case of boredom with each other than any real problems in our so-called relationship. I would go back to him soon enough but for now life had other kinds of fulfilment for me.

As she sleeps, I take the camera from its cradle on the tripod and heave it quietly onto my shoulder. Only one of the studio lights are still on, pointed away from us and illuminating the bricked-up rear end of the underpass. I pan across her prostrate form, her posture designed to avoid the uncomfortable spots created by McLaren's attack. (I know that 'attack' is the wrong word but can think of nothing else more appropriate right now.) I let the pixellating screen absorb the contours of her neck and shoulders for me, the shadows of her spine and the smooth slope where her torso twists into her hips.

I recognise the man as he reaches out a hand to me so hesitatingly take it in my own. "You were at the fight last night," I say suspiciously.

His body is toned in such a way as to suggest his muscles are born of gymnastics or yoga rather than weightlifting, his bright blue eyes locking onto me beneath a small explosion of darkly curled hair. "Fight? That was no fight," he says, glancing at Emma and I can't tell whether he is smiling or grimacing. "*That's* a fight."

I look to where he is pointing, two men wrapped around each other and ravaging blows on one another. Their grunts echo around the warehouse we are in that is nothing but four enormous walls with windows lining the very tops of them and a thinly-plated flat roof overhead. The same scene is repeated a half-dozen times across the dusty concrete floor as if it were the scene of an illusionist's trick, mirror upon mirror reflecting each other.

"Salvatore," the man says and I realise we are still holding hands.

He reminds me of X. slightly, possessing similarly beautiful forearms.

"Elizabeth Afterlife," and he releases my hand slowly, poetically. Emma has left our side, walking across to some old gymnastic equipment that had been set up in one corner and standing between a pair of suspension hoops.

"What's with the camera?"

"I'm a docu. Freelance."

"Anything I might have seen?"

"I'm not exactly prime time."

"Aahhhh," he says, placing a hand on my back and leading me towards Emma, now hanging from one of the rings. "We're talking about the pirate stations, right? The Media Virus guys?"

"Sometimes. Whatever pays."

"Whatever pays, right," he says, then shouts up at Emma, "Your lady here says whatever pays, Em. That's they what its about, right? Whatever pays?"

"That's right, Sal. Life's just a ride. It doesn't matter."

She was heaving herself up and down on the ring and I imagined that her freshly damaged muscles must still have been screaming in pain.

"Ain't nothing that's not for sale, right Em? Dignity, pride, self-respect. It all has its price."

I was aware that the fights have slowed or stopped, that attention was on us and that something was probably brewing.

"Right, Em?" Salvatore shouts up at her again.

But before the sentence is out she has spun from the hoops, pirouetting in the air and landing on top of the man, her knees tucked in so that the full length of her shins connect with his chest and force all of the wind out of him. Despite the surprise Salvatore manages to grab her ankle and pull her down with him as he crashes to the ground, lashing out with one clenched fist but Emma is too quick, ducking out of the way of the blow and scissoring her arms together around his elbow then connects her hands at his wrist so that his entire lower arm is encased and snaps it back at the joint. He seems to bite down on the pain, reaching around and grabbing her by the waist, spinning her around. The other fighters are slowly converging on us and instinctively I draw the camera onto my shoulders and begin filming.

Salvatore rolls backwards, throwing his torso across Emma's, his arm still locked tight in her grip as she uses her legs to defend herself, kicking him once on each side of his head even as he stabs his fingers into an exposed bruise on her chest then forces her heel into his thorax. Despite his relative bulk she manages to throw him up off of her with a thrust of her hips, simultaneously releasing his arms as he spins and then forcing them behind his back as she landed on top of him and punched him once, hard, in the face.

Salvatore lets out a massive grunt as if he has been holding in his breath the entire time, spits blood from his mouth. There is a smile on his face as Emma climbs off of him and I notice her grimacing as she limps away, sucking in deep breaths, her tired limbs noticeably quivering.

"There's a couple of events next week, Em," Salvatore calls out after her, coughing halfway through the sentence because of his bruised larynx. "You're welcome to come along—like old times?"

She demonstrates for him the latest advances in middle-finger technology, mumbling irritably to herself as she stalks towards the trays of medicinal supplies stacked by the warehouses' sole fire exit.

And I realise I have been allowed a glimpse into just how much Emma Larson can look after herself.

It'd taken me three weeks of watching and filming her discreetly as I walked by the bridge she lived under to finally go talk to Emma. And it had taken me about seven minutes of her company for me to realise I had a brand-new obsession going here. It is my personality, and always has been, to be obsessive about things and more than once it has caused me problems. On the other hand, more than once it has brought me great pleasure.

And two nights after witnessing her tussle with Salvatore, an event I now saw as more akin to two puppies play fighting than anything more serious, I am able to add another notch to the latter category.

She is as enthralling during sex as I had imagined her to be—beguiling and gentle and playful in that way that only women can be with each other. We are so far removed from the brutality that surrounds her normally, from the threat of masculinity. She traces my tattoos with her fingertips and at times I forget to involve myself in the act, instead leaning back and watching her move, observing the ripple of tissue beneath her skin and the shape of her bones as if it were a ballet of flesh—until she pulls my mouth onto her and everything is forgotten.

Even the camera, recording quietly behind us.

Afterwards I rise and go to the exposed water pipe that she has fixed a rusted tap head to and wash off the smears of her blood from her opened wounds. Her medicine bottles and needles lie in a long metal box that she has only recently begun left open and unlocked, a sign of her growing willingness to reveal herself to me as well as the camera. The bottles are small and made of glass with pinpricks in their plastic lids where she sucks the fluids out, a variety of hypervitamins, nutrients and painkillers that she doses herself with regularly so that she might go on doing what she is doing just that little bit longer.

I turn and she is asleep, her back to me. The single contour of her spine, like a brushstroke, engraved onto the pale skin, her hip a sharp crescent rising away from her. I find myself wondering how much more space there is on her body for more damage and what will happen when it runs out.

*Arizona Bay* is still looping quietly on the stereo as it had been through the entire sex act and I watch her silently as Hick tells me for the sixth or seventh time that life was just a ride.

Several days later I sit patiently as the underpass is readied for another night. Salvatore and three others whom I also recognise from the crowds from previous fights are busy clearing a space and delineating uneven borders on the grounding chalk. Salvatore himself is talking with Emma in the opposite corner and I can tell just by looking at the them that there's been something between them. He notices me watching then places a hand on Emma's shrinking waist.

We'd had a small argument earlier after I found her injecting a third dosage of painkillers, asking her to stop just for a few nights but she had refused to hear my pleas, particularly when I could provide no good reason as to why she shouldn't.

The others move around me, joking with each other about fights they have had as if in a deliberate attempt to exclude me and so I retreat to my camera, secure, at least, behind its mechanical eye. Near the time when it all starts Emma come across to me and I notice how her skin seems to hang on her in places as if the muscles beneath are so battered they are collapsing in on itself.

"You okay?" she asks me. She barely seems to notice the camera now even with it nestled between our intimacy like a dog between a married couple.

"Fine."

"I'm not going to call it off, so don't bother asking."

"I wasn't going to."

She nods. "I promise you I won't get hurt. You know I can take care of myself. Just let me do my thing and maybe in a couple of days I can afford to take a night off."

"Okay," I say somewhat unenthusiastically. She touches my arm with a hesitancy that only seems to taint her actions when Salvatore is around. As she turns I stop her. "You're bleeding."

She looks down at the tear of blood and its accompanying slug trail running down her forearm out of a fresh needle hole, quickly grasps it more in shame than any attempt to stop the leak, then leaves me alone. Over her departing shoulder Salvatore fixes me with a flat stare.

Over the following half hour a small crowd gathers, nervously crowding into the underpass like shell-shocked cockroaches. They each lay a minimal fee in the jar that one of Salvatore's friends is watching over, the odd one leaving his details so that an appointment can be assigned. It's one of the few occasions when my camera feels like a hostile entity amongst them rather than a welcome one and I find myself standing next to Salvatore as he watches Emma limbering up. She seems to be fighting her own body with each stretch, arguing with her tired and damaged muscles.

"She shouldn't be fighting tonight," I say to Salvatore, using his broad shoulder as a rest on which to support the camera. "We both know that."

"Why don't you just leave that decision up to her," he replies calmly without looking back. "She doesn't need you getting all maternal on her."

"Is that what she thinks?"

"She's had enough people telling her what to do, including me when she first started this shit. Let her have what time is left to herself."

Salvatore ducks away from me and I have to catch the camera's extra weight as it is transferred back into my hands. I spend the rest of the time leading up to the fight standing atop the bridge that runs over the overpass, trying to find poetry in the way the smog clouds from the factories disperses in the air. I hear the cheers begin and listen through the concrete to the muffled sound of blows landed and Emma's few possessions clattering around as she is thrown into them.

I feel like I am walking backwards and forwards at the same time, my head straining under the pressure of whether I should go watch over her and just leave her to die like she so obviously wanted. As I descend the rubble that has been arranged into a small set of steps the voice of the crowd changes and I sense that something is wrong. I force my way through the collection of overweight white collar workers, spaced out body builders and bruised rednecks and Emma is swaying strangely before us, as if suspended from a wire too thin to see.

Her legs are half-collapsed beneath her, the man who has been unleashing himself upon her looking uncertainly at her, trying to assess whether he could or should hit her again. Emma's eyes are completely unfocused and there is a stream of blood running from her head, down her neck and between her breasts. When she falls, its happens in slow motion. I see the individual particles of dust that rise into a cloud around her and the flecks of blood that splatter across the stone.

I find myself entranced by her prone form, unmoving as Salvatore and his friends force everyone out including the fighter and I think to myself *this is what she'll look like when she's dead*. I'm bumped to one side as Salvatore goes to her, kneels down. She's like scrap in his arms as he lifts her towards the mattress she calls her bed, as if someone has made a plaster cast of her body and lifted her from it, leaving the limp bandaged shell behind.

Salvatore issues instructions to one of the others who retrieves Emma's metal box.

As I see him suck liquid from one of the bottles into a needle I snap out of my reverie and collapse to my knees beside him, grabbing his arm. "What the fuck are you doing? The last thing she needs is more fucking drugs."

Salvatore snaps his hand away, glaring at me. "Don't be stupid. Of course she needs them."

I make another grab but his reflexes are lightning fast. "But look what they're doing to her! Look how thin she's getting!"

"Is that a joke? Are you trying to be funny?"

The words confuse long enough for him to place the needle in Emma's shoulder and squeeze its glutinous contents into her. "Of course I'm not trying to be funny. What's that supposed to mean?"

He looks at me and something seems to pass through him, a realisation. "Fuck," he says, disbelieving. "She never told you did she?"

"Told me what?"

Salvatore sighs, caressing the point on Emma's arm where he injected her. She groans lightly and I notice that her entire arm is quivering minutely. "Fuck it. If she hasn't told you by now she never will. It's her issue. None of my business."

He stands, throwing the needle at a plastic bag full of them in one corner but missing. The glass chamber shatters against the wall. One of the fighters is in the archway of the underpasses entrance, his broad chest and shoulders and shaven skull lined with silver moonlight.

"We're ready to go," he says, dangling keys in the air.

Salvatore reaches down and scoops Emma into his arms and despite his strength I know the ease with which he does it means she is in an even worse state than I first suspected.

"Salvatore? What are you talking about? Where are you taking her?"

"She needs to go to a hospital," he says, brushing me aside and I'm still too confused to do anything. "We knew this would happen sooner or later. Just look at the bottles."

Then he is gone and I am still standing in the middle of the underpass, alone, listening to the sound of a car speeding off. I stare at the footprints in the concrete dust, the specks of Emma's blood against the wooden chest where she keeps all her clothes and the metal pharmaceutical box. I bend down and pick up one of the 15cc bottles, turn it over in my hand.

Codeine.

I pick up another bottle, examine it next, wondering why Salvatore pointed me to them—then notice that one of them has a label that is peeling partially at one edge I carefully pull it the rest of the way, revealing another label beneath and its far more than a simple painkiller. I don't recognise the brand name but I know the compound from a piece I worked on a few months back about viral infections. There are only a few drops of the clear, shiny liquid left inside. And I know without examining them that Emma has replaced the labels on at least some of the other bottles in the box, her opening up to me merely a charade; a gesture.

I put away the bottles, slam the lid of the box shut, and leave the underpass wondering what else she has lied to me about.

If X. hadn't chosen that night to page me for help I probably would have gone to the hospital soon enough despite my decision to let Emma Larson die if that's what she wanted. But he did and so for a week and a half I was several hundred miles away from the web I had become entangled in. He and his crew had raided an animal laboratory but things had quickly gone balls up and it had taken us a while to get things safe enough for him to leave the city. He had wanted me to stay but by that time my anger had faded to nothing and all I wanted was to get back to Emma and so I had made my excuses and promised to catch up with him later.

On the train back I had wondered if I would make it in time.

Now I sit uselessly on the steps of a building near the underpass, amidst the clatter of skateboarders grinding and kick flipping off of the railings, staring down at the sign that first attracted my attention.

Emma Larson. $30.

The virus is not only eating away at her but her value too, it seems.

Salvatore and a few of the others are milling around, getting things ready and I'm not surprised she is still offering herself up to anyone willing to pay.

Finally I stand and walk down the embankment that leads to her home. We see each other at the same time and both hesitate. Salvatore nods at me then says something to the others and they all disappear into the shadows of the underpass.

"You're back," she says, an accusation, an expression of relief. Her arms are wrapped around her as if she is trying to hold herself together. There are goose bumps on her skin despite the temperature being in the high 90s.

"A friend of mine got in some trouble. I had to go help him."

She nods. "Salvatore told me. You left your camera. I kept it safe for you. But I don't want you to use it anymore"

There is a moment of silence and I take another couple of steps towards her, aware of how tentative I was being with her. "Shit, Em. How much weight have you lost?"

She shrugs. "I'm not keeping a chart. Call it three pounds for every day you were away."

"Maybe if you'd told me in the first place I wouldn't have gone away."

"I don't need you to look after me. What would you do anyway? It's Strain 6, resistant even to the third-generation drugs."

"I've got contacts. My friend X., he knows people that have raided labs working on chemicals that we won't see for thirty years . . . "

"It doesn't make any difference. It's going to happen. I'm just lucky enough to have a better idea of time and place than most—what would I give that up for?"

She turns and leaves me in the scorching chemical winds and, like the self-replicating virus that is consuming her, each day I have been away from her has turned into a lifetime.

Until the event starts assembling itself I wasn't sure if she actually still fought or if the sign was just a piece of bravado. Now I am in that terrible place again, any pleasant memories of us making love now buried under concrete dust and spray paint, standing like a ghost as people move around me and through me. She watches me from across the room as a young woman with bleached hair and bad skin wraps bandages around her calves and knees to give her weakened legs extra support. The woman wears a lab coat and is most likely the drug-dealing med student that Salvatore has mentioned in the past where Emma gets all her medicines from.

Once the crowd starts gathering I can sense that it's not only her body that has changed. They seem angrier, more filled with bloodlust and whatever rage has brought them here. I wonder just how many people there are out there that are willing to pay $30 to beat the shit out of a dying woman and where that anger comes from. And I know that the only thing stopping her destroying herself is the growing number of street fighters asked or hired by Salvatore to watch over the crowd.

I'm no longer scared that she cannot control the fights—I'm scared that she might be tempted to not bother trying.

I follow her over to the metal box, now filled with empty bottles and cracked needles. "Let me," I say and take one of the hypodermics, squeeze it full of the biological agent that has salved her thus far. She holds an arm out for me that is littered with bruises and welts, constantly bleeding scratches and brilliant white scars.

Somebody turns up the stereo, increasing the sound of Bill Hicks' machine gun preaching to the most the battered old system can handle.

*I had a great time on drugs. Never robbed anyone, never shot anyone. Never beat anyone, never stole a car ... got rreeeeaalll fuckin' high ...*

She turns for me and lifts her shirt, presenting me with a relatively clean piece of flesh near her left kidney. "I can't believe you're still fighting," I say, and inject her. She sighs with the pain of her now hyper-sensitive nerve endings. "You're *dying*, Em."

"We're all *dying*. We're all dead. We just haven't realised it yet. Emma Larson is dead. Salvatore Mellina is dead."

She looks straight at me with eyes that seem twice as big because of the immense dark rings that circle them. And as she walks away from me, she holds both hands to her breast, to her heart, and tells me, "Even Elizabeth Afterlife is dead."


Watching her fight after my return is like sitting by someone on life support. Each movement is the spike of a pulse beat; each grunt the hiss of a pneumatic lung; each drop of fibrous blood a few more cc's of morphine or saline.

She seems to be clenching herself so tightly that each muscles wraps itself around the next in a vain effort to keep her standing. She moves into the punches and kicks, the headbutts and elbows, chasing them down, at times lurching after her opponent, always demanding more. I become aware of the crowd's own frenzied state rising alongside her as they make some secret pact to tear her to pieces. Salvatore's men are bustled and jogged and I wonder how much longer they can hold it all back.

I take what time I can with her during the days because I know I would regret it if I didn't. We no longer have nights because she offers herself each time the sun goes down. She keeps taking her medicine not because she thinks it will help but because she knows it won't.

And each time I hold her she gets smaller.

When Hannah, the renegade med student, doesn't turn up with more stolen bottles of drugs for a few days Emma can't even get out of bed. Salvatore comes by one day and says the girl had been shot in the head by one of the others she dealt to and was currently receiving a handsome dosage of her own medicine, so to speak. He acts differently towards me now and I wonder what Emma has said to him since I've been away. He waits outside the underpass all day every day except when there are streetfights taking place, I suppose protecting our privacy in the damp shadows of the bridge.

Emma constantly asks me to get her more medication and I know it is because she wants to be able to stand up again. She wants to be on her feet when it comes. I contemplate giving her just enough to keep her going yet not so much that she can bring herself to fight but I know this would be a cruelty beyond that of which I was capable.

"Tonight," she tells me. "Please."

I hesitate, now that we have finally got our nights back and her sign has been put to one side. Now I know how necrophiliacs must feel, clinging to the corpse of their lover or child, believing it to be the real thing; or better.

"I want to be with you again."

Her eyes are bright and clear, a dizzying reflection of her mind. "Please."


It doesn't take me long to find a dealer.

As I walk back I can't resist the creeping feeling that Armageddon is upon me. I imagine the sky is darkening not because of twilight but because we have suddenly become detached from the solar system like an errant vertebrae. I start noticing how all the buildings seem to be in a half-state—either unfinished or falling apart. Those that are complete architecturally are vacant and silent, stillborn monstrosities of concrete and iron. The roads are cracked, the pavements torn open in places by the roots of trees long since felled. And then there all the junkies, the drifters, so many that it seems there is nothing else in the city. Has everyone found themselves a place in this vast crumbling framework? Inside great rusted tanks like giant lungs or in the cradle-holes of skyscraper foundations? Or in disused parking lots, layer upon layer?

I'm walking along the ridge of an aqueduct when my pager goes off. It's a message from Salvatore. *I need to talk to you. Now.*

I think of Emma and of how time has taken on the form of a chemical filter lately, squeezing the seconds through at an ever-quickening pace into finer and finer points. But I know the sedatives I gave her before leaving will be enough to keep her still for another few hours and so I make the slight diversion necessary to get to the training warehouse.

The walls have been tagged since I was here last, bright green and blue lettering that sparkles like metal, warping along the walls and ending in a dragon's mouth where the door lies open. Salvatore is sitting within it, long legs stretched out in front of him. His broad, tight shoulders are kinked up around his neck as he leans back on his beautiful gymnast's arms.

"How is she?" he asks, moving over to make room for me beside him. His body smells exquisite.

"She wanted me to get her more medication."

"You left her by herself?"

"She's sedated. Until I bring this to her I don't think she could move if she wanted to. Her wounds are no longer healing anymore. There's just nothing left."

The wind that blows is strong and warmed by the heat of the factories. You can always hear them in the distance as if they are a single great machine under our feet.

"You think I should have stopped her long ago don't you?" he says.

"It doesn't matter any more."

"She's lyrical, Elizabeth. She's like a poem—or a prophet. She can convince you that anything is the right thing to do, that it's the *only* thing to do, and she doesn't even realise she has that power. I could never resist her. Never. She sees past all the shit. We're all dead? Yeah. Maybe just some more than others."

"She thinks she's providing an outlet for all that aggression but you can tell she's just stoking it. But it's not about the ones who fight is it?"

Salvatore sighs. I can see in his eyes how much he cares for her and I suddenly feel like a thief, like an impostor, for taking her from him this last month or so.

"Did you know there are others now? That's why she dropped the price to thirty bucks. Motherfucking *competition*."

We smile awkwardly because there is nothing funny about it.

After a short while I asked, "What was it you wanted to see me about?"

"You came to me, Elizabeth."

"I know but your page . . . "

He's staring at me and his eyes are a weapon, a knife thrust into my forehead to the hilt.

"What page?"

"The . . . page . . . "

I begin to show him the device but pause in mid air.

"Where the hell would I get you pager number from?"

And he doesn't even need to say it.

We take one of the fighters' flatbed trucks, Salvatore shouting for the small handful of fighters to follow and drive straight to the underpass, cutting through a caravan of eighteen-wheeler oil tankers and the accompanying military escort. When we arrive the first thing I see is the sign posted at the foot of the steps leading down to the bridge.

*Emma Larson is dead.*

And beneath it, in smaller text—*It's just a ride.*

The crowd is roaring, vicious, mercenary—I can feel it even before I have descended the steps. They spill out of the bridge's shadowed archway, jostling with each other and I'm horrified to see blood splatters on some of them as I force my way in. Salvatore follows, shouting for Emma, elbowing men in the face and chests when they don't move for him. We converge on a lump of limbs sprawled on the concrete like something out of Lovecraft and pull it apart until Emma is visible underneath.

"Back the fuck up!" Salvatore screams and it then that the other fighters arrive and one of them must have had a gun for there followed the cataclysmic explosion of a shot being fired in the tunnel's confines. Like a nailbomb that has been set off they scatter almost immediately but still there are sporadic, confused tussles going on.

I grab one short balding man wearing a uniform of some sort and drag him backward by the neck, squeezing his trachea between thumb and forefinger to stop him struggling, then dump him to one side. I glimpse Emma's face as another punch is landed upon it, her features dowsed in blood that is both her own and of others. I know she has invited this chaos upon herself and I hate her for it.

Finally we free her, Salvatore liberally applying unnecessary force to spectators and participators alike and suddenly I am doing it too, stamping on their faces a they lie prone, revelling in the sound of their nose and cheekbones breaking as if it were a cheap orgasm, anger flowing from me in a torrent. Emma is torn from her own execution and yet for almost a minute she lies there, untouched, as we lash out at those who have done this to her because we know, deep down, that the one person responsible is the one person we wouldn't dream of attacking.

Then I go to her side, her clothes torn from her, her matchstick body mapped with cuts and gashes and puncture marks. All of her trackmarks have reopened as if in celebration of the event, purging her system of the final few remaining millilitres of drugs and I almost can't stand the beauty of the plasmic tattoos thus created. I lift her to me but her eyes have already settled back in her head.

The underpass has been cleared and only Salvatore stands with me, two-stepping in argument with himself about whether he should leave us alone or not—until I look up at him and he sees in my eyes that it's okay.

"It's just a ride . . . it's just a ride . . . " the stereo says and it's the first time I even notice it has been playing that same endless loop.

Salvatore kneels next to me, close enough that I can smell the rage like chloroform on him, places his beautiful hands around me in substitution for touching Emma's corpse.

"It's just a ride . . . it's just a ride . . . it's just . . . "

Stops when it is smashed by the brick I throw at it, a brick loaded with blood. Salvatore starts crying and I feel like I should too but I don't. I'm looking at my camera set up on the tripod in the far corner, the tape inside clicking away rhythmically.

The hospitals have been raided; the morgues ransacked. Every inch of pavement is a grave if you want it to be.

We stand before the pyre, a miniature one of the all those of infected cattle burning on the horizon, and I wonder, is it still just a ride?

We've put all her stuff, the needles, the CDs and tapes and posters, her training gear, into the flames, setting her life on fire piece by piece. All that is left is her sign pinned to the top of a metal pole protruding from the centre of the pyre. Neither Salvatore nor I know why we put it there exactly, it just seemed appropriate—or, at least, what she would have wanted.

We just stand there in silence as she drifts into the air, now so much grey dust, and I think that is as close Emma Larson would ever get to having wings. Eventually Salvatore walks away without saying anything and I listen distantly to the sound of his truck revving them driving off. I'll never see him again.

Daylight trails off in tandem with the withering smoke as the fire dies down and still I can't leave. In my hands I hold my camera, the on-board miniature screen frozen with the image of Emma. This is the pixellated gift she made for me over the week or so I was away. It was why she had refused to let me record anything else over it but had been unable to say why and with that realisation comes a further one—that even then she was initiating her plan. I can tell from the timecode that the recording takes place over a number of nights right up until her last, when she had sent me away then retrieved the drugs she had been stockpiling as part of her plan.

She has left this for me and I'm still not sure whether it is a loving gift or an accusation of some sort. I haven't been able to watch it yet, instead leaving it on pause perhaps with the vague notion that the cassette inside will jam.

*Emma Larson is dead* the sign reminds me and through the oily air I see my own name flicker through it.

*Elizabeth Afterlife is dead* it tells me and I whisper back, "I know, I know."

# RAGE AGAINST THE MACHINES

Before the riots, there was the audition, which you could say was the touchpaper that lit this particular dirty bomb. And this is how the audition went down . . .

She walked in from the rain utterly drenched, her liberty spikes semi-limp from the weight of the downpour and her kohl running like bloodstains down her cheeks, dragging a chipped and heavily stickered Stratocaster by its neck. Dragging a murder victim, dragging her self-esteem.

Her neck was punctured by a little plastic spout that emerged from her throat.

She froze when she saw three faces staring back at her. "I'm here for the audition?"

A question, like she thought she'd gotten the wrong place.

"No shit," one of them said. Tall, thin, a mostly-shaven head with a slim strip of green running up the middle. "We were just about to split, had nothing but fucking timewasters so far. You're not a timewaster are you?"

One of the others, shorter and with tattoos taking the place of a t-shirt, smirked, swaying slightly against a mike stand. His hair was teased into a ball of spikes, a padlock draped around his neck, a withered cigarette stuck between his lips. Hiding behind the drum kit was another man, this one more heavily built than his fellow band members, thick arms folded over a snare. Almost invisible in the darkness of the corner of the room were two woman slumped on the floor, arms around one another, watching her blankly. One blonde, one dark haired.

"Only one way you're going to find that out isn't there?"

The man shrugged. "Plug up."

So she did and the rest of the band did too and Travis kicked out a wicked beat on his kit just as he had with the ones who had come before the girl, fast and trippy to try and catch her out. But she kept up and started screaming vocals into the mike as if she were trying to murder it sonically, stumbling around once they had gotten going and thrashing the guitar into a static mess. Finally Fincher dropped his own guitar and signalled for the session to stop.

The woman was choking for breath, raindrops now replaced by sweat, spikes slumped to one side. She continued to grip the microphone, guitar slung low by her hips.

"Okay," Fincher said, reluctance tattooed on his face. "Two things. First, you're on rhythm—I play lead. This isn't a fucking orchestra."

The woman stared back at him for a moment. "Okay."

"Second, our last vocalist has just been sentenced to fifteen for a supposed armed robbery and we're not interested in finding another replacement in a month's time. You got a record?"

" . . . ."

Fincher waited, turned to the others. Travis remained peacefully perched on his drumming stool, sticks in hand. Sid was grinning vaguely at the opposite wall.

"Well?"

"What is this, an audition or a fucking interrogation?" the woman snapped, yanking the cable from her guitar. "You Policie moles or something? Fuck this shit . . . "

She stormed past them, swinging the guitar over her shoulders so that it almost connected with Fincher.

"Hey," Fincher said. "Hey!"

The woman stopped, turned. "*What?*"

Fincher held up one hand. "Public nuisance, three counts. Two counts assault. Eight for destruction of private property but only one for trespassing. Theft of a vehicle. Resisting arrest."

He turned to Sid. "Sid?"

"Ummm . . . disturbing the peace, arson. Grievous Bodily Harm. Three counts theft. Ummm . . . something else. Assaulting a police officer, couple of times. Resisting arrest. Yeah."

"Travis?"

"Disturbing the peace, assault, making threatening phone calls. Vandalism of public property. Destruction of public property. Destruction of private property. Arson. Resisting arrest."

Fincher turned back to the woman, one eyebrow raised. "Well?"

She hesitated for a moment but then thought better of it. If this was a trick, she was close enough to the door to make a quick exit. "Possession of a deadly weapon. Common assault. Aggravated assault. Theft. Handling stolen goods. Arson. Criminal damage. Violent disorder. Breaking bail." A pause. "Resisting arrest."

Sid snorted a laugh, eyes rolling around in their sockets.

"You sure you'll have time to fit in gigs in between all of that?" Fincher asked.

"I think so."

"I'm Fincher. This is Travis, Sid."

"Katja," the woman said.

"Well, Katja . . . welcome to The Stumps."

Straight after that, Fincher had told her to help start loading the equipment into the van that was parked in the alley alongside the building.

"What for?"

"The gig?"

"What gig? *Now?*"

"Have you got other plans?"

"Well . . . no . . . but . . . "

"Then get loading. We're due there in half an hour."

I press my face to the windows at the back of the van, ignoring the new girl, can't remember her name. We drive fast to avoid getting stopped by the Policie patrols that are sweeping the area, chopper searchlights flashing across us occasionally.

I stare out into the streets, searching for any sign of the intruders. They're growing in number, I can feel it.

We turn a corner and I can see the shore in the near distance behind an outcrop of storage warehouses. The great creatures loom mockingly against a descending red sun, towering over even the tallest skyscrapers, unmoving, pretending to be nothing. Pretending to be harmless and inanimate.

But I know better.

Shouts of *Oi!* and the stink of stale sweat and the cocktail of anger and excitement and impatience and frustration. The previous act staggered off the stage dragging with them a severed guitar, leaving the shattered pieces that made up the rest of it for The Stumps to walk across. Feedback blends from one act to the other and they walked out.

Katja slung her guitar around her neck, slapped the amp cable into her instrument and sparked up a chord. As the ragged noise rang out she turned to the others, assuming their places on the stage. Something came flying over her shoulder and struck Sid on the head but he didn't seem to notice.

Fincher gave her a heads up.

"What the fuck am I supposed to play?!" Katja shouted above the noise. The tube in her throat moved in time with her words, mesmerising.

Fincher smiled and shrugged, then cut into a deep, heavy riff that grew quicker with each note. Travis started a drum beat and Katja grabbed the neck of her guitar and began to shadow them. The crowd cheered and everything fell into place, a manic rhythm, a heart attack filtered through stacked speakers and with nothing else to do Katja started screaming out lyrics randomly, filling the gaps as best she could.

The crowd was pogo'ing and bouncing off of one another like a seizure. The security at the front of the stage would pick crowd surfers up and throw them back again for more and Katja found a chorus from somewhere, shouting *this is it, this is it* over and over until everyone was shouting with her.

Through this first song then the next, a rampaging frenzy of noise and Travis never stopped, only slowing the beat in between songs like a DJ blending beats per minute. Katja staggered around the stage, her skin glowing with sweat and reflected light, spiked hair lashing around like a weapon. She fell against one of the amps at the back of the stage then sprinted to the front again, launching herself into the crowd, her guitar cable snapping free of the instrument suddenly and lashing through the air in front of Sid.

She wriggled across the sea of hands beneath her until one grabbed her and pulled her back. She kicked out but the grip was too strong and was quickly followed by another hand on her ankle. She managed to look up and saw it was one of the security men dragging her towards the stage and instinctively she renewed her resistance afresh but it was no good, she had no leverage.

Above her, Fincher bounced up and down, slamming his guitar in time with the huge, chunky chords he let fly and he was smiling at her struggle.

"Fuck off!" Katja cried out as the security man grabbed her around the waist and she lashed out with the guitar and struck him across the head. His grip on her wavered enough for her to struggle free and clamber back up on the stage, searching for the loose amp cord and slapping it back into her guitar. A line of blood trailed along the butt of the instrument and the person it belonged to had just followed her up onto the stage.

"Katja!" Fincher's warning lost amongst the white noise and epileptic lighting.

The security guard powered into her, knocking her to the ground against the drum stand, fisting his hands around her liberty spikes and then shoving her face into the beer-stained stage. She kicked, kicked and finally made contact, catching him across the jaw and then swinging the guitar again into his stomach.

Fincher grabbed the man's bomber jacket and pulled him away moments before another guard jumped on-stage and punched him across the back of the head. Fincher plummeted to the ground beside Katja, who scrambled to her feet. And Travis's rhythm still kicking out, a dark fucking frenzy of snare and hi hat, Sid's menacing bass underpinning it.

Katja jumped at the guard that had hit Fincher, hooking one arm around his neck and letting her momentum tear them both to the ground. She kneed the man in the face before he could do anything then kicked him in the groin for good measure before being pushed to one side by some of the crowd who were wanting in on the action. She still had her guitar slung around her neck and started up with a few more chords, befriending Travis's beats for only a few moments before something flashed in front of her and it was a Molotov cocktail.

The device smashed into the amp stack and immediately exploded into flames and Sid's bass dropped out. More of the crowd were pouring onto the stage and more security followed, fighting them back where they could but there was too many and now the fire was spreading, up the fabric curtains at the side of the stage, sparking the electrics as it went.

A hand grabbed Katja and she was already halfway through the motion of lashing out when she realized it was Travis, his drumming finally ended.

"Go!" he shouted over the cacophony, over the mutating spirals of feedback and burning anarchy. His arms were bulging from the set and he led her through the chaos and towards the fire exit to one side of the stage.

The van was fired up and waiting, Fincher leaning out of the driver's side. There was a young girl beside him, a nicotine-thin groupie with clamshell eyes and wide, thin lips.

The back doors were open and both Katja and Travis dived in beside Sid, sprawled out on the bare floor looking decidedly unconscious.

"Fuckers!" was the angry shout from one of the security men who chased them out but the van kicked up dust in his face as it moved off.

Katja raised her middle finger to the man then pulled the doors shut.

And so that was the end of her first gig with The Stumps.


I'm battering around inside the back of the van as Fincher speeds through the rain-slicked streets and I can see flashing lights in the distance. The new girl is thrown across me as we swerve abruptly to one side.

"Shit!" Fincher blurts out. The groupie that he pulled out of the gig with him is clinging to his leg.

In front of us is a swarming crowd of rioters that quickly converge around us and the whole vehicle is being shook and clambered upon. Fincher revs the engine then kicks it into reverse and something smashes against the metal arm that separates the side window from the windshield. He brings us around back the way we came and then takes a hard right when Policie vans appear at the end of the street.

"Are they coming?!" he shouts at me.

I scramble to the rear windows and peer out and I can see some of the rioters splintering off, chasing after us. The sirens and lights of the Policie flash past the street's end.

"They've gone past," I tell him, gripping the steel mesh across the glass with the top joint of my fingers.

The new girl is next to me now, watching the small group chasing after us. One of them throws something but it falls short of the van and explodes into flames just behind us, momentarily illuminating the face of the one that threw it and I realize . . . *it's one of them.*

"*No*", the word escaping from me. Then louder, "NO!"

I throw myself away from the door, as far from the creature as I possibly can because it must be after me, it knows that I know.

"What's wrong with him!?" I hear the new girl shout at Fincher.

And Fincher, he shouts back, "How long have you got?!"

A large anarchy sign was sprayed on a wall next to where Fincher had parked the van so that Katja's liberty spikes merged with the legs of the A as she smoked her cigarette. The wall belonged to one of several grubby warehouses that led towards the bay a few hundred yards away.

"Someone needs to stay with him, make sure he doesn't do anything stupid," Fincher said, nodding at Travis.

"Yeah," Sid mumbled, still sprawled out in the back of the van. "Yeah."

The groupie was pulling Fincher towards a crumbling building nearby, her stride like that of a newborn gazelle. "You coming?" he asked Katja.

"I'm fine," she said, and let the cigarette smoke roll off of her tongue. "I'll stay with Travis."

Fincher hesitated. "Sid will be with him. You can come inside."

"No. I'm good here," she insisted, not really looking at him or his limpet.

The man shrugged then ducked through a metal door that had been bent back in one corner and into the building.

Katja spiked her cigarette into the loose dirt and slowly approached Travis.

"You okay?"

He was crouched by a pile of concrete slabs, knees up to his chest, head pressed downwards as if he was trying to crawl into himself.

"Yeah."

"So what did you see back there?"

Travis shook his head without looking up. "What do you mean? Nothing."

"You saw *something*," Katja insisted.

"Ignore him." Sid now, looking blearily up at her, eyes still half closed. "He sees lots of things. The guy can drum like a beast but he's a loon."

"Shut the fuck up," Katja snapped, moved across to Travis, close enough that her shadow fell over him. "What did you see, Travis?"

"Sid's right. I see lots of things. But they're not real."

"Why don't you tell me anyway?"

"They're not real," he said. "I hallucinate. I didn't take my medication."

"What are you meant to take? Chlorpromazine?"

He looked up suddenly, meeting her eyes for the first time. The side of his shaven head was stained by dried rivulets of sweat.

"I was prescribed it not long after this thing was put in," Katja explained, fingering the tracheotomy tube. "They had me on so many meds I guess things got a little fucked up. Why aren't you taking it?"

He sighed heavily, like a child being forced to apologise for something they'd done wrong.

"Fincher sells it. He can get good money for it on the street. We need the cash for equipment, for food."

"And what about you? Don't you need the drugs?"

Shrugged.

"If I can get you some meds without Fincher knowing, will you tell me what you saw?"

He looked at her warily and she sensed it was from many years of being the punchline to someone else's joke. "Come to the shore," he said.

I stop several metres from the chainlink fencing that runs along the edge of the walkway with a six foot drop into the thick black waters of the bay on the other side. The loading cranes are working further along the walkway, pulling cargo from rusted trawlers and transferring them into the storage warehouses that line the shore. Workers scurry amongst the great beasts in little yellow or white hardhats and further out into the bay are the rigs.

"They come out of the water," I tell her. "They're born or made on those rigs out there and they swim to the shore and climb out and disappear into the city."

"The creatures you see?"

"Yeah. The ones with empty faces."

"That's what you saw back there? One of them?"

I nod. "They hide in amongst us, waiting."

"Waiting for what?"

"For them."

And I point to the rigs, to the great monsters. I tell her that they're not moving just now, of course, but that I can feel their presence from where we stand. I tell her that their warning lights will become eyes, their huge metal legs will walk them to the shore and the destruction will begin. I tell her that I've seen them moving in the early hours of the morning, before the first shift begins on the docks.

"When will this happen?" she asks.

"Soon," I tell her.

She takes a step closer to the water and I shout at her to stop.

"They're in there," I say. I can see the familiar dark shapes moving beneath the water, ready to drag her in.

She looks down, then up at me.

"You don't see them, do you?" I say.

And she surprises me when she shrugs instead of ridiculing me. "They're probably laying low just now," she says. "Until they're ready, like you say."

And I'm not quite sure how to respond. I can't think of anything to say to her.

"Am I interrupting something?" Fincher says out of nowhere. He's standing behind us, the waning light exploding around him. The girl, the groupie, is slumped against him, sex-dazed.

"That was quick," Katja says, arching her eyebrow. Then, "We're just talking."

"Yeah Trav is good at that," Fincher says, a squint smile on his face. "So what was it this time, Trav? The radio waves that the broadcast pirates use to control us? The bugs that have truth serum instead of poison? The oil rigs that are going to come to life? The old building that . . . ."

Stopped. Smile broadened. "So it's the oil rigs again is it?"

"It's none of your business," Katja warns him.

"Well I'm sorry to have to break up your little *tet a tet* but we'd best not stick around here long enough for the Policie to find us. I'm going to hook up with a guy who can arrange some new equipment for us across town."

So we stick low for a couple of days, moving from squat to squat, slumming it. Katja gets me some Chlor-P and sneaks it to me whilst Fincher and Sid have gone out to pick up the new equipment he's sourced. I hide them under the mattress that will be my bed for the next few days and promise I will take one later.

I lay awake later that night, staring at the cracks in the squat's ceiling. I refuse to go to sleep. I'd seen one of them earlier, amongst a rabble of graffiti artists that are currently living on one of the building's upper floors—one of the invaders. It hadn't seen me, or at least it had pretended not to, but I know how clever they can be, how devious. They are waiting for the right time, the right moment.

Not yet.

I get up, go to one of the windows and wipe away the grime. I stare out at the behemoths lurking offshore and I can feel them staring back.

Not yet.

Four gigs in six nights, that was what came next for The Stumps, and with each one things seemed to escalate in the city.

At Wild Jacks, surrounded by latex waitresses, the stage encased by fencing that went almost to the ceiling, firing out the songs they had played that first night, gelling now, moving sweetly together. The crowd slammed against the fencing and Katja screamed back at them with a voice of fire and cut glass.

At an impromptu street festival with pallets dragged from the loading bays used as stages. They broke through another set, adding variants to the songs now, stealing from the other bands, ripping and remixing and throwing it all back at the crowd. Katja sang until she bled from her trach. tubing, writhing on the ground in an endless wail.

They stole equipment from the other bands and had it stolen back.

Repainted the van twice in case the Policie were looking for it. Even developed a small fan base that appeared at each subsequent gig and sprayed graffiti on the walls to spread the word.

Fincher drove them to an old filling station, the garage adjacent to which had been taken over by a mullet-haired promoter named Azrael only to find the place slowly burning to the ground. There were fragments of body armour littering the ground and there was Azrael's body, folded into an oil drum.

"Fucking Policie man!" shouted one of the teenagers from the crowd that had gathered. "They fucked the whole thing up!"

"What happened?" Fincher asked and someone else stepped forward.

"SWATs," the boy explained. "They just . . . just fucking *lynched* us. Went nuts. We weren't even *doing* anything, man."

"You might as well just go," another from the crowd says. He's older, thickly set, skin like that of a rhino and a face to match. "Fuck all happening here tonight now. Maybe ever."

Fincher nodded, turned, and the others were already heading back to the van. "Where you going?"

Katja stopped, so did Travis. Sid kept walking for a few more moments before realising what was going on. "Back to the van," Katja said.

"What for? We've got a gig to be getting on with."

"You serious?"

Some of the crowd that had been starting to leave hesitated, listening in on the exchange.

"We've got our equipment. Got our songs. And if these losers hang around for another hour we've got a crowd. What the fuck else do we need, exactly?"

Katja snorted, shook her head, and headed off towards the van again, the heat from the dying fires warming her back.

"You're going to let a little fucking fire get in the way of our gig?!" Fincher shouted at her. "You fucking . . . "

His words drifted off as he watched Katja lifted one of the stack amps out of the van. "This shit won't plug itself in, you know," she commented as she carried it past him.

And so the gig went ahead despite the Policie's best efforts to crush it and even though everyone was a little more jumpy than usual when the sound of chopper blades were audible over Travis's drumming, it all clicked into place like it had before.

Stomping across the rubble from one of the garage's smashed walls, Katja hurled aggression at the crowds, dropping her guitar temporarily when she reached the end of the cable's line and losing herself amongst the crowds. Fincher tried to keep her in sight but she quickly vanished beneath the grabbing tattoo'd hands and it was only her constant barking pitch that ensured she was still okay.

She emerged a few bars from the end of the song, triumphantly staggering back towards her bandmates and pulling the guitar on again in time to launch them quickly into the next track. Some of the crowd were stoking the fires, raiding the semi-demolished garage for anything flammable and throwing it on, the blazes taking over the role of the spotlights that were lying shattered on the ground.

It was all energy, pure energy.

They were heading towards the final third of the set when Fincher and Katja both noticed something had changed about their sound, quickly realised that Sid had stopped playing. Whatever he had taken before the gig was now in full effect and he was swaying from side to side, her arms loosely flopping against the guitar, his knees ready to buckle.

Just in time Fincher grabbed him, catching him as he was about to collapse, looked around for an idea of what to do. Katja picked up the extra guitar duty, turning to one of the amps, knocked onto its side by the rioting crowds, and bleeding feedback into the air. Fincher pulled Sid towards a mike stand and let him lean forwards onto it, the crook of the stand resting under the man's chin and taking his weight. Fincher stepped away cautiously, ready to catch the man again but Sid stayed put. His eyes had rolled shut and he was hunched over at an unreasonable angle but he was standing and that was all that mattered.

The track ended and feedback trailed off into the air along with the smoke from the fires.

Katja turned back to Travis, smiled at him, but Travis was looking straight past her. She followed his gaze and saw, at the end of the street that led to the gas station, a set of headlights getting increasingly closer.

"Shit."

The word was carried through the air and everyone seemed to turn at once just as the streetlights illuminated the SWAT van more clearly.

"They're coming back!" someone shouted and the crowds quickly dispersed.

The Stumps grabbed their gear and threw what they could into the van, Sid being jolted to a reasonable approximation of consciousness by the sudden panic, enabling him to jump inside the vehicle just before Fincher chucked in a stack amp after him. Mic stands and Travis's drums followed, the thud of the SWAT van's door sliding open nearby spurring them on. There was still enough of a crowd more interested in fighting than running to provide enough of a barrier for the Stumps to get the remainder of their gear into their own van.

As Katja and Travis climbed inside, something exploded next to them.

I shove the last of my drums into the van and chase Katja around the side and we both jump into the front beside Fincher, already there. She screams out in pain and I realise she hasn't quite made it in and one of the Policie officers, in full SWAT gear, has a hold of her ankle. He smashes his baton across the back of her knee over and over and so I grab her t-shirt by the neck and jerk her away from him. I grab a brick from the footwell, its been there ever since we loaded ourselves up with projectiles a few weeks back, and throw it at him, catching him across the helmeted head with enough force for him to stumble away. I pull the door shut and Fincher has already sparked the engine and kicked us into gear but the SWAT man, he grabs the door handle and I have to pull against him and he's lost his helmet and I realise he's one of

ΓΓ

the intruders.

There are cables and soggy, rotten flesh where the helmet was once fixed to his head, not merely a safety device but a part of him. I look down into his wet, dark eyes and feel myself spiralling into them in the same way I feel myself about to spiral into the dark waters of the bay and then he is gone, tumbling from the van as we pick up speed and we are so out of there . . .

"We can't go back to the squat—not yet," Travis says.

Smoke from the fire at Azrael's is filling the night sky like a cancer and across the city similar spillages join it.

"Should your knee be pointing that way?" Sid asked, peering over Katja's shoulder.

She tilted her head to the side, wincing as she traced a finger along the swollen mess of her leg. "I can't even tell which lump *is* my knee."

"We need to split up for a while," Travis continues, sucking up a cigarette in one go and dropping the roach to the ground. "If they're looking for us, we're better off that way."

He'd pulled the van into a scrap yard whose owner had nodded briefly at Fincher as they eased past, parking it amongst 10 foot high piles of tires. Now they lurked amongst the chainlink fencing, the engines and the drive shafts.

"But Katja—she can't walk," Travis says, the first words he'd spoken since piling into the van back at Azrael's.

"I can walk fine," Katja protested, pulling her leggings back down over the damaged knee and then standing up as if to prove it to them.

"See? No problem there," Fincher said, already backing away. "Keep out of trouble, avoid any riots. We'll meet back at the squat at dawn once things have calmed down."

"Sounds good to me," Sid murmured, staggering after the guitarist.

Travis tried to protest but they weren't going to listen. As long as their own asses were saved.

"Don't wait around on my behalf," Katja said and began to hobble away.

"We should stay here. It's safer."

"Nothing safe about standing still."

"But . . . they're *out* there. The Policie that grabbed you, he was one of them . . . "

Katja kept walking, putting as little weight on the damaged leg as possible. "That's great, Travis. Let me know if you see any more of them, won't you?"

Travis swallowed. He wanted to warn her, to make her understand—but the tone was in her voice, the tone that they all used on him sooner or later and so he knew it was useless.

She shuffled to one of the junkyard's gates but stopped as she was about to step through.

Turned back to him and shouted, "You coming or not?"

I can feel the moment getting closer, a burgeoning tension in the air, swelling like Katja's knee. Where once the riots would explode in a sudden burst of activity that quickly burned itself out, they now tumbled on endlessly, sparking new battles as the embers from a large fire would birth a smaller one.

We're both starved and follow the smell of oil-soaked meat to a trailer up on bricks at the side of a road with a moustachioed man leaning out across a makeshift counter. We order up a couple of burgers and eat them as we walk, the streets glistening from a brief rainfall and spilled fuel.

We don't even notice him at first, not until it's too late.

We're in the middle of the road, chewing on the last of our meal in mutual silence, and we spot him at the same time.

A single Policie in SWAT gear emerges from an alleyway, his truncheon gripped firmly in one hand. We can't see the rest of the patrol but know they are around somewhere, can hear the crackle of their voices through his shoulder-mounted radio.

"Stay calm," Katja says softly. "Just keep walking."

I do as she says but already my heart is racing. I hear a creak of metal and I don't want to look to the shore, I don't want to see one of the creatures flex its muscles or stretch itself to life but I don't want to look at the Policie trooper either and so my eyes roam spastically.

The trooper holds his truncheon out to signal us to stop, turns down the volume on his radio. He wears goggles over eyes I know to be black and endless.

But I trust Katja.

"I want you to line up against the wall over there, spread your arms and your legs."

"What for?" Katja says. "We're just grabbing a bite to eat. What's going on?"

"Do as I say—*now*, " the officer barks and starts to remove his goggles but I can't bear to look at those chasms again and I shout out at him and lunge, grab him, I can feel the burning rage deep inside him and I won't let him hurt her, I *won't*.

The creature lashes out with the truncheon and catches me across the arm but I don't feel it, not yet, I tear his helmet away and elbow his sallow, empty face. I'm vaguely aware of Katja shouting something but the words are lost amidst the sounds of the intruder's muffled cries as a I he falls to the ground and I jump onto his neck with my knee. He lets out an inhuman gargle and I reach down towards that throat and I don't really know what happens next but suddenly it's Katja that I'm looking at and we're on the ground together, she's hunched over me and the wetness all over my hands and arms, it's not just rainwater . . .

Katja felt paralysed as she watched Travis beat the man, tearing into him as a wolf would a deer, unable to say or do anything to stop him because she was so stunned by the sudden fury of the attack. Her bandmate tore at the man's uniform as readily as he tore at flesh, shredding a major artery in his neck with the sharp edge of a piece of punctured armour.

It was only when Travis's own rage seemed to burn out that she was able to move again, to react, and by then it was late, so, so late.

She bent down next to him, her hands trembling as she reached out to him.

"Travis."

It was all she could manage. Then;

"Jesus."

"I had to," he said as he watched droplets of blood fall from his hands. "He would have killed you."

"Shit, Travis, this is bad. *Really* bad. This is going to fucking set things off."

"He was going to kill you . . . "

"Bullshit! Fuck, Travis what was that all about? I told you to stay fucking calm!"

"You don't understand . . . "

"I understand you're fucking *nuts!*" she screamed, glancing around to see if any more Policie were coming. "We have to get out of here *now.*"

"Katja."

And she turned and Travis was pulling away the blood-soaked vest the man wore from his chest. "Don't you see?"

"See what?"

And his expression melted, his face became consumed by a sudden, echoing sadness. "The . . . wires . . . "

Katja breathed, her throat thick with emotion and she wanted to scream at him but she just couldn't bring herself to do it. The memories of her own hallucinations were still there, the ghosts of the anger and frustration she felt at seeing what nobody else was seeing.

She nodded. "I see them," she said. "I see them, Trav. But we still have to get out of here. Right?"

"Okay," he said and she helped him to his feet and together they hurried off back into the alleys that run like clogged veins through the city before any other Policie can arrive.


They make it back to the squat without incident but there is something tangible building in the air, a dark energy that permeates the crumbling walls, the sodden streets. There was a group of graff artists lingering in one of the doorways, unloading a pick-up with lots of little tube-shaped packages wrapped up in black bin bags, heads down, no eye contact, straight past them.

Up the staircase to the second floor, counting four strung-out bodies on the way, three arguments that were about to spill over into violence, a single act of sex but mainly people just sitting there as if waiting for awful news.

"You'd better take that off," Katja said, nodding at Travis's blood-stained shirt. He did as she asked, stuffed it in a holdall at his feet that could have belonged to anyone.

Katja grabbed a cigarette from a half-crushed pack that was lying on a table and lit up. She lay down on a ratty mattress, clearing it of someone's possessions first, rubbed at her damaged knee. Travis just waited for her to say something.

"We're going to need to up your fucking dosage, man, if shit like that is going to happen again."

"I've not been taking the meds," he said, quickly, simply.

Katja snapped upright like the jaws of a beartrap. "*What*? Why not?"

"I want them to go away. The . . . thoughts . . . "

"That's why you need to take them, Trav!"

"You don't understand."

"Too fucking right I don't!"

"What if they *don't* go away, Katja? What if I take the medication and the . . . and they're still there? It's easier to just go along with what everyone says and think that I'm crazy. But what would happen if it turned out that it was everyone else that was wrong? What then?"

Katja took a drag on the cigarette then passed it to Travis, who promptly finished it.

A couple of the graff artists they saw unloading the van outside came into the room carrying their little packages, placing them carefully in a box in the corner. One of them glanced at Katja as they left again, perhaps a challenge of some sort, and brushing past them, Fincher.

"So you made it back," he said, grinning, eyes sparkling with chemical brightness. "Any trouble?"

"No," Katja said quickly. "Everything was quiet."

Fincher's eyebrow arched. "Really? All hell is breaking loose out there. There's some rioting across the Lower East side, near the bay, caught it on the radio a minute ago. It's spreading across the city."

"Where's Sid?"

"I propped him up against one of the doorframes downstairs. You okay, Travis?"

"He's fine," Katja answered before the drummer had a chance to.

Fincher's eyes tightened on her and it looked as if he was going to say something else but was interrupted by a sudden rush of noise from down below, like a crowd erupting in a sports stadium. He went across to the grimy windows at the front of the building, swiftly followed by some of the other squatters who had been roused from their collective trips.

"Holy shit, will you look at this?"

Katja got up and peered out to the streets below and to the crowds that were emerging there, hands full of metal poles and small knifes, of Molotov cocktails and sticks spiked with nine inch nails like the prongs of their Mohawks. They were rushing forwards, swarming around the trash cans and parked cars and at first it looked like they were charging *at* something but it quickly became clear they were instead running *from* something – namely the thick line of Policie SWAT troopers forcing them forwards like a road sweeper trawling for rubbish.

Something sailed through the air and exploded next to one of the cars, bursting into flames that quickly engulfed the vehicle before it was overturned by the rioters. Its alarm went off for a few brief seconds like the final cries of a slaughtered animal before grumbling to an electronic halt.

"Fuckin' a," Fincher grinned, "it's Sid!"

And there he was, stumbling around like a zombie, swinging a plank of wood around, heading towards the Policie as everyone else ran away.

"What the fuck is he doing?" Katja murmured.

"Oh man, I've got to get in on this!"

Fincher barged past Katja towards the stairwell, grabbing the strut of a disassembled bed as he went.

"Wait!" she cried but he was already gone. She lingered just long enough for Travis to reluctantly join her before they chased after Fincher out into the street. Scores of other squatters were also pouring out armed with whatever they could find but amongst them Katja noticed the graffs lingering at the corner of the building as the crowds washed over her and she was consumed amongst the sweating, hair-dyed masses.

Something whistled past overhead and a moment later there was another explosion, the whole crowd sweeping to one side suddenly as if they were disturbed bathwater and Katja lost her balance as her weight went onto her bad knee, she rolled, bounced off of someone and began falling.

A hand grabbed her and it was Travis, thick and calloused fingers wrapping around her and pulling her up again. They managed to break free of the crowds just as another cocktail exploded against the wall next to them and there were SWAT officers right up ahead, smashing rioters over the head with batons, dragging them by whatever limbs could be dragged, pressed beneath plastic shields.

"Can you see them?" Katja shouted over the noise and Travis shook his head maniacally and she wasn't sure if he was answering her question or not.

She ducked out of the way of some dark object that had been thrown through the air, pinned herself into a doorway.

"They're coming, Katja!" Travis shouted before being uprooted by the force of the crowd's tow, stumbling away and this time it was Katja's turn to pull him free.

As she steadied him she spotted Fincher up ahead, grinning as he hurried towards a SWAT trooper that was on his knees, facing the other way, raising the plank of wood he was armed with and about to bring it down—but he didn't see the second trooper to one side, stun gun raised and ready to be fired.

"Fincher!" she shouted, too late, far too late, the electrified cord exploding from the weapon and embedding itself into Fincher's side, jolting him so severely that both feet left the ground and he came crashing down again at the sort of awkward angle that would ensure broken bones.

He had barely landed before six or seven Policie swarmed over him, nothing more than a flurry of truncheons and fists and boots, a shining Kevlar assault. Katja grabbed a Molotov cocktail that had been dropped by one of the rioters, touched it carefully to the burning car and hurled it at the Policie troopers. It exploded just short of them but the blast knocked most of them backwards and away from Fincher's bloodied and utterly still body. Even through the confusion she could see the mess that his head had become, the impossibility that she could do anything to help him.

Now vicious jets of high-powered water were being aimed at them, sweeping rioters aside as easily as skittles and greasing the ground beneath their feet.

"We have to get out of here," she said to no one in particular, then louder and straight at Travis, "*We have to get out of here!*"

Another explosion and then a rumbling and she looked past the rioters to see a huge chunk of wall from one side of the squat missing, flames pouring out of it and bodies lying around it. Bricks continued to tumble from the opening and she could see a steel beam that had become exposed starting to bend under the strain. The flames licked up the side of the building as high as the second floor, towards the very window they had been staring out of minutes before and she thought of the graff artists and their stash.

"Oh *shit.*"

I just stand there as Fincher is beaten by the creatures, unable to move and I can hear the guttural noises that they make as if they are feasting upon him. I panic that they can smell me, that they'll recognise my scent from earlier that night and Katja screams at me, "*we have to get out of here!*"

The ground shakes beneath my feet and I know that the moment has come, this is when the creatures in the bay will begin to rise, that they're already stretching their muscles, shaking themselves clean of the sediment that has built upon them whilst they have been waiting.

I follow Katja as she pushes her way through the rioters and we have to arc around a mass brawl that has broken out and suddenly a car is upturned, a white pick-up that spills its cargo across the street. We run past it then Katja doubles back, snatches a couple of the bag-wrapped packages that have fallen from the truck, someone shouting at her but we're already gone.

Then there's another crashing *boom* and the ground shakes beneath our feet enough to unbalance us and throw us against the crumbling walls of an alleyway. We duck into a recessed doorway and catch our breaths, now far enough away from the main body of the rioters that their shouts are a blurred echo.

"What are those?" I ask her as she unwraps the packages.

She doesn't answer, instead holds one of them up for me to see.

A pipe bomb.

"We have to defend ourselves," she says.

And I know what she's thinking, I know what she wants us to do. Of course we have to defend ourselves, to stop the creatures before they cross they bay.

"Okay," I say. "I know where we need to go."

She doesn't know where he's leading her but right now it doesn't matter.

They glimpse another riot spilling out across a parking lot in the distance, Molotov's like falling stars tumbling through the night air and bursting into a sudden, brief life moments later. The crowds are chanting, singing, calling out *Oi!* as if this were nothing more than one big gig, the show to end all shows.

A chopper swings overhead but they've got bigger targets in mind than a couple of stray punks with a handful of pipe bombs and it sweeps away into the distance.

They emerge out into an open lot just as she feels her knee about to give way, has to grab at Travis for support.

"I can't keep running," she tells him, her voice crackling and she coughs up something sticky from her throat, spits it out.

"We're almost there," Travis tells her.

"Almost where?"

And he steps to one side and she realises that they're at the bay, the bulk of a loading crane looming overhead, the ground slick with engine oil and spray from the tides. At the edge of the water there was a line of small boats like corpses lined up in a mass grave. Further along the curve of shore she could see the area of beach that he had led her to previously, pointing down into the waters at the shapes that he saw there and then across at the rigs.

"Shit," she muttered with sudden realisation. "We're going out there aren't we?"

But her words were lost amidst the deafening sound of another explosion, the sky filling with orange and black clouds a few blocks away and sirens are set off like a chorus of screams. Figures in the distance—a group of rioters, tumbling through the streets towards them, Policie water cannons chasing them all the way.

They couldn't turn back now.

They ran to the boats and Katja jumped down onto one of them, grabbing a rail to soften her fall to favour her knee. She looked up and Travis was hovering at the edge, fingers clenched around the rail, teeth grinding against one another as he stared out towards the rigs.

What was it that he *saw*?

"Travis come on, we have to go! The riots are coming this way!"

Another explosion some way further along the bay, kicking the water up into a rolling black mass that rocked the boats.

"*Travis!*"

Great legs being stretched, the vibrations of their movements echoing through the water of the bay, sending signals across the sea bed that will awaken more of the invaders, beckon them. The rigs haven't revealed themselves yet but I know it's not far off now. I want to run, but where to?

The invaders are already taking control of the city, preparing it, and the water is choking with more of them down below. We have to stop this now, I know this.

And yet I can't move.

"Travis!"

Katja, on the boat somewhere beneath me.

*"Travis!"*

I jump before I change my mind, dropping into the boat. We undo the docking ties and she starts the motor. A piece of flaming debris flies overhead and hisses as it hits the water, the rioters are at the docks now, right behind us. Katja keeps the throttle fully depressed until we are well clear of them and they drop into the water behind us, pressed on by the Policie fakers.

The boat is battered on its course, debris thudding against the hull and I look over and I can see them there, lurking just beneath the surface. I move away from the edges, next to Katja as she steers us towards the first rig.

She aims us at the mooring and the ladder which leads up into the metal mass but we're going too fast, far too fast and she swings the boat around, slams it into the concrete base sideways, throwing me sideways. I tumble to one side, collide with the railing and topple over.

Katja grabbed Travis just as he was about to fall over board, snatching enough of his t-shirt to steady him and there's a split second where she was leaning over the edge too, staring down into the dark waters, and saw something moving down there, a flash of ice white skin. Then it's gone and Travis was upright again and the boat was beginning to tip—the impact must have damaged its hull.

"Go! Move it!"

She shoved Travis ahead of her and he resisted at first but the lapping of water across his ankles quickly gave him the encouragement he needed. He pulled himself up onto the ladder, began to climb, Katja following, a pipe bomb in each of her hands.

The entire structure creaked and rocked above them, most of the bolts and fixings that she saw rusted and misshapen, covered in dried algae. She had no idea how long it had been since the rigs had been in use but certainly not since she had been alive—they were nothing more than immense lumbering relics.

But not to Travis.

They reached the first platform, rolled onto what remained of the steel plating that floored it.

Across the water Katja could see the city as it burned itself away, intermittent explosions peppering the scene. They just needed to hold out there long enough for the main fury of the riots to calm down but from the noises that the rig was making, she wondered if that was now going to be impossible.

Travis clung to edge of the platform like a child would its mother.

I can feel the beast's motions, the rumble of its musculature vibrating through my fingers and across the back of my neck, down my spine.

Great legs about to pull free from their moorings and take off towards the city, great arms that will crush all that it finds. Fincher dead and Sid probably dead too—and how much longer before Katja and I joined their ranks? And the rest of the city?

"Give me the bombs," I say to Katja as I get to my feet.

Travis hold his hands out to her. "Give me them. We have to stop this thing before it reaches the shore."

"Travis, man, get a fucking grip! Of all the times to . . . "

And he lunges at her suddenly, taking her by surprise, but she's quick enough to evade him.

"You stay the fuck back," she tells him, waving one of the pipe bombs at him threateningly.

There's a huge, echoing creak that seems to come from the very base of the rig and then a sound like something metal snapping.

"We have to *do* this!" he shouts. "We have to stop them!"

"Travis there's nothing to fucking stop! We just need to wait here long enough for the everything to calm down."

"Wait *here*? You think we're safe here?"

Another echoing creak and the platform shuddered. She could almost picture the bolts popping loose and into the water below, disturbed by the impact of the boat moments before.

"We have to stop them!"

And he jumped at her, grabbed her before she could fully avoid him, spinning together, crashing to the ground. One of the bombs rolled from Katja's hands, came to rest against a piece of framework. Travis had her pinned, his muscular drummer's arms holding her down as he pulled the other bomb out of her hand. She lashed out at him with one heavily-booted foot, caught his shoulder and threw him backwards.

Got to her feet, went for the loose pipe bomb, grabbed it.

Turned and Travis had the other bomb in his hand.

They stared at each other across the platform, an old-fashioned stand off.

"Travis . . . "

But he was gone, she could see it in his eyes—the same look that had been there when he'd pointed into the waters back at the shore; when he'd looked out the back of the van after their first gig; just before he'd ripped the SWAT trooper to pieces. He was in another world, one of his own creation.

He pressed the fuse of the bomb against the metal wall beside him and dragged it down once, twice.

"Travis . . . "

And the third time it sparked.

She came to on the shore amidst the other debris, hair tangled around her face, her skin burned in places. The sky had faded from black to grey-blue and gulls were swooping overhead.

She pulled herself out of the surf and up onto the beach, looked out across the bay.

The rig had collapsed, taking out another two in a domino effect as it had fallen, their dirty yellow skeletons only just visible above the water level in places. Metal shards, pieces of packing crates and fragments of torn fabrics drifted onto the shore beside her—the city, torn to pieces and thrown into the ocean, now being returned anew.

She began to get up, felt pain rush through her leg and remembered the wound to her knee and then remembered a lot more. Peered along the jagged sands but there was no sign of Travis, walked up to the concrete siding of the docks. That's when she began to notice the bodies.

They lay amongst shattered crates, pinned beneath half-demolished walls and upturned loading cranes and as she weaved her way back into the city their numbers thickened. There were groans of discomfort and pain, pleading wails and calls filling the air like the last of the thick smoke. SWAT gear crunched underfoot as if it were the carapaces of giant insects and yes she noticed the wires that stuck out from beneath some of them but no she didn't stop for a closer look.

More survivors trudged through the aftermath as she did but some tacit agreement meant they passed each other as one ghost would another. She had difficulty finding her way back to the squat for the landscape had changed dramatically—buildings now gone, piles of rubble replacing them, new styles of edifice. Roads blocked; others created. It was as if a new city had formed itself overnight.

When she finally got there, she found that half the building was gone, sliced away by an explosion that had blackened the bricks and mortar that lay at her feet. The pile was high enough for her to climb up to the second floor without using the stairs. She dragged herself onto the landing, around an upturned corpse that hung off the edge like a proudly-displayed flag.

She noticed a couple of the graff artist's pipe bombs laying on the floor, nudged them to one side, and as she did so revealed another object. Katja bent down and picked up the small plastic pill bottle, still stuffed with medication. She opened it up and dropped two into the palm of her hand, hesitated.

She crossed back to the torn edge of the squat, sat down with her legs dangling over.

The smoke was beginning to clear, the returning tides swallowing the last visible remains of the rigs. She watched those that remained moving amongst the choked alleyways and her breath caught when she saw something emerging from one. Its movements were slow and jerky and water trailed behind it. It appeared to be naked, ice-white skin gleaming in the new light. It turned around and, in a moment, was gone again.

Katja raised her palm, considered the pills, then dropped them both.

Just in case.

# EMOTION SICKNESS

His gait was slouched, always slouched, and he didn't look like a murderer as he walked towards me but that was what he was. That was what we both were.

We were outside a building that passed as a biker bar down by the loading bays that fed the ships coming into the docks. Nestled under the protective buttress of a giant loading crane, the place was like barbed wire manifest, all edges and latent aggression. Bikes littered the small parking area like sleeping insects.

"You've not given up already have you?" he asked me, crossing his skinny arms across his skinny chest and leaning back against the half-height wall I sat on. A smug smile on his face.

"Be patient. So how was your night?"

"Wonderful," he said. "Dziga took me to this club, showing me off I think. I didn't mind. He was so happy there."

I laughed, just a little. "So what did you do to him?"

"Don't be so crude. I didn't do anything."

"Yeah, I know. They do it to themselves."

"Always."

"So what did he do to himself?"

"Guess."

Guess. Why did he make me fucking guess?

"Auto-erotic asphyxiation," I said because it was the first thing that came into my head.

Wiktor was silent for a moment and when I looked at him I could instantly read the expression on his face.

"Lucky guess," he said huffily. Then, "I think he loved me. Really loved me."

"So he's dead *and* desperate?"

"Fuck you, Vanya"

"And you too."

"Once he'd decided to go through with it, he wanted me there. He wanted me to be a part of it."

"You did it for him?"

"Of course not," he snapped. "He wanted me to watch."

"Really," I said. Suddenly more interested. "You ever watched before?"

Wiktor shook his head. "Not up close like that."

"How was it?"

Wiktor shrugged. "A bit of an anticlimax, really."

"Usually is."

"Speaking of anticlimaxes are we going to be out here all night or are you going to get to work? It's fucking freezing."

"Already done," I told him. Now it was my turn to be smug. "Did I ever tell you about binary poisons?"

"No, you never told me about binary poisons," he sighed. He was bored now, had had his fun already. Fucking child.

So I told him. I told him how certain chemicals were perfectly benevolent by themselves, even in very high quantities. And I told him that those certain chemicals could be mixed with other certain chemicals which were in turn mostly harmless. And I told him how when those two mostly harmless chemicals mixed . . . they were no longer mostly harmless.

"Like Sodium T.D.C.," I said, as shouting became audible from within the bar. "And alcohol."

And the door was blasted open suddenly, six or seven bikers stumbling out and colliding into their bikes, toppling both themselves and their machines. They were being violently sick, their bodies battered by spasms that threw them around as if they were fitting.

More followed, another handful, spilling past those already prone in front of them, tripping over them.

Wiktor straightened up, hands gripping the wall until his knuckles went white.

"There!" one of the bikers shouted at us, this one obviously not amongst my victims—I hadn't been able to slip it into all of their drinks so I knew I'd miss a few. No big deal. They must have recognised me from when I had been in the bar, the novelty of a new piece of tail having worn off and suspicion replacing it.

"Time to go," I said and Wiktor needed no more encouragement as the bikers that were capable of it charged towards us. He was already over the wall and sprinting across the industrial trash that lay beyond the car park as I pulled myself up onto the ledge, stood up and proudly displayed to my victims, in the bright moonlight, my middle finger.

And so this is now but before the bikers, before the bar—there was Anatoli.

I'd used a tiny dose of ammonium chlorate on one of my friends, an injection of potassium dimethylsulphate on the next. While the AC had merely triggered immediate unconsciousness, the dimethylsulphate had made pink froth spill from the mouth and he had almost fallen on top of me as he realised something was wrong.

That moment.

That moment when their eyes say to me *what have you done?*

That moment when I smile.

Anatoli had been a longer term project. He waited for me on the ratty sofa we had just finished fucking on, his body corroded by beads of sweat like submerged bullets. I handed him a glass of black vodka and knelt next to him.

"What's that?" he asked me, nodding at my own drink.

"Just water."

"You don't want anything stronger?"

"Not for me. Drink up."

This had been at the start of the week. At the end of the week I'd gotten a call from him. Anatoli said he had been violently sick all night and there was blood in it now and he wanted to go to the hospital. I told him to wait and went straight round.

His floor was slick with vomit and yes there was blood in it. Good.

That meant that there was enough V12 crystals in his bloodstream that they were starting to tear through his internal organs, mainly his liver and kidneys. The particles formed because the propyldiathylpropate solution I had been feeding him slowly over the past few months had bypassed his body's natural defences and begun to crystallise in his veins before being fed to his organs.

I wondered how long he would have left as I helped him off of the floor and onto the sofa, laying him on dried pools of his own regurgitate.

"I can barely move," he told me. He tried to grip me, shake me, but he was too weak and slumped backwards. "You need to take me to the hospital."

"It's just food poisoning," I said, wiping my hands on my skirt.

"Fucking food poisoning!" he shouted and sprayed my with saliva mixed with bile. "I'm fucking dying here Vanya!"

The propyldiathylpropate had too strong a taste to put in water without anyone noticing which was why I had been feeding it to him in the shots of black vodka but now it no longer mattered. I gave him the glass.

"You need to drink. Keep your fluid levels up."

"I *need* a doctor."

"Stop being such a baby," I snapped. "You *need* to calm down".

I ran a hand along his bare stomach and under the waist of his trousers. "Besides . . . if you get stuck on a ward who knows how long you'll be there. I'll *miss* you."

Wrapped my hand around him, well lubricated with his bile and a little blood. Stroked.

The vaguest of smiles drifted across his mouth and I tipped the water into it.

"No doctors for you," I said.

And there weren't.

That night had been a busy night.

On my way back from seeing Anatoli I had stopped off for an hour or two at one of the bars downtown to look out for any potential new friends. A few possibilities, a few phone numbers and some unnecessarily direct offers later and I was heading along the winding roads that led up into the hills and the large houses that dotted them.

I always felt like I was ascending into a better world when I went over to Kristian's, or at least a world that promised to be better. There were sure as hell no gypsy camps allowed anywhere near there.

I wore a black cocktail dress that I had shoplifted the day before because Kristian acted like he wanted class, refinement. I knew better, that underneath it, just like all the others, what he really wanted was a slut—so the dress only came a quarter way down my thigh, almost enough to see some of my scars.

Kristian had the penthouse in an exclusive block of apartments at one of the highest points on the hills. I took my usual route, an emergency exit stairwell at the back of the building, so as to avoid any issues with the doorman but had only gone up one flight when I heard footsteps descending. I ducked into the recess of a doorway that had been cemented over and watched as a young man, certainly no older than me, walked past. He looked stoned, didn't see me.

I waited until he was out of sight before hurrying the rest of the way up.

I had felt teased by Anatoli's nearness to death then, as if someone had been stimulating me to orgasm then stopped at the very last minute and I was still looking for that final release. It was Kristian's moment tonight and I had a very special concoction waiting for him in my handbag.

It first looked like something was wrong when I noticed his door wasn't closed. I thought perhaps that he was ready and waiting for me, strung out on the bed like he had been once before but although his bed sheets were ruffled he wasn't there. I called his name. Again.

There was a strip of light visible under the en suite bathroom door. Something new, this time?

I tried the handle and the door was unlocked.

And there was Kristian, waiting for me—naked and slumped in the bathtub, one long leg and one arm hooked over the porcelain rim. Blood seeping from the slashes across his wrists.

*Motherfucker.*

This didn't make any sense, no sense at all.

I dropped to the floor beside him but I already knew he was gone. A straight razor lay on the tiles amidst the growing pool of blood.

I touched his head because it was something to do.

This ruined *everything*!

"What the fuck have you done!" I shouted at him, beat his chest with my fist. "Why would you . . . ?"

I took out the poison I had prepared for him and poured it into his mouth anyway, an act of defiance. I had been working for weeks for this night and he goes and . . . .

Wait.

The boy.

He'd come down the stairwell and in the dozen times I had been to Kristian's I had never seen or heard anyone else use the passage. As far as I knew it only supplied access to the penthouse.

That little bastard.

I spotted him walking dreamily along the private sidewalks that wound back down to the grubby tenements of the city below. He didn't seem aware of the car until I pulled up alongside him, angling it slightly in front of him before stopping. I opened the passenger door.

"Get in," I told him.

He was as young as he had first looked, though he emphasized his youth with a close-fitting top and shiny jeans that highlighted his spindly figure. He had the passive-aggressive stance of street trash.

"I'm not interested," he said and started to walk on.

I jerked the car forward, blocked his way again.

"I'm a friend of Kristian," I told him.

"I don't know any Kristian. I don't know what the hell you're talking about."

"Get the fuck in now or I'm calling the police."

The threat seemed to deflate his nonchalance a little. "I didn't do anything," he said guiltily.

"Then get in."

He wouldn't tell me at first how he had done it and I pretended not to care but of course I did and I think ultimately he was desperate to be sharing it with someone. Perhaps that was true for me too.

"Imagine you're standing on one of the bridges in the bay over there. One hundred and fifteen foot drop. Just one step, that's all it would take. One step over, a moment's thought. A moment's decision. It's that easy."

"If it's that easy," I challenged, "then why we aren't all killing ourselves?"

"Fear, mostly." He shrugged. "Maybe we just need a little encouragement."

"And you're the one to provide the encouragement?"

Again a shrug.

"You know I'd really rather you hadn't encouraged Kristian to be perfectly fucking honest with you. He was mine."

"Your boyfriend?"

"Hell no."

"Then what?"

So I told him, I told him because I thought, fuck it, he's the same as me, more or less.

"Well how was I to know?" he said. "You should have been quicker off the mark."

"I didn't think I needed to be!" I shouted at him, then had to slam on the brakes as some asshole pulled out in front of me. It looked like a gang car so I let it go. I'd had enough trouble already that night.

"Poisoning," he said and was that derision I heard in his voice? "How crude."

"Fuck you is it crude! I spend a lot of time and effort finding and mixing the right shit to get each dose exactly right. There's nothing crude about it."

"If you say so."

"You prey on the weak, the suggestible ones—what is that if not crude?" I countered.

"First of all, I don't *prey*," he snapped at me. "And secondly they're no more suggestible than anyone else."

"Bullshit."

"Is it hell. And I can prove it."

"How?"

So skip the drive across town towards these little shacks that I guess count as houses and then to the tower blocks that loom over them. About thirty stories high, the poverty levels getting steadily worse the higher you climb. The ones at the very top are probably high enough to give them a great view of Kristian's luxury apartment across the other side of the valley.

He takes the stairs to the fourth floor and I can smell urine in the air, old stale urine.

He knocks on the door and this balding guy with a barrel chest and military tattoos down one arm answers. Wiktor introduces me as a friend and we step inside, though the guy barely acknowledges me. He looks pleased to see Wiktor, however. The apartment is grubby but well organised, the remnants of a regimented upbringing. There is homophobic graffiti on one wall and I don't know if this guy put it there himself or not.

We sit on the floor because there is no furniture to speak of and still the guy ignores me. Wiktor talks with him, laughs with him, caresses him and I just sit there mostly. I don't touch the drink he gave me out of habit. Then they go off into the bedroom and I'm left for a few minutes before Wiktor comes back out.

"Why don't you go down the car," he tells me. "I'll be there in a few minutes."

I nod because it seems like the thing to do, sneak a look behind him and see the guy sitting on the edge of the bed, his face in his hands.

It's just when I'm starting to feel like the boy has pulled some con job on me that he emerges from the broken doorway of the high rise and climbs onto the car's hood, slaps it for me to join him.

"What's going on?" I ask as I do so.

"Just wait," he says.

I follow his gaze up, up, up and then there on the ledge that splits the first twenty five floors from the final five, there's a figure.

"Is that . . . ?"

Wiktor stops me from getting up, presses a finger to his lips. "Don't disturb him."

And the man way up there, I can see him spreading his arms and I wonder if he is thinking of fighter jets or birds of prey as he leaps from the ledge and into the air. It seems to take an awfully long time for him to hit the ground and it also seems like no time at all. I've never heard a noise like it when he makes contact.

"*Shit!*"

"Come on, we'd better go," Wiktor says, and climbs into the car.

For a few moments I can't move and I want to go see the body, at least I think I do, but already people are looking to see what that terrible noise was and I know it's not safe. I start the engine and Wiktor says, "Do you have a place? I don't have a place. Just somewhere for tonight?"

I don't answer him. I just get us out of there.


And so it's not exactly a competition, what developed between us, although I guess that is an aspect of it. Although neither of us would admit it, I think it feels good to be sharing what we do with someone.

My place was one of the smaller trailers in the camp, the wheels removed and replaced by concrete blocks to keep any dampness from rusting the undercarriage. There was abusive graffiti scrawled all over it but that's no big deal, everywhere we go the hatred follows us. I felt Wiktor's hesitation as I pulled onto the wasteland we'd been on for the past few months and that was natural, I guessed. Over the weeks he'd gotten used to it.

He made decent money doing what he was doing, before he killed them off of course, and split it with me in return for allowing him to stay with me.

We crossed paths irregularly and would trade stories to one another like a married couple discussing their work days and these tales were part boast, part confessional.

He told me about Olivio, a Latin American man in his forties who had blasted the top of his head off with a shotgun and about Nico, a DJ with a speech impediment who lay down on the train tracks under a tunnel at the edge of the city. In return I told him about some guy I'd picked up in a metal club whose eyes didn't leave my legs, encased as they were in stripy thigh-high socks, and how he had grunted orgasmically as I had shoved the hypodermic into his back and pumped all 100cc of the special concoction I had formulated the night before. I told him about the secret shack out in the nearby woods that acted as my lab and workshop but I never took him there.

One night we lay next to one another on the fold down bed and he was in a bad mood, I could tell, though he wouldn't say why. I'd made some new friends that night and had already decided that I would test one of my new compounds on a pair of them at the same time, a kind of field trial.

"Are you listening to me?" I asked him. "Like an LD50 test."

"A what?"

"Lethal Dose 50%. It's a test they do on animals. They dose them with increasingly stronger amounts of a substance and see how longer it takes for half of them to die from it."

"What are you going to use on them?"

"I'm not sure yet. One of the orals anyway—but this time I want to see if they'll drink it willingly. Maybe the herbicide mix."

"The green one?"

I nodded, passed him my cigarette.

"Can I ask you something?"

"If you want to," he said.

"What do you say to them?"

Wiktor took a long drag, held it, the let the smoke unfurl from his mouth. "It depends."

"On . . . ?"

"On them. On me. On the situation. I usually just make it up as I go along."

"But what do you actually say?"

"Whatever I have to. It's usually not that difficult to figure out what would work best on a person."

"What about me? What would you say to me?"

"That would be telling," he said, and for the first time that night he smiled.

"Does it always work?"

His jaw flexed with tension and there was a momentary pause before he spoke next. "Most of the time. Some people, however, are more resilient than others. I almost always get them in the end."

"Almost?"

Again a slight pause. "There is this one guy I've been seeing for a while, ever since I first came to this city. He just . . . nothing I say seems to phase him for some reason."

"Who is he?"

"No one special. His name is Rollins, Tariq Rollins. He's an artist that apparently has a bit of a reputation in the underground scene. He paints and makes sculptures of out of junk and I'm constantly trying to tell him how terrible he is. But he just doesn't seem to care. He usually calls for me when he's finished work on a new piece like I'm champagne or something. I always make a point of criticising the new work but he just smiles. All that work, all that effort and in a fucking hooker walks and tell him it's awful. And he fucking smiles."

"Was that where you were earlier tonight? With him?"

He nodded and took a final drag on the cigarette.

I'd watched the blood settle in this one's veins before I had finally left his apartment, sneaking out the fire escape because it was busy in the corridor outside. I already knew from previous nights that he liked rough sex but he wanted it rougher than ever before. He had broken the skin when he had bitten into my shoulder so I hadn't felt that guilty when I lashed out and fractured his jaw in response. I hadn't planned on finishing him so quickly but I was pissed off at him and hurting when I sprayed the stuff into his face and chest.

It had been absorbed directly into his bloodstream through the epidermis, a technique I'd read about in some journals I'd stolen from the library and one that had been employed by South Africa to deliver weaponised biological poisons to leading anti-apartheid protestors. It went straight to his nervous system and ignited every nerve ending along his spine simultaneously, overloading the pain receptors until they had all just shut down and his body had gone limp. The shock must have killed him because he was already dead when he slumped to the ground.

Then the blood settled.

Twenty minutes later and I was back at the camp and listening to the sounds of a fight. Someone from the city must have felt like a go at one of the family and around the back of a burnt out flatbed truck I saw one figure beating the shit out of another. I grabbed a piece of wood that had been staked into the ground and shouted at the aggressor and it was only then that I realised it was Wiktor he was attacking.

"Stay out of this you piece of trash!" the man looming over him shouted at me.

"Get the fuck away from him!"

"This is none of your business!" And he kicked Wiktor in the head, hard.

"This is our home, this is our business." Yvgeny, one of my cousins, emerging from his caravan, armed with a machete. His wife Maria, swollen with another child, glimpsing out from the doorway, a shotgun at her side.

"Get back," the stranger warned, waving a switchblade in our direction as we converged on him. "Back!"

And Yvgeny was on him in a moment, as lightning quick as his father before him had been, his immense hands around the man's neck and the two fell to the ground beside Wiktor's prone form, random limbs flailing. The man screamed as Yvgeny dropped the machete into his shoulder and I shouted at my cousin to get back, the spray I had used earlier in the night in my hands. One quick dose into the intruder's face, and another.

His screaming suddenly stopped and his body went rigid, then limp.

Yvgeny booted the man in the head and retrieved his weapon before telling me, "You'd better check on your friend there. I'll take care of this one."

I nodded, went to Wiktor's side. "I'm sorry, Wiktor, this shouldn't have happened to you. He must have thought you were one of us."

His eyes were bloodshot and unfocused, a large split welt rising on his left cheek.

"Come on, I'll get you cleaned up," I told him.

"You don't understand," he mumbled. "This is my fault."

So it was his pimp he told me, that man, as I traced the edge of his facial wound, collected up the blood on the tip of my finger. Or ex-pimp.

"He found out I'd had something to do with the deaths of some clients back home and . . . and so I ran. I didn't think he'd still be after me after all these months."

"Apparently he was," I said.

"What's your friend going to do with him?"

"We don't ask questions like that," I told him, dabbing the wound with a cloth soaked in antiseptic solution.

"I'm sorry. I should have told you. I didn't think he would find me."

"It's none of my business."

"I still should have told you."

"This isn't a fucking marriage. You can keep secrets from me if you want. There's no obligation."

"But I wanted you to know."

And I thought to myself, if this is a night of secrets, should I tell him one of my own in return?

Maybe just the one.


Turned inside out, plastic veins, flickers of metal clasps to hold everything in place, squirts of light to describe the motions of her internal systems, a new decadent hum through which it is all filtered and it is my sister, lying there on the bed.

"How long has she been here?" Wiktor asked me. He looked down on her prone form, examining her as if she were a piece of art.

"Five years," I told him. "She was transferred here after intensive care, once she'd fallen into the coma."

"What happened?"

"She tried to hang herself." I thought of telling him about our father and what he had done then changed my mind.

"She isn't getting any better?" Wiktor asked.

Her skin was now the colour of the sheets laid across her. I could almost see the blood sliding through arteries laced with the medicinal additives that had hijacked it. Riding her like a machine. She wore a neck brace to cover up the wounds that refused to heal.

"No," I told him. "Not so far."

The hospital seemed to make him nervous and I wondered if it was something to do with the fact that the building was full of people who were dying and whose deaths he had no control over. I wondered if it was purely control that he sought.

Back in the car he asked me how I paid for her continued treatment and so I told him about the break ins and how I would take valuables from my friends after they had died.

"Like a serial killer taking a trophy," he commented but I didn't respond.

I figured we knew enough about each other already.

Things escalate, that much is obvious. My life has been an escalation, from its start to this very point. A upward spiral, ever tightening, towards some point of singularity—but then that's true for everyone. Wiktor included.

The night the end began we'd both gotten ready together. I watched him apply mascara with more precision that I could ever manage and helped him struggle into a ridiculously tight pair of PVC trousers and he returned the favour by pulling my hair into a tight braid. I told him about the friend I was going to visit, a young self-styled guerrilla-slash-terrorist who was like a gene-splice of Che Guevara and Kurt Cobain. Wiktor's mood was still sour from that morning when one of his own projects had backed out of an overdose at the last minute but he had already arranged to go back and see them that night and was intent on finishing the job.

"Losing your touch?" I teased and got a one fingered salute in return.

So sensitive.

We went our own separate ways and I took with me two vials containing a clear liquid, the glass decorated with a black lipstick kiss. It had taken me a week to prepare it thanks to the fact that it needed several days of fermentation but I felt certain it would be worth it. I didn't know exactly what the consequences would be or what the best dosage was but I couldn't wait to use it.

And then it had all gone wrong somehow. I don't know what had happened, if I had gotten the dosage wrong or if the heat of carrying the stuff around had affected its potency somehow but either way it hadn't worked. My friend had just laughed after I had jumped him and forced the stuff down his throat. Laughed at me so I knifed him with the switchblade I kept on me. Just a little slash, enough for me to escape and nothing more—it was the least I could do.

I'd ended up back at the caravan with only a few hours of the night gone and no ball for this Cinderella to go to. I called a few friends but it didn't lead anywhere. So I figured I could borrow one of Wiktor's maybe, just for a short while, and as soon as I'd seen the name I'd felt that little tug of pressure you get when you know you are going too far. A tug I knew well. A tug I liked.

I wrote down the name *Rollins* on a scrap of paper. And his address.

A few hours later and I called Wiktor. He was pissed at me because he was still working his friend and I told him I didn't want to bother him for too long but that Rollins and I were having our own little party over at the artist's private studio and perhaps he would like to join us later?

There was silence on the other end of the phone, long enough for him to hear Rollins shouting on me what I wanted to drink.

"Don't do this," Wiktor said, through the static. "This isn't fair."

"You're owe me one, remember? You're owe me for Kristian."

"That was different. That was before. I didn't know . . . "

"It doesn't matter. You took one of my friends before I could get to him . . . I'm just returning the favour. I'm helping you out here."

"Fuck you," was all he had left to say.

"Maybe when I get back," and my words were drowned out by Rollins shouting across the room again.

"*What you want to drink?*"

"Don't bother, honey," I called back, more into the phone than across the room. "I'll fix the drinks myself."

I listened for a few moments longer to the sound of Wiktor's silent rage, a rage like sexual energy.

And I hung up.

But then the question is how did it get to this point, where we are both lying on the floor, covered in each other's blood and me with an empty gun in my hands. How did we go from that small argument to this moment, right here, right now? This is what I ask myself as I hold him.

After the argument, after I'd hung up. When the phone line went dead and Wiktor sought his revenge.

When he took his revenge.

Rollins was sprawled across his bed, his densely-haired chest motionless. I went through his closet, sweeping aside the clothes that hung there, looking for any hidden boxes of valuables but there was nothing there. Under the bed—nothing. No safes, no hidden stashes.

Damn it, this guy played the starving artist bit to a tee.

In the end I had no choice but to tear out a couple of framed paintings and hope that I could fence them on somewhere. If this guy was as hot-shit as Wiktor said he was (and Rollins himself thought he was) then I should have no trouble getting at least something for it.

I put my clothes back on, grabbed the rest of my stuff and was just about to leave when the phone rang. I glanced back at the bedroom, glimpsed Rollins's rapidly paling foot, then answered it.

"You're still there?" Wiktor asked me.

"I was just leaving."

"Uh huh." He sounded strange, drugged up or something. There was a lot of background chatter.

"Where are y . . . ?"

"Did you have fun?"

I hesitated before answering and realised that perhaps I was feeling a little guilty about what I had done. "Not really. The guy was a pain in the ass. You could have warned me."

"I never thought I'd have needed to, did I?"

I wasn't really hearing his words, I was too busy listening to the noises that were surrounding his voice like a gang of poltergeists. I asked him again, "Where are you?"

"Nowhere."

My spine was tingling and it felt as if there was something moving amongst the ganglia of my brain.

Too quiet for a club. But familiar.

Nerve endings fired, neural impulses ignited and the answer made its way towards me.

"Wiktor . . . "

And then I heard it, the sound of someone being called over a public address system and echoing through lonely corridors. Asking for Doctor Warislav to come to room 242, urgently.

My jaw clenched, my heart began to swell up.

"Wiktor, no . . . "


He would have been able to get past the nurses because they didn't care about the long-term patients that were nothing more than a drain on their time and resources. He would have closed the door behind him for privacy and then sat down beside her in that chair that I had been sitting in for five years and then what would he have said?

He would have asked her why she clung so hard to such a worthless life. He would have taken her hand in his own and told her that it didn't have to be such a struggle, not if she didn't want it to be. He would have told her that death was not fear but peace and didn't she want to be at peace? He would have whispered this to her, as gently as he would have offered his love to her, and he would have watched her heart monitor's readout begin to slouch.

Her lids would already have been closed but her eyeballs might have fluttered a little beneath them. Would her semi-rigid limbs have softened? Perhaps.

I had spent most of the early nights and days wondering whether she was able to hear me or not as she lay nestled within the coma, but after a while I had stopped caring because I realised it made no difference. Was there a point in being a part of the world if you couldn't react to it?

I knew all these questions that he would have put to her because I had already posed them myself. I knew how this scene played out because I had already imagined it a thousand times, only it had been me that had been with her and not Wiktor.

And I didn't know whether that made it better or worse.

Brought the car to a screeching halt right outside the ER and leapt out without even switching the engine off, my vision distorted by spent tears, and Wiktor was already there waiting for me. He grabbed me and I screamed at him and didn't care that people were looking at us and he just took the back of my head and pressed my face to his chest and I cried into him like just another fucking grieving relative.

Then I pushed him away and stared right at him, forcing what I was feeling at him like a gunshot and hoping that it hurt him as much as it did me but he just blinked. Once. Twice.

"What have you *done* . . . ?"

Not a question but an accusation.

"I didn't do anything," he said. The same as always.

"They do it to themselves," I finished for him. I felt limp, empty, wasted. I knew she was up there but I couldn't see the point in going to see her. What was left of her.

"I hate you," I told him.

And he didn't say anything.

The silence remained as we drove back to the camp because there was nowhere else for us to go. A brooding, heavy rain fell, turning the world into a reflection of itself. I sat at the table and he made me a black coffee with enough sugar to make my teeth sting then sat across from me.

The rain and children screaming made it sound like a war zone outside.

"What did you say to her?" I asked after a long, long time.

"Does it matter?"

"Yes." Then, "No." Then, "Yes."

He leaned forwards until his hands and forearms were in view, me with my eyes down turned, too heavy to hold them up any more.

"Why, Wiktor? That was just too much."

"You told me yourself, life is an escalation. Ours more than most."

"But not *that*."

There was a sudden noise like an explosion—I looked out the trailer's small window to see it had been one of the kids dropping chunks of a rotten engine into a deep puddle. The image made me think of genocide victims being rolled into a mass grave.

"Come on," Wiktor said, "we both know we couldn't have kept on like this indefinitely. What you did just speeded the whole process up."

"What *I* did?! What *you* did."

"You went behind my back and killed Rollins!"

"Only because you killed Kristian!"

"But that was *before*! That was *before*!"

I was grinding my teeth in frustration and anger. "Wiktor . . . "

"What?" he urged, lifting my chin so that we looked into each others eyes. His face held the strangest expression that I found myself unable to read.

I thought of injecting him with sodium pentathenol and watching him fit and foam at the mouth.

I thought of throwing a glassful of polychloroxyl onto his neck and watching as it soaked into his bloodstream and burst his heart.

Or tying him to the bed and hooking him up to a drip laced with one of the many gentle, persuasive poisons that I had for months on end.

"You don't know what you've done."

"I know," he told me, leaning closer until I could feel his hot breath on my cheeks. "You used her as an excuse to keep going, Vanya, to resist the urge to give up. That's all. As long as you had to pay for her expenses you had a reason."

"A reason for what?"

"To put up with all this shit," he said, raising his arms. "Whatever gets thrown at you. Or has been thrown at you."

The pressure was growing, filling me. I thought of all those nights I spent by my sister's side and I had known it was pointless, of course I had. She would never recover—they had told me that right from the start.

"What else should I have done, for fuck's sake?" I asked him.

"Let go. You just let go."

He slid out of the chair, knelt next to me as the rain battered the metal walls of the trailer. Took my hands in his.

"You stand next to a busy road—*just step out into the traffic.* You have one of those poisons of yours—*just take a small drink before you give it to your friend.* Tell me what you feel."

"I feel like I'm holding a loaded gun but don't know where to fire it."

"You're holding that gun and all you need to do is turn it. Just turn it so that you can see the little scrape marks on the inside of the barrel where past bullets have burned their way out. That's all it takes."

Stroking my face where the tears have stained.

"Why hold it back? Why struggle so much? If it was easy, if you didn't have those feelings then perhaps you wouldn't be so tired from fighting. If it takes so much *just to keep going* then is it worth it, truly worth it? What is that you keep going for?"

I shook my head. I fought more tears. I wouldn't let them out, despite his urging. Too many already.

"It's okay," he soothed. "You don't have to fight it."

I jumped as something cold touched me and I looked down to see him placing a gun in my hands.

Suddenly I realised what was happening and the worst thing was it didn't feel wrong. I knew what he was doing but his words still made perfect sense to me.

"Please don't . . . "

He stroked my hair, squeezed my hands around the gun. "I won't make you do anything you don't want to. This has to be your decision."

"I know."

It felt natural, holding the weapon. I raised it into the light. My father had owned many guns but always shotguns. This felt different.

I stared out into the rain, even heavier now. The kids had gone, the camp was silent. Everything was being washed away.

"I need some water," I told him. "My mouth . . . I can't . . . "

"Sure. Let me get it for you."

He went to the bathroom and came back with a glass for me. I sniffed it first, touched it with my tongue and I noticed him smile.

"Habit," I explained, then drank the whole lot in one go. "You don't know what she meant to me."

And then I looked at him and there was something in his eyes and I realised he knew *exactly* what she meant to me. That was the whole point wasn't it?

A tear spilled down my cheek and he looked genuinely sad for a moment.

"I don't know if I can do this," I told him.

"Of course you can," he said, kneeling beside me once more. My knees were slightly parted and he placed himself between them, a hand on each exposed thigh. The gun in my hands, in my lap.

"I feel so numb, Wiktor . . . "

He moved closer, close enough that his breath was on my neck and I could see the reflection of myself in his eyes. "And what's the point in being a part of the world if you can't react to it?"

I smiled slightly at him feeding my words back to me.

"She's gone. She's safe. At peace. Don't you want that too?"

I looked at him, then nodded.

"Okay," I said to him. "Okay."

Wiktor licked his lips and as he did so I leaned forward and kissed him until I felt his mouth open for me, his tongue beyond. His hands lifted from my thighs, up my torso and cupped my face and I cracked open the capsule I'd slipped into my mouth while he was getting the water and let the poison spill into both of our mouths.

It took him a moment to realise that something was wrong and when he did he jerked away from me so suddenly it was as if a grenade had gone off between us. Saliva swirling with dark purple threads spilled down his chin and he didn't even spit for a few seconds because he was so absorbed in his own surprise.

"What was that?!"

"You must have bitten me."

"Bullshit, that's not blood." He wiped and examined the stuff on his fingertips. "What the hell is it?"

I told him flatly, "Chloroproxymyl. Or an approximation of it, anyway. It's an alternative to cyanide."

"Jesus, Vanya, no . . . "

"I told you my methods worked better." I could feel my stomach beginning to react against the serum already. "Don't worry, there's not much pain. You'll feel some cramping and it might get pretty bad but within a few minutes . . . "

"You stupid fucking . . . !"

"Don't shout at me!"

"Don't tell me not to shout! Do you know what you've done?!"

He doubled up abruptly, as if someone had folded him, slamming his head off of the ground. When he looked up at my his entire face was creased with pain.

"You fucking killed my sister! That's what *you've* done!" I shouted back.

"I didn't kill her!"

A surge of pain shot through my stomach, as if someone had just grabbed my guts and twisted them. I almost dropped the gun. "Don't start with that shit, Wiktor," I said through gritted teeth. "You killed her. You killed all of them. Don't fool yourself."

"I'm serious," he pleaded. He made a vague swipe at the gun, I don't know what for, but he fell well short. "I didn't kill her. She didn't kill herself. I tricked you Vanya . . . "

When I coughed there was blood in it. I spat doughy phlegm onto the carpet at my feet.

"*What*?"

"I wanted to prove to you that I could make you step over. I didn't touch her. I couldn't even find her fucking room!"

My head was growing fuzzy, as if it were filling with blood. "Wiktor . . . I . . . "

"I was going to, at first, but . . . I couldn't do that to you. Vanya, I can't see. My eyes . . . "

"The . . . CPX has reached your optic nerves . . . "

"*Do something*!" he shouted at me.

"I can't . . . there's nothing I can do . . . "

"FUCK!"

He slammed his fist into the ground. "The gun isn't even loaded!"

I flipped open the barrel and he was right, there was nothing in there. "You stupid bitch! Why the hell did you . . . ?"

"I didn't want to kill you! I didn't want you to kill yourself. I just wanted to prove . . . "

His words were lost in a sudden surge of blood that spilled from between his lips and he slumped to the ground and a moment later I joined him, my arms unable to hold me up any longer. We lay there together, haemorrhaging in unison, a perfect and toxic Romeo and Juliet.

"This is the way . . . this is the only way it could have gone for us . . . " he told me.

I tried to answer but my throat was as full of hot blood as an Ebola Marburg victim.

I think he said *damn* but I couldn't be sure.

I pulled myself over to him, slumped onto his back and pressed my face close to his.

"It doesn't matter," I said. "This is how it is."

His hand closed around mine and my vision went in one sudden blink as my eyes filled with blood.

And in the darkness, I found myself wondering what would happen to my sister now. Would she hold on, now that there was nobody left for her to awaken to? Or would she step over? Into the water, off of the ledge. Bring it to an end.

I would never find out.

# PUBLICATION HISTORY

"Notes Towards the Design and Production of the Protohuman," is original to this collection.

"Devastation," is original to this collection.

"Pretty," first appeared in *Chiaroscuro 12*, 2002.

"Fuck Punktown," first appeared in *Punktown: Third Eye*, ed. Jeffrey Thomas, 2004.

"Her Love For Me Is Oxyacetylene," first appeared in *debug*, ed. Kenji Siratori, 2004.

"Elisabeth Afterlife Is Dead," is original to this collection.

"Rage Against the Machines," is original to this collection.

"Emotion Sickness," is original to this collection.